TOKYO LOVE

Visit us at www.boldstrokesbooks.com

TOKYO LOVE

by

Diana Jean

2020

TOKYO LOVE

ISBN 13: 978-1-63555-681-0

This Trade Paperback Original Is Published By
Bold Strokes Books, Inc.
P.O. Box 249
Valley Falls, NY 12185

First Bold Strokes Books Edition: March 2020
Previously published by Crimson Romance (2016)

Credits
Editor: Ruth Sternglantz
Production Design: Stacia Seaman
Cover Design by Tammy Seidick

I wish I could dedicate this book to all of Japan. I wish I could dedicate this book to the young girl who led me around Mitake mountain, who knew very little English (and I even less Japanese). To the grave of Honinbō Shusakū and the group of local boys who brought me there. To maguro, konbini rice balls, fried chicken bento, and mountain stream fish on sticks. To hanami, hanabi, and every local festival with good music, great food, and cold beer. To KA International School and the students who taught me what it meant to live on both sides of the world. To Shinto cave shrines, Daibutsu, and cool summer forests. If I could I would dedicate this book to Tokyo humidity, which could never be escaped or forgotten.

However, I cannot dedicate this book to anyone or anything unless I first dedicate this book to my sister, Colleen. My sister who has found in Japan love and heartbreak, friendship and loneliness, foreignness and familiarity.

Colleen, this one is for you. Thank you for lending me a piece of your life.

CHAPTER ONE

K athleen made a mistake.

She was standing in the middle of a crowded train station, people swirling around her like leaves in river rapids. Kathleen was stuck in the undercurrent, being pulled straight to the bottom, trapped from moving forward, drowning.

She looked around at the people; most avoided making eye contact with her. Holo ads floated above, their colors and noise battling the straining overhead announcements. There were official signs around too, scrolling in a bold red font. They probably could have helped her, if she could read them.

She had been too naive. She had been too trusting in her self-confidence and assurance in her place in the universe. She shouldn't have taken everything for granted. She should have been careful, keeping her feelings, her tender heart, locked safe away from prying eyes and hands. She should have been more prepared, ready for anything, ready to take on the shit whenever it hit the fan.

She should have taken that Japanese language course in college.

She had never felt this white until she moved to Japan. She had never felt so foreign until she realized that while many people in Tokyo had a passing level of English, it was definitely not the same as being fluent in English. She had never felt more lost than when she fell asleep on her evening commute back to her apartment. She had missed her transfer. She had missed it by at least ten stations. She had no idea where she was.

The station was huge. Just from where she left her wayward train, she could see at least ten other trains leaving. Which direction where they going? Where should she go? Where was she?

She hurt all over. She had been wearing her heels all day and had been on her feet at meetings. She had been trying to give optimistic presentations on the new developments with her project goals. Manager after manager had barraged her with the same questions. *When will it be done? What are the setbacks? Why are there setbacks? What is the cost? How will you optimize profit and time? Can we make your life more difficult? Please elaborate.*

She used to be a simple programmer, sitting in a small cubicle in Champaign, Illinois. Her life had been simple. *Write this code. Check this code. Check it again. Send it out for beta. Rewrite code.* She hadn't appreciated the monotony then. Now she was a project leader. Now she had a team of programmers who answered to her and, goddammit, she was jealous of their tedious lives.

She was tired and wanted to take her shoes and skirt and bra off. She just might, here in the middle of the train station during busy rush hour. She should start bringing comfortable walking shoes with her to work. Or maybe sweatpants.

She looked around the station again. She needed to ask for help.

Three years ago, Japan Railway introduced a new type of station manager. *Have a question in the train station? No longer will you have to track down a busy employee. Instead, walk to the nearest Help kiosk and press the friendly green button (red button for emergencies only). Located every five feet, Help displays a friendly hologram station manager, ready to answer any question in over seventy-five languages.*

That was how they were advertised, but Kathleen often found herself to be the lost foreigner in the train station and had learned to dread using the Help kiosk. She stomped over to the nearest console—her feet were too heavy for grace—and slapped the green button. "English," she spat, before the computer would ask her in each one of the over seventy-five languages.

A flicker, and then, in a small ring on the floor, a glowing blond woman stood, smiling pleasantly. "Thank you for using JR Help. How can I help you?"

In terms of holograms, she was shoddy. Kathleen could see right through her and just about every pixel on her flawless pale skin. The hologram also wasn't looking directly at Kathleen—her gaze was fixed a little past her left shoulder. Really, it was quite simple to program an eye-tracking device to focus on an individual's face.

"Where am I?" Kathleen asked.

"This is Omiya Station." The holo's voice changed abruptly on the proper noun, as if she had suddenly suffered a stroke.

"Okay…how do I get to Matsudo?"

The hologram stared at her with a blank, smiling expression. "Please repeat?"

Kathleen bit her lip. "How do I get to Matsudo?"

"Did you say Shibuya?" A glowing train map appeared. "First, take the JR Shonen-Shinjuku line to—"

"No!" Kathleen waved her hand. "Matsudo."

"Did you say Shibuya? First, take—"

"*Mat-su-do.*"

"Did you say Shibu—?"

"Matsudo, you hack piece of—"

"Excuse me?" A soft voice came from behind Kathleen.

Kathleen whirled around, afraid she had attracted the attention of some official. A woman, probably in her late twenties like Kathleen, wearing a soft, ruffled blouse and a stiff pencil skirt. Not the JR station manager uniform. Her sleek black hair was carefully parted and pulled into a side ponytail.

At once, Kathleen was both grateful that she hadn't upset the machine so much as to call over a real worker, and also deeply embarrassed that she had alarmed this poor commuter. "Ah, sorry. I mean—" Dammit, what was the word? "Shumisen." She gave a hurried bow.

The woman only looked concerned. "Don't worry about it." She spoke with a flawless American accent, and Kathleen could have cried. The only people she knew who spoke fluent English were people at the company, and half of them spent their days questioning her every decision. "You're trying to get to Matsudo Station, right?"

"Yes," Kathleen exclaimed, grateful and still very near tears.

The woman smiled, but in that sort of strained please-don't-let-this-stranger-cry-on-me way. "I'm heading there myself. I can show you the way."

"Thank you. Thank you so much. I'm Kathleen Schmitt, by the way." She reached into her bag, digging out a business card. One of these days she really needed to grab some of those cute cases that most businessmen and women carried in this country. She handed it over, bowing again. She might suck balls at the language, but she had learned the whole bowing thing within a week. Mostly because every person seemed to bow at her, and it was getting awkward just standing there taking it.

The woman smiled, handing over her own business card with a

little more grace. Hers came in a lovely sakura case with an actual GIF of petals falling from the cover. "Yuriko Vellucci." A foreign last name…maybe she was married to a foreigner? That was probably why she spoke English so well.

Kathleen looked down at the business card: Yuriko Vellucci, Mechanical Engineer–Quality Control, Mashida Intl.

Yuriko worked for the same company as Kathleen. "I didn't know you worked for Mashida."

Yuriko frowned at her. "We are in completely different divisions." She held up Kathleen's business card like Kathleen needed the reminder.

Kathleen felt a little peeved. Maybe it had been a dumb thing to say—Mashida was a global company and had tens of thousands of employees—but Kathleen had never seen anyone from Mashida outside of work. Which was a little pathetic, considering she lived in company housing.

Yuriko didn't seem to care about Kathleen's excitement. Instead, she looked up to the train times, red letters traveling across the platform in floating ribbons. "Come on, we'll miss the next train." She quickly turned around, weaving back into the rush hour crowd.

Kathleen could only concentrate on keeping track of Yuriko's sleek black hair in a sea of…well, sleek black hair. Hair coloring was popular in America, even with unnatural pigments. Most people she'd met in Japan just generally didn't seem to like the idea of standing out from the crowd. Not that Kathleen didn't see a few redheads or purple-heads floating around.

"Come on. The doors are closing," Yuriko shouted over her shoulder, stepping into a jog to the ringing music on the platform. She leapt into the crowded train, forcibly pushing several people aside.

Kathleen dove after her, squeezing and panting.

"Sumimasen," Yuriko murmured, working her way to the far door where a little space could still be found. Kathleen realized then just how much she had botched up the word earlier. It was a dumb word anyway. What was the point of saying *So sorry, excuse me while I shove you against total strangers*?

Kathleen managed to stand in front of Yuriko, holding her briefcase at her back. She used to hold it to her chest, worrying about someone being able to easily pickpocket her. However, the priority had quickly shifted to making sure no strange dude could, even unintentionally, feel up her butt. Besides, while perverts existed in Japan, petty theft did not.

Even before the door chimes ended, about ten more people

shoved their way onto the train. Kathleen was pressed against Yuriko's flouncy blouse. She gave her an apologetic smile. Yuriko shrugged it off, looking away. She was probably just as grateful as Kathleen to be shoved up against at least one person who wasn't a sweaty man. Not that Kathleen was a pile of roses after Tokyo humidity and her hard workday, but at least she wasn't wearing a three-piece suit.

The doors closed and the train started moving. Kathleen couldn't even feel it jerk into motion, half because the trains partially floated off the tracks, and half because there were about a thousand pounds of flesh cushioning her. The thought that didn't comfort her.

The train was quiet. No one spoke on their phones, but they tapped on their wrists, playing games or answering texts. A few people whispered to one another, and she could hear someone's headphones on high volume, the tinny music escaping. She looked up to Yuriko. "Which building do you work in?"

Yuriko's eyes were on the holo maps of the train line, floating above everyone's heads. Kathleen realized that her eyes were a startling shade of blue, and she wondered if it was natural or cosmetic. "I travel between work sites." Her voice was short.

Kathleen wondered if she had done something to piss her off. Probably just by being an annoying foreigner. "Oh, I see." She shut up, looking away.

Yuriko sighed, closing her eyes. "Sorry. I had a difficult day. My main office is in Shinjuku."

Kathleen still wasn't sure if Yuriko was going to be friendly now. "I work in the Shinjuku office as well. I guess Engineering is on another floor."

Yuriko looked like she was holding back a smirk. "Undoubtedly."

Kathleen knew she should shut up while she was ahead, but it was just so damned nice to talk to someone in real English. "Your English is really good."

"Thank you. My father is American."

That explained the last name, and the accent. "I'm from America too." That got her a *No shit, Sherlock* eyebrow raise from Yuriko. "I mean, I'm from Illinois. Champaign. Where is your father from?"

"I was born in Milwaukee."

Now Kathleen was feeling like an ass. For the first few months she was here, she used to call back home, complaining how every Japanese person treated her like a stereotype. Just some dumb American who spoke too loudly and couldn't be bothered to learn Japanese. Not that it wasn't true, but Kathleen thought she was pretty good at the bowing thing. Of course, not every person in Japan was from Japan or even Japanese. Kathleen had just gotten too used to it, considering all of her coworkers fit the mold.

"Well, that's cool," she finished, hoping it didn't sound as lame as she thought.

Yuriko was hiding another grin, so it probably was. She closed her eyes and took a deep breath, causing her chest to press gently against Kathleen's. "Sorry, I'm just really tired, and we had a crisis at the test site in Saitama today."

"Crisis?" Kathleen couldn't help but be curious. Mashida was a huge corporation with thousands of products and departments. The crisis was unlikely to affect her.

"Yeah, the new PLCs were malfunctioning. Apparently, this new coding has managed to mash up the wires. When prompted with the new programming, it freezes all movement for about thirty seconds until it can reconfigure."

PLC—*Perfect Love Companion*—was Mashida's premier line of AI life-size dolls. Computer sim lovers and sex dolls had been around for decades. It was only a matter of time before Mashida finally perfected the physical synthetic lover. No more touchless holograms. No more dull-eyed mechanical dolls. The Perfect Love Companion was to be the ideal blend. A lover you could talk to, go on dates with, and who would look just like any other person.

For decades, people—mainly men—had been carrying around their virtual girlfriends on their phones; now they could hold their hand. No more would men have to settle for a lifeless doll. This one would be just as attentive, just as loving as your computer.

PLC was the reason Kathleen had left her safe job in Illinois. She'd been programming the virtual lovers for five years now, and her big break was to program a sim who was destined to be more than a holo image.

Kathleen suddenly groaned, rubbing her wrist against her leg to pull her sleeve up to look at her bracelet mobile. She had set it to silent after leaving work, not wanting the distraction while she attempted to navigate the trains, but Yuriko's words had given her a bad feeling she had probably missed an email.

Lo and behold, an urgent email was waiting for her. "Damn," she murmured. She touched her middle finger to her palm, opening up the email: *PLC 10.6 beta malfunction. S/A code movement compromise hardware in Saitama. Full report attached. F*

Yuriko raised an eyebrow. "Software Development, right? Let me guess, you're a part of the new PLC project?"

Kathleen didn't have the movement of her other hand to send an email, nor did she want to voice one in front of Yuriko. Instead, she tapped her fingers and sent an automatic text. *Will report later. K*

"I'm running the new PLC project."

Yuriko actually looked a little impressed. "Explain to me, then, why you had to change the old code for, of all things, a simple shoulder movement?"

"A shrug. It's to make them shrug."

"A shrug? What was wrong with the old code?"

Kathleen shrugged herself. "It was stiff, robotic. PLC has the potential for smooth, minute movements. Why not take advantage?"

"Because it crashes the hardware."

"Maybe the hardware needs an update as well."

Yuriko no longer looked impressed. Kathleen flushed in embarrassment. She blamed her day for her rudeness. She was constantly criticized by Engineering for pushing the limits of the technology; it seemed she had finally run into her limit.

"Look, I'm—"

"We need to change trains here." Yuriko pushed past her to exit the packed train.

Kathleen was temporarily thrust into the throng of strangers but quickly recovered enough to follow. Luckily, Yuriko's force managed to forge a path in the sea of bodies. Together, they crossed the platform to the next departing train. While it was still full, at least they weren't pressed against each other like the last train. Yuriko settled with one shoulder against the door, staring out the window. Kathleen stood awkwardly in the aisle, holding a seat bar for stability. She stared at Yuriko, wondering if there was any hope of salvaging the conversation.

Unfortunately, this train ride was shorter than the last. When they entered the station, Yuriko turned to Kathleen, flipping her hair over her shoulder. "Look, I've got to stop at the konbini. I assume you know where you are now?"

Kathleen nodded. "Yes, thank you. I mean…" She bowed, feeling a little ridiculous, but she knew it was the right gesture. "I'm sorry."

Yuriko sighed, tugging at the end of her ponytail. "Don't worry about it. And if you find yourself lost again, just text me, okay? We obviously live in the same area, so it probably wouldn't be too inconvenient." She gave a small smile, but it looked a little impatient. "Try not to overhaul the code again tonight. I'd like to get to bed early."

Kathleen smirked, feeling a little better. "Thanks, Vellucci-san."

Yuriko waved a hand. "Yuriko is fine. Vellucci-san just sounds weird with your accent."

CHAPTER TWO

When Yuriko was eleven, she found her dad working in the shed out back on his old 2022 Trinix Hybrid. It was one of the last cars ever made that still used fossil fuels to help it run. It was terribly clunky and loud and dirty. Her dad liked to tinker with it, trying to improve the technology but keep that classic style.

He used to work on it whenever he fought with her mother.

So Yuriko, whenever she felt upset or torn or confused, used to go into that shed and bang around that old car. She loved being up to her elbows in oil, practically inhaling the toxic fumes. It was amazing. Her dad had been working on that junker for ten years with little progress. Yuriko turned it into a fully automated electric car within nine months. She even gave it a new wax.

She loved to see how machines worked, from the delicate modern nanotechnology to clunky antiques. They were all fascinating and beautiful. They all deserved a bit of tinkering and improving.

When she first saw the Personal Love Companion project, she thought it was creepy, if not insane. Love simulations had always been virtual reality based. Anything hardware-based made by those same companies was a sex toy. Yet the PLC promised so much more. The programming might be weird, but the machines, the dolls, were like art. They were beautiful and refined. They were the cutting edge of robotics, and she hadn't cared that she would be helping to bring more perverted computer programs into the world. She wanted to be on the ground floor of those machines.

She examined the hydraulic tubing of the PLC 10.6. The PLC was laid before her, all wires and tubes and valves and lightweight steel boning. It did not have a skin on. Since that would be customized, only a few were given default skins for the purpose of testing. The skin would only get in the way of her work. She didn't need it. Even without eyes or eyelids on the PLC, she could see the fine motors moving synthetic pads to widen or narrow. Even without teeth or lips, she could recognize a smile or grimace. She had been with these PLCs since the 2.0 beta, and she didn't need all the bells and whistles to understand them.

The hydraulic tubing would pump cooling water to overheating areas, simultaneously heating itself to make the synthetic skin warm to the touch. It had been faulty since the PLC 5.3. The more complex the mechanics got, the more the bulky hydraulics failed.

She poked at a junction point, trying to visualize a way to make it more streamlined and secure.

Her wrist buzzed with a new email. It was a mass email sent to her department. She tapped it. *New patch from SD on the S/A malfunction. Testing in Shinjuku.*

Her eyes widened in disbelief. Software development had already sent in new code for the shoulder malfunction? It was only yesterday that it broke down. The whole situation was still under review, and Yuriko had expected an email about it in the afternoon. Then the real drama would unfold of how the problem would be fixed and, more importantly, *who* would have to fix it.

For software to just send out new code without prompting was nearly unheard of. She stepped away from the PLC, turning to look around.

Mitsu was standing at one of the computer stations, entering a report. She was wearing a white lab coat as was required in the testing sites. The stark whiteness was offset by a rather large glittering red bow in Mitsu's hair.

"Mitsu-san?" Yuriko called.

Mitsu turned, pouting. Even her lip gloss was glittering. "Mitsu-*chan*," she corrected.

Yuriko rolled her eyes. "People will think you're my favorite," she replied in Japanese.

"I am your favorite."

Yuriko couldn't help but grin. "Okay, okay. Did you see the email for the new patch? Can you input it into this model?" She motioned to the PLC lying in front of her.

"Hai-hai." Mitsu turned back to the computer. A few taps and Yuriko could see the diagnostic display for the PLC in front of her. A couple of warning signals popped up, and Yuriko reached over the

PLC and closed a couple valves that she had opened while testing. The screen went green and Yuriko nodded to Mitsu.

Mitsu typed a couple of commands into the computer. Yuriko stepped back as the PLC before her twitched. The eyeless eyes opened, and the retina lights flickered on, scanning the area. Since this PLC wasn't programmed with a cortex scan, it wouldn't be able to process much besides anything that might be in its path.

Following Mitsu's instructions, it sat up and swung its legs over the side of the table. It sat straight and stiff. A light blinked on in its head, just behind the ear, reading the next instruction.

Then it slumped its shoulders, cocking its head to Yuriko. The muscles in the lips pulled back into a lazy smile. Then it shrugged.

Mitsu came to stand beside Yuriko. The PLC repeated the motion. Then used its other shoulder.

"No issues?" Yuriko asked.

Mitsu shook her head. "It looks…good."

It did look good. The movement was slight, but all the mechanics in the shoulder moved in time with a slight tilt of the head. Minute and precise. Nothing jammed up, nothing tried to compensate or obstruct the movement.

The lazy smile was new. Yuriko supposed that was just the simulation the development team decided to send out as an example. She remembered Kathleen Schmitt's words: *PLC has the potential for smooth, minute movements. Why not take advantage?*

There had always been a mutually antagonistic feeling between the software and hardware development teams. They both worked so separately while needing to come together to make a full product. Yuriko's team often felt that they were the ones who needed to pick up the pieces of a mess made by software. They always had to adapt to the code, never the other way around. They had to fix the problems made by the programming. They were the ones criticized when it failed.

She suddenly wondered if something she said to Kathleen had prompted her to pick up the slack on this problem. She felt a mixture of guilt and satisfaction at the thought.

She hadn't been very impressed by Kathleen. She had known that a foreigner had been brought in three months ago to take over Product Development. She'd had a vague vision that they would be like the previous head, Osada Renjiro, a CEO type with too much confidence and too little talent. Of course, that was why Osada had been removed from the project.

Kathleen was…pathetic.

Well, she had seemed that way to Yuriko. She had been screaming at a Help kiosk like a madwoman, then turned to Yuriko like she had just given up all hope.

It was hard to describe why some foreigners seemed to take up so much space. Kathleen was certainly curvier than the normal Japanese woman; her breasts and hips seemed barely contained in business casual clothing. Kathleen had curly reddish-brown hair, the sort of hair that would break any comb or brush that tried to tame it. She had tied it back into something that looked like a literal knot, loose curls haloing her face and neck. Her eyes were wide, a warm brown, and she had a prominent nose and full lips.

Nothing about her appearance was demure. In the train she had leaned against Yuriko in the crush of the commute. Her body had been heavy and warm.

Yuriko didn't deny that she was attracted to the female figure, and Kathleen was a lot more figure than Yuriko was used to encountering.

Then Kathleen had opened her mouth.

She was overeager and a little too desperate for conversation and connection. This woman had been living in Japan for three months, yet she acted like the freshest of tourists—too loud, and with too much presence.

It probably hadn't helped that she was directly responsible for Yuriko's problems that day.

Yet watching the PLC with its perfected movement, not a warning error or troubling mechanical failure in sight, Yuriko wondered if maybe there was just a little more to Kathleen than a hopeless foreigner.

CHAPTER THREE

Kathleen had heard rumors that in Beijing office workers got to take naps in the middle of the day. At the designated time, it was perfectly acceptable to take out a pillow and sleep at your desk.

She didn't have time to sleep—she had about ten incoming reports and at least three proposals to write—but she would have been very grateful to rest her head on a soft pillow while she scrolled through her three thousand emails.

"Director?"

She looked up. "Fukusawa-san?" One of her subordinates. Hopelessly polite and terribly efficient. He was sort of her secretary, keeping track of all the tasks she was forced to delegate. Even though a portion of his day was spent running around the office for her, he had all the same skills as she did.

He was a practical genius when it came to computer software. In fact, when she first met him and realized that he would report to her, she wondered why he hadn't been promoted. Sometimes she still did. She guessed what she possessed, and Fukusawa lacked, was creativity. Give Fukusawa any task, and he would complete it efficiently, but he was incapable of creating his own tasks or finding those rough edges in the code. Those little opportunities for reimagining were beyond him.

Though, it seemed to Kathleen, every time she tried to bring up a new opportunity for innovation, her superiors spent all their time just trying to find its weaknesses. Life used to be so simple before she had to think about personnel management, deadlines, and budget evaluations.

Fukusawa stepped forward and handed her a tablet. "Tamura-san requires you. It's about the PLC 10.6 beta."

She stood up, taking the tablet and flipping through the files

Fukusawa had brought up for her. She bit her lip, feeling the blood drain from her face. "Shit."

"Excuse me, Director?"

She waved him aside. "Nothing, sorry. Can you text me whenever Sugiyama-san's report is finished? This might take a while."

"Of course."

She swept from the office, scanning the pad on her way down the hall. *Preliminary evaluations completed...proceed ahead of proposed schedule...begin 10.6 beta tests.* She looked from the pad as she opened the door to Tamura's office. Tamura was the assistant vice president to the entire company. She wasn't technically Kathleen's direct supervisor, but since her office was so close to the PLC development project that Kathleen was currently running, she tended to weigh in on important decisions. Like this obviously ill-advised one.

Tamura's secretary looked up at Kathleen. She was a pretty, thin woman with black hair that shimmered purple and blue in the light from the window behind her. The trend in shimmer colors had recently gotten popular, and at first glance, it made most people's hair look a natural black. Kathleen knew that if she was to try it, it would probably turn her reddish-brown hair an ugly gray or green in the sunlight. Natural redheads did not agree with most color pigmentation.

The secretary smiled. "Schmitt-san." Her accent was very thick, and she couldn't quite get her tongue around Kathleen's name. It sounded more like *Shu-mi-tsu.* "Assistant Vice President Tamura-san will see you now."

Tamura's office door opened automatically, and Kathleen attempted not to storm inside. The office was lavish compared to Kathleen's. Kathleen had been impressed, upon moving to Japan, that she got her own fancy work space with large windows and a desk, all to herself. However, Tamura's was about three times in size, with lush oak furniture and soft carpeting. Kathleen was pretty sure she was served lunch on a silver dolly. She also guessed that the other door in her office led to a private bathroom.

Tamura's appearance was typical businesswoman. Her no-nonsense hairstyle was pulled into a sharp bun, and probably hair-sprayed into submission. She always wore suits with pointed shoulders and elbows, all black or slate. She wore thick black glasses, and Kathleen could see a newsfeed projecting from the rims. When Kathleen stepped into the office, Tamura blinked several times to close the feed. She tapped her wrist, bringing up a visual on her desk of the document Kathleen had just been skimming.

"Always so prompt, Kathleen," Tamura commented, smiling. Her English was perfect, though she had a slight accent. She did much of her business with foreigners and had gotten used to informality in the workplace—hence her use of Kathleen's first name. Not that she had ever invited Kathleen to reciprocate.

"This is a joke, Tamura-san."

Tamura arched a brow, tapping at the holo document, making it flicker. "I'd thought you'd be excited."

"Beta-ing wasn't supposed to being for another *six months*." Kathleen held up the pad. "This says by next week candidates will be screened. Just last week I received an urgent text that the cortex readers wouldn't be running until next month. We haven't even gone over the mainframe failures from Tuesday."

Tamura leaned back, her black eyes sharp as they assessed Kathleen. "The schedule has been shifted. PR has come back that Lian-Yeh has already started the beta for their companion product."

She really wanted to shout, *I don't care about China!* Instead she said, "We aren't ready."

Tamura tapped her glasses, blinking through her emails. "Medical has assured me that the cortex readers will be ready by next week. We won't be able to screen many applicants, which is why we have decided to choose a very particular few with the skill sets required to properly assess a product that will, obviously, be a little rushed through production."

"A little rushed? If we send out the product now, it's bound to have numerous problems. Crashing, coding failure, mechanical failure." She knew it would be better to let Lian-Yeh have six months on Mashida than to put out such a faulty product.

Tamura frowned, all forced politeness gone from her features. She rested her hands on her desk, long nails tense on the wood. "Mashida is the world's leader in love simulation technology. We are the pinnacle of innovation in the field of AI and robotics. Ms. Kathleen Schmitt, you were brought here three months ago to jump-start our most exciting product to date. So you will make sure it's ready by next week, and you will be very careful in choosing our beta testers for this exciting opportunity."

Kathleen took a step back. She shouldn't argue with one of the highest ranking people in the corporation, but she had a feeling Tamura didn't care about the product she had poured her soul and stress into for the past three months. Tamura just cared about numbers, which China was apparently beating.

So she took a deep breath. "We need to come to a compromise."

"Compromise?"

"The product isn't ready for beta. Not to the general public. Just let me choose some people in the company, one or two, who know this product. They can test it outside the lab and send back reports. It would be incredibly helpful data and unlikely to damage our reputation. In fact, it could speed our progress, so that we could put out an even better beta than planned."

"Give me a timetable." Tamura was already pulling up a new document, quickly writing notes with one sharp nail.

She, feeling a little overwhelmed, attempted to run numbers. "Okay, so we choose a tester by next Monday, give them two months—"

"Four weeks, maximum."

She gritted her teeth. "All right, four weeks. If they send detailed weekly reports."

"Daily."

"*Daily* reports. Then we can simultaneously develop the real beta in...oh, probably two months?"

Tamura looked up at her, eyes still unrelenting. "You have six weeks. That is my final offer. You will take charge of this pretest, and I will cover with PR."

Her head was swimming. *Fuck, six weeks.* At least it wasn't next week. "Okay, I'll find someone to test—"

"No, you will perform the pretesting."

It took her a moment to register what Tamura meant. "Wait, no. I will find a suitable tester. Possibly Fukusawa-san." She threw out the name. "I know his work ethic. He would be a very good candidate for..."

Tamura was ignoring her. She finished writing her note and tapped the edge of the document, storing it. She stood up, the polite fake smile back in place. "No, Kathleen. If you insist that this product isn't ready, then you will be personally responsible to make sure it is, within my graciously extended deadline. Please make an appointment with Medical by Monday, so the prototype can be fashioned for you by Wednesday." Her eyes glimmered. "I expect your first report to be forwarded to my secretary by Thursday."

CHAPTER FOUR

Tamura had to be punishing her. She was probably pissed that Kathleen was just about the only subordinate who dared to challenge her. She knew her other Japanese coworkers could be stubborn, but they tended to have that silent, passive-aggressive attitude. She was anything but passive. It was probably why most of her review meetings had ended up being sort of a disaster.

At least they hadn't fired her yet.

Before she came abroad, the PLC project had been falling way behind schedule. When she arrived three months ago, the beta had been slated for two years away. She thought they had been impressed with her six-month improvement. She had slaved away for that result, countless nights bringing code up to par, arguing with Engineering. During that time, if she wasn't in her apartment sleeping, she was at work.

She pressed her thumb against the lock, and her door snapped open. Despite the modern lock, it was an old metal door, heavy and loud whenever it opened or closed. She leaned against it, stepping into her apartment and kicking off her shoes at the entry. The hardwood floor felt too good through her stockings. She only took enough time to grab a can of beer from the fridge before she practically skated over to the low table, falling to her knees beside it.

Living in company housing meant she hadn't needed to buy furniture. However, it also meant that everything was a little more Japanese than she was used to. Her table, which she kind of always thought of as a coffee table even though it was probably closer to a dinner table, was low to the ground. She'd been given flat cushions to sit on, but even after so long, she still wasn't quite used to eating and working on the floor. She had a TV, which she barely used, considering she couldn't even properly pronounce the few words she knew in Japanese. She would kill for a couch.

Her kitchenette was only separated by a counter, but at least it was sizable, with a fridge, oven, and two burners. She was grateful to have a separate bedroom with a Western-style bed. She probably would have cried in that first week if she had to both eat on the floor and sleep on a futon. She also had a small bathroom with a separate room for the toilet. She'd even gotten something of a crazy deep tub, though it wasn't long enough for her to stretch out. She knew Japanese people tended to soak in bathtubs, but Kathleen only knew how to work the shower.

She leaned heavily against the table, pressing the cold can of beer to her cheek. It was cheap Japanese beer, but it was tolerable. On nights like this she needed it. Her back and legs ached from sitting at her desk for the rest of the day, desperately trying to make a format for the reports she would soon be filing. She pulled her computer from her bag.

The small black cube with a power button and some access ports was surprisingly heavy for its size, simple, and a little outdated. She had been using it since she was a programmer in America. Mashida would provide her with an upgrade, but she wasn't quite ready to get rid of the device that had started her career. She placed it in front of her, tapping it so her screen and keyboard displayed over her table.

Her document was up, slightly translucent—she was able to see her kitchen behind it. She flicked it aside, looking for a better distraction.

Her wrist buzzed, and her computer, automatically synching with it, displayed that she had a call from her brother.

Sitting up, Kathleen opened it. "Good morning, Dave."

He looked like he had just gotten in from one of his ungodly early morning runs. His curled hair was damp, and his cheeks were flushed. He smiled at her, and she felt her heart squeeze. With all her family living at a thirteen-hour time difference, it was hard to find good times to call them. Dave had done better than her parents. That was probably because he seemed to only sleep four hours a night. "How is it in Japan-land?"

"Humid, all the time." It had gotten significantly worse in the past couple of weeks. No matter how much AC the trains pumped in, they still smelled like an elephant enclosure. "Rush hour is rancid."

He laughed. "You know, I saw a vid of Japanese rush hour with people with white gloves helping to push commuters in the train. Have you had that?"

"Not that exactly. It's pretty cramped in there. Last week I got pressed against the door. When it opened, I thought I was going to smack into the platform. But luckily some of those attendants were there and caught me." It was actually pretty embarrassing to have a total stranger catch you as you were squeezed like toothpaste from a crowded train.

Dave was laughing loudly, which made her feel a little energized again. Dave's wife, Juliet, must have overheard and stepped in from the kitchen to chat with her, all of it small talk and some not-serious news about her parents. Kathleen soaked it in. She didn't have friends in Japan. Her coworkers treated her with distant respect, and her superiors obviously didn't want to spend more time with her than required. She used to have so many friends. They went out drinking after work or did stuff on the weekends. She'd even had Brandon for a while, but they had broken up long before she was given the promotion.

She saw Juliet kiss Dave as she went off to work early. She was lonely, but she knew that might happen. She had suddenly moved to another country without knowing how to speak the language. At least work kept her busy most days of the week.

"So"—Dave turned back to her—"anything new at work? Still making sex dolls?"

She frowned, though she knew he was just joking. "They are not sex dolls."

He smirked. "Ah, and all the single men who buy them just want to dress them up?"

"Sex dolls are inanimate. Nothing more than large, expensive toys. The Personal Love Companions are much more complex."

"Ah, so they can talk to you while you're having sex with them."

If Dave had been in the same room with her, she would have smacked him. "It means they can walk and talk and interact with you. You can take them on dates—"

"In public?" He sounded horrified.

"The point is that you can develop a relationship with them. It doesn't have to be about sex."

"Yeah, and would you have a relationship with a computer?"

She had been programming love simulations for years. Even before she was taken on by Mashida, she had been coding holo dating sims. Most of the time she was required to stick to a pretty close script. Each dating sim had a distinct personality and quirks. The user was pretty restricted on how much input they could give.

The PLC project was much more. Not only were they individually programmed to match each user personally, but the companions could actually listen to the user. They could figure out responses that weren't just canned lines. They could react and learn. With the holo dating sims, the user had to input to the sim *I am sad*, and then the sim would act accordingly. With PLC, the doll would *look* at the user and understand that they were sad.

She thought it was an amazing project, but she also knew she wasn't the demographic for them. Sure, she might be lonely, but she could never take a relationship with a doll seriously. She would look at the AI, at the mechanics, and be impressed. She knew she would enjoy testing the doll's limits. She would go on a date with one, if only to witness how many strangers could tell if the doll was real or not. She would talk to it about complex issues, if only to see if the doll could respond appropriately. She would be a good tester for anything preliminarily, but she would be a terrible beta. She just wouldn't be able to commit to the doll like their customers would.

"It's not my job to have a relationship with a computer."

Her wrist beeped and she looked down to find that Medical had scheduled her cortex exam. Her heart sank a little. Maybe it *was* her job to have a relationship with a computer.

The cortex scan was the newest innovation for programming AI. In the years before its development, customers were forced to fill out hundreds of pages of surveys and go through extensive interview processes, to have a doll whose personality and appearance would align with the customer's. It was all very tedious and never very accurate. What people said in surveys and interviews could be completely contradictory to their lifestyle. For instance, a customer might say they exercised a lot, while in reality they were just being optimistic. Then they got a holo sim who constantly talked about exercising or the customer's personal regime, and they found their interests didn't match.

Now, all a customer—or in this case, Kathleen—had to do was show up for a cortex scan appointment. The scan was painless and only took fifteen minutes. Then she had to fill out a brief form, mostly personal information like her age and gender, and that was it. The data was sent to her team, who would synthesize a chip that would be given to Engineering. The chip would contain the perfect personality and appearance for her ideal companion. Then it would take a mere forty-eight hours for the PLC to be made and programmed. Ridiculously fast.

She was overwhelmed. She paced outside her apartment door, constantly staring down the railing to the parking lot outside the complex. Her PLC was due to arrive tonight, and she really didn't want her neighbors to see. If she could catch the delivery truck, then she could usher the PLC inside her apartment as fast as possible.

She looked down the rows of apartment doors. She didn't know her neighbors, but they all worked for Mashida. Would they know she was doing this preliminary beta test? She had found most of the people here tended to keep to themselves. Surely not everyone who worked for Mashida was familiar with or even aware of the PLC project. After all, it was an international corporation with many different departments and products. Maybe they would just think she was getting a couch or a new table. Maybe.

"Lost again?"

Kathleen turned toward the stairs to see Yuriko Vellucci towing along several bags from the convenience mart. Yuriko arched an eyebrow at her in question.

"Oh." Kathleen raised her hand, which was holding a half-forgotten beer. "I was just…The apartment is a bit…stuffy." People drank on the balcony all the time, right? It wasn't illegal, right? She totally wasn't waiting for a life-size personalized semi-sex doll…right?

Yuriko seemed to accept it without much thought. She was wearing slacks this time, and a vest covered another ruffled blouse. Her hair was pulled into a ponytail again, and even though she looked sweaty and tired, not a strand had fallen out of place. Kathleen was insanely jealous.

Yuriko just shrugged and made to pass around Kathleen.

"You live here?" Kathleen asked.

Yuriko hesitated. "Of course."

Kathleen struggled to make herself not seem like an idiot. She already knew Yuriko worked for Mashida; living in company housing was hardly unique. "Oh, I mean…on this floor? I haven't seen you around."

"My work hours are a bit random."

She was walking away, and Kathleen knew she should probably let her go. The package should arrive any minute, and it would be hard, after starting a conversation, to convince someone to leave immediately. Yet this was not Kathleen's first beer of the night, and she was so strung out on nerves that she couldn't help but try to reach out to someone. "Do you want a beer?" she blurted out.

Yuriko hesitated, eyes narrowing at Kathleen, as if trying to see if Kathleen had some weird ulterior motive. Then her expression softened. "Sure. I wasn't really hungry for these onigiri anyway. Just let me put this away."

Kathleen suddenly felt a little giddy. She watched as Yuriko opened her apartment door, only a few down from hers. Then Kathleen rushed into her apartment and grabbed a couple beers. She would need to stock up on more soon. If the past week of work was getting to her, this new week was bound to get even weirder.

She stepped outside to find Yuriko waiting. She was still wearing her black pants, but she had taken off her vest, showing off the rather breezy blouse that made her look both professional and cool in the stifling humidity. Her hair was still pulled back, but she raked her nails across her scalp, as if she itched to take it down.

Yuriko accepted the beer. "Thank you. Rough day?"

Kathleen gave a nervous laugh. "I'm actually a lot more worried about the rest of the week." And the next five weeks. "You?"

Yuriko leaned on the balcony railing. "Today was not so bad, but last night we received a last-minute project." She tugged at her ponytail. "We were out so late that the trains had stopped running. Had to take a cab back." She sipped her beer. "Anō, I wonder if I can get corporate to pay for that?"

Kathleen had a feeling she knew exactly what last-minute project Yuriko was talking about. "You know, before I accepted this position, I had always heard about the crazy hours business people run here in Japan. I thought it was just an exaggeration. Now I think I should have been grateful for the nine to five that I had in America."

Yuriko's lips quirked. It wasn't quite a real smile, but it was the closest that Kathleen had seen in their brief interactions. "I had a job in America for a while, in Milwaukee. But I wasn't satisfied there. In terms of engineering AI, Mashida is a world leader." She shrugged. "Even if their projects tend to be dating sims. But I suppose that is the largest market." She sipped her beer, staring out to the opposing apartment building across the parking lot. "Why did you come to Tokyo, Kathleen?" She actually looked a little interested.

Kathleen toyed with her now empty can. She kind of wanted to open the spare, but she also didn't want to look like an alcoholic. "I actually worked for a US branch of Mashida. It was a good job, but when they offered me the promotion...I guess I wanted a change of pace."

Yuriko was staring at her now, drinking thoughtfully. "Let me guess—you broke up with someone?"

Kathleen decided that it was definitely okay for her to open the other beer. "Ah, well, yes. Sort of. Probably." She attempted not to chug it down. "How did you guess?"

Yuriko gave her a soft smile, not condescending in the least. "Not many Westerners come to work in Japan. The culture here is just so different."

"You're telling me."

"So either the foreigner has some invested interest in Japan, like they're married to a Japanese person, or maybe they're an otaku or something. If not that, then, well, usually they are running away from some personal problem." She paused. "And if you don't mind me saying, you don't seem like the type to have more serious baggage than a heartbreak."

"It wasn't really a heartbreak. We just had been going out for a while. And then he realized one day that he didn't want to go out with me. So we broke up."

Brandon was one of those guys where it all seemed just a little too easy. They met through mutual friends, started talking, and then they were hanging out alone. They never truly argued, not about anything important, and they dated for three years. They had the type of relationship where everyone just assumed that wherever one went, the other would follow. When Brandon asked to break up, Kathleen wondered if he had found someone else. She almost wished he had. She felt like it would have made her feel better, to lose to another girl, than to just...*lose.*

It was thoughts like these that made Kathleen think moving across the world was a good idea.

Kathleen knew Yuriko was still looking at her. "Okay, maybe it hurt a little. But I was in a rut. For a lot of unimportant reasons. Thought it would be a good change."

"And is it?"

"I'll get back to you when this hellish humidity dies down."

Yuriko choked back a laugh. Kathleen felt immensely proud of having provoked it. "Well, I'll give you one word of advice. Don't date Japanese men. There is a reason Mashida makes billions selling fake girlfriends here."

"I'm guessing you'd never try out a love sim or even the PLC for yourself?"

Yuriko grimaced. "I synthesize them for a living. I have to test skin textures and hair fibers, and I can't tell you how many times I've seen them, halfway through production, with all their inner wiring spilling out and metal skeletons exposed." She shook her head. "No, I think if I saw one in real life, it would only disturb me."

"Well, when the PLC is released, you might not have a choice."

Yuriko raised an eyebrow. "One of those dolls costs as much as a luxury car. Even in a city this big, I think I can avoid them."

Kathleen laughed, hoping she didn't sound too nervous. "Well, you never know when one might crop up."

Yuriko shrugged and finished her beer. "I guess we'll see then." She turned, probably to head back into her apartment. Then she stopped, looking over her shoulder to Kathleen. "Hey, thanks for the beer. And I hope this change of pace works out for you."

For a moment, Kathleen thought Yuriko was referring to the imminent arrival of her PLC. Then she remembered her own words from early. "Ah, thanks."

Yuriko smirked. "Ja ne." Then she went into her apartment.

Kathleen looked over the balcony and saw a Mashida van pulling up to the parking lot.

CHAPTER FIVE

Yuriko closed her apartment door behind her and leaned against it momentarily. Her apartment was just as she'd left it: a huge mess. Various tool kits were strewn across her floor. Part of a reject PLC leg was on her table, where she had been tinkering with it for a week. One corner of her living room was filled with random parts, some even with skin or hair flaking off. A box of PLC eyeballs was on her kitchen counter, minuscule delicate parts spread across the white surface. Her bag of konbini dinner was on the floor. Her mother constantly complained that she should learn to cook for herself. The problem wasn't that she didn't know how to cook—it was that she lacked the space to cook.

She toed off her shoes and stepped into her kitchen, bending over the bag. She realized that she was still holding the empty beer can she had gotten from Kathleen. She tossed it in her recycling bin.

Talking with her had been nice. Nicer than she expected anyway. Kathleen still looked like a nervous wreck, though honestly, Yuriko had no idea why. It could have been the sudden order for a custom cortex scan PLC that was put into production earlier that week. Rare as those were, they had been made before for various tests.

Kathleen had said she had come to Japan looking for a change of pace. That wasn't surprising. She knew too many foreigners with the same idea. They'd come running to Japan, expecting to be swept off their feet by the cutting edge of technology or the charm of a completely different culture. They never seemed to expect the stress of culture shock or the realization that they were moving to a country where they were the minority. Where they were always the odd one out in the crowd.

She remembered when she moved to Japan with her mother.

She had visited plenty of times before the divorce, but nothing quite prepared her for living here. The school, the kids, just *being* here and knowing she wasn't going back to America at the end of the summer.

She hadn't realized what it meant to have an American father. She hadn't realized that it meant she was different from most of the people in the country that she had to call home. That even though she was fluent in Japanese and had a Japanese mother, it wasn't the same. It wasn't enough. She was half, not whole.

The story of how she came to find her place in Japan wasn't dramatic. She simply learned to be a little more Japanese than necessary. She spoke softer than she had in America. She kept her hair black and straight, and she kept her clothes modest and unassuming. She did everything not to stand out and never talked about how much she missed American sized couches or yards. Or American mac and cheese or ranch dressing.

At the time, it seemed a trivial thing to give up, but she wondered if it had done more harm than good. She had learned to keep her emotions close to her, locked up and away from scrutiny, away from judgment.

She wondered if Kathleen would learn that.

Chapter Six

Kathleen wondered—if some neighbor or stranger or maybe policeman were to walk into her apartment, what would they think of the giant box lying in the middle of her floor?

Probably a body.

Her table and cushions were pushed to the side. The box was slightly dented—from when the deliverymen attempted to get it through the door—but nondescript. White cardboard with her address and *Personal Love Companion* stamped on the side. She had to dig around for a pair of scissors to open it. Inside was a foam casing, wrapped with more tape. Then the body, wrapped in clear plastic, half covered in manuals and information pamphlets.

She was quick to slice through the plastic. Not because she was excited to see the product; it was more that seeing a realistic body wrapped in plastic was disturbing. Maybe she should talk to her design team about sleeker packaging. Something a little more organic than what you would find your computer packed in. Packaging aside, there was a major problem.

Her PLC, her personally made, very expensive love companion, was…a girl.

Kathleen stared at her for a good ten minutes, trying not to go into a panic. This was a disaster. The cortex scan was supposed to make the customer a doll to perfectly fit their interests and needs. She had spent months working with Medical, trying to get the complicated nuances smoothed over. Making sure the companion was calm for a calm person, active for an active person. If the scan couldn't even tell that she was exclusively interested in men, then this project was already in the grinder.

She took a few deep, even breaths. Then she tapped a small memo to be incorporated into her report for tomorrow. Maybe it was a blip in the system. Maybe it was an easy fix. When she had to fill out the forms about her name and age, they could also add a small section for sexual orientation. Their process would still take a fraction of the time other companies had proposed. Maybe this wasn't a total disaster. Maybe she wouldn't be fired by the end of the week.

Crisis temporarily on hold, she decided she should probably make more observations, if only to help distract herself from the glaring flaw.

The PLC had long straight black hair, shimmering in the setting sun coming in through Kathleen's living room window. She touched it to find it soft and completely tangle free. The PLC had a simple cut with bangs that hung low on her forehead. Her lashes were dark and short, eyebrows thick beneath the bangs. Her nose was flat, cheeks round, but she had a pointed chin and full lips. She was wearing a standard white shirt and shorts, made from a cheap, nearly translucent material. She was very thin, with pale olive skin.

The PLC looked Japanese, though something about her face structure seemed unique. Kathleen knew the body should reflect her personal tastes, but she knew the physical appearance was already flawed, considering she was the wrong gender. She had never looked at a beautiful woman and felt more than just passing admiration for her appearance. She couldn't even begin to comprehend how she should be judging this PLC that was supposed to be designed specifically to please her. Trying not to freak out, she touched the skin, finding it pliable and warm.

Kathleen immediately stood up, wringing her fingers. This was insane. This was creepy. She understood why Yuriko would find it disturbing to see a PLC somewhere outside the Engineering facilities. The PLC was incredibly convincing, but she knew that this was not a person. This was a computer she had been programming for over three months. This was a project funded and run by hundreds, if not thousands of people.

The PLC looked so *real*. Like she had just opened a box to find some unconscious woman lying in the middle of her apartment.

She took another few steadying breaths and wrote another note into her wrist unit. *Make higher quality default clothes.* She was truly uncomfortable that she could practically see through the shirt. She knew underwear was not included. *Make undergarments a default.*

She went to her kitchen and pulled out another beer. She was starting to get a little dizzy, and she knew she should probably be clearheaded for the critical stage of turning the PLC on. She could run through that system check later. Right now, she sort of felt like running screaming from the apartment. She needed some liquid courage to make her stay.

She wasn't sure if it was the gender mix-up that was terrifying her, or the fact that she was simply extremely put off by the technology she had worked so hard to prepare. *Dammit*, she hadn't even tried talking to the PLC, and she was already questioning her entire career. She had never run up against this with her other programs. Holo dating sims were nothing compared to this. She had always been able to separate herself from those. This was a whole new level of realism, and she found herself draining the beer.

"User Kathleen. Turn on," she practically shouted. Full instructions were included, but she had drafted them herself. She didn't need to read the manual when she had practically written it. The PLC was voice activated for the particular customer. She could say the words in any language, and the PLC would recognize her from the cortex scan.

The PLC opened her eyes. They were a glassy blue and she blinked up at the ceiling, reading the environment already. Assessing that nothing was obstructing her, she sat up and looked around until her eyes landed on Kathleen, who felt like cowering under the steady gaze.

The PLC was breathing now, and Kathleen felt like she was going to hyperventilate.

She *knew* her.

This had to be a joke. The eyes, the face, the way she was grinning slowly at Kathleen. It wasn't just a PLC. It wasn't just a robot. Kathleen could count on one hand how many people in Japan she knew personally. *This* had to be a goddamned joke.

The PLC blinked slowly. "Doing okay there, Kathleen?"

"Yuriko," Kathleen breathed, surprised she could speak at all.

The PLC stared, no change in expression. "Would you like that to be my name?"

"No. God, *no*." Kathleen closed her eyes and ran a hand through her hair, uncaring that her fingers tangled and pulled at the strands. The pain distracted her slightly, and she forced herself to take in a few deep breaths. She had to get control over herself. She was just overwhelmed. She had to be mistaken. She looked at the PLC again.

The PLC was staring at her, blue eyes wide with concern. "Are you all right, Kathleen?"

Kathleen's mind felt numb, but she attempted to focus on what was important. The PLC seemed functional and she recognized her instantly. That was good. She could obviously assess the situation and understood that Kathleen was freaking the *fuck* out right now.

"I'm just...I'm just fine," Kathleen answered. She wanted to lie on the floor and give up now.

The PLC gave her a shrewd look, but then shrugged, flipping her hair over one shoulder. Then, quite fluidly, she stood up. She brushed off some of the remaining plastic, and then took a step away from the box. Kathleen remembered, in her youth, how robots used to be jerking, stuttering things that were constantly falling over simple obstacles. The PLC seemed to have no problem exiting her box. Then the PLC turned around, put everything back inside it, and pushed it to the corner of the room. She even went as far as putting down Kathleen's table and arranging some of the cushions back around it.

Kathleen just stood and watched, feeling stupid. She should be feeling a sense of great pride. The PLC was performing perfectly, better than she could imagine. She was stable, strong, and able to make decisions without prompting.

All Kathleen could think, watching her tidy her meager living room, was *Why the hell does she look like my neighbor?*

Then the PLC sat at her table, legs folded under her, and motioned for Kathleen to do the same. Kathleen sat down, with much less grace, and resisted the urge to slam her head repeatedly into the surface.

The PLC smirked at her. "Tell me what you're thinking."

"Why do you want to know what I am thinking?"

The PLC rolled her eyes. "Because I can't read minds and you're about a stiff breeze away from a total meltdown. If I have to call an ambulance to save you from catatonic shock, then I would at least like to give them a reason why."

Anyone else might have laughed at the PLC's dry wit. In fact, in any other situation, Kathleen probably would have been impressed by the nuances in the synthetic voice. "Who programmed your features?"

The PLC's eyes went unfocused for a second. "Analysis from cortex scan of Kathleen Schmitt."

Kathleen swallowed, feeling it stick in her throat. "Specify analysis."

"Probability of physical attractiveness to subject, 97.9 percent. Eye shape, 96.9 percent. Eye color, 99.8 percent. Structure of nose and cheekbones, 87.9 percent. Structure of chin, 95.6 percent. Voice intonation, 99.6 percent. Structure of—"

"Stop, please. Just stop." It was just the data from her cortex scan. How could that make a replica of Yuriko? What did that *mean*?

The PLC's eyes focused again. "Is there a problem?"

It could be human error. Yuriko did work in Quality Control. She undoubtedly had gone through every skin graft and hair fiber and eye color and face structure available and signed off on their quality. She probably hadn't intended for it all to culminate in a PLC that looked exactly like her, but subconscious human bias could have played a role.

Granted, it wasn't Yuriko's job to look at every finished product. If she had looked at this PLC, wouldn't she have been surprised? Wouldn't she have realized it had to be some mistake? When they had talked earlier that evening, Yuriko hadn't looked like she had the freakiest day of her life. She didn't look like she had come from work after seeing herself as a PLC.

Something was wrong. A mistake, a glitch in the system.

Kathleen stared at the PLC again. Maybe her face wasn't the same? Yuriko's hair wasn't that distinctive from other Japanese people she had met. Blue eyes weren't common here, but she did admit she liked blue eyes. Brandon had blue eyes. She was still probably suffering from the dumb foreigner stereotype of thinking every Asian person looked the same. Maybe the hair and the eyes just reminded her enough of Yuriko to mistake the rest of it for her. She had to be freaking out for no reason.

She sucked in more air and, quite calmly, attempted to push away those alarming thoughts.

Of course, it only brought to the forefront that the PLC was still a woman. That brought her back to the edge of a spiraling despair. "I've made a terrible mistake."

The PLC didn't speak, but her expression was open, waiting for more.

"I need to...I am not a good candidate for a beta. This was way too personal for me to accurately judge. I should have insisted someone else perform this test. This is a total disaster. I'm going to lose my job." She clutched her beer. It wasn't helping her. She probably had too much adrenaline coursing through her for it to relax her.

"Why would you lose your job?"

Her voice reminded her of Yuriko's, but Kathleen forced herself to ignore that. It was just a coincidence. That wasn't the real problem right now. "Because I can't interact with you like a customer would. This test is totally meaningless and flawed, and when we release you to the open market in six weeks, it will be a disaster."

The PLC frowned. "Why can't you interact with me?"

"Because you're severely flawed."

Now the PLC looked a little affronted. "Flawed?"

"You're a woman! I'm interested in men."

"Bisexuality is a real thing, you know."

Kathleen glared. "I'm *only* interested in men. Besides, *you* are a robot, a Personal Love Companion. I cannot love you. I'm sorry, but I'm really freaking out." She pressed her forehead into the table. She took a few steadying breaths, and when she was sure she wasn't going to start crying, she looked up.

The PLC was resting her head on folded hands on the table. She looked at Kathleen curiously, her blue eyes contemplative. "Kathleen... did you want to fall in love with me?" Her voice was soft, and something about it soothed Kathleen's frayed nerves.

"Well, no. I just need to collect data."

The PLC smiled slowly. "Then why are you freaking out? You just need to test me, figure out my kinks and rough edges, right? I know you've played your own love sims before. Aren't I just a more complicated one?" She reached out, her fingers closing around Kathleen's wrist, giving a gentle squeeze. "It'll be okay."

It was very strange to have a computer that she programmed comforting her from the brink of a total meltdown. Her fingers were soft and strong, and her voice was calm. Kathleen knew she was getting more than a little hysterical. The PLC had a good point. Sure, maybe she wasn't as personalized as Kathleen had expected, but some of her first dating sim tests had turned out even worse. This was something fixable. Something easy to see and easy to explain in a report.

She sat up. "How do you know about my love sims?"

The PLC grinned, tapping her head. "The cortex scan and basic information. I don't know every personal thing about your life, of course. I know you headed my project, and I know you're in my code."

Kathleen frowned. "That's weird."

"Is it?" The PLC propped her chin up on one hand. "What would be weird is if I called you Creator or God. Or maybe goshujin-sama?"

Kathleen shuddered. "No, my name is just fine." Then she hesitated. Did she really want to know? "What is your name?"

"Do you want to give me one?"

"I want to see what name you'd come up with." Kathleen knew that no PLC had a default name. Would she be able to problem solve and pick one for herself?

She tugged at a strand of her hair. "How about Ai?"

Kathleen paused. "Eye? Like an eyeball?"

She snorted. "No, *Ai*," she exaggerated, like it would help Kathleen understand. "It's a Japanese name." She grinned. "It also means *love*."

Kathleen wrinkled her nose. "Fitting, I guess. Are you Japanese?"

"Well, I was made in Japan." She grinned. "But I guess with your cortex scan, I am a bit more worldly."

Kathleen had no problems with Ai as a name. In fact, it somewhat helped that Ai hadn't named herself Yuriko. Not that Ai was Yuriko. That was just a coincidence. She had to convince herself of that.

With her freak-out ebbing away, she was starting to feel extremely tired. This day was just a little too much. She set aside her half-finished beer and stood up. "I think I need to pass out now before I conduct any more tests."

"Okay, then," Ai said.

Kathleen stopped. "Wait, where will you sleep?" Then she stopped and rubbed her forehead. She knew that PLCs had a sleep mode. It hardly mattered the position or place they entered it.

Ai grinned at her, as if she already knew what Kathleen was thinking. "I'll be fine out here. Unless you want me to join you in bed?" She arched an eyebrow.

Kathleen waved a hand. "No, definitely not. Okay, I'll see you in the morning, I guess." She practically stumbled into the bedroom.

Ai's voice, soft and almost sweet, drifted after her. "Oyasumi."

CHAPTER SEVEN

Kathleen decided, after a full night of rest, that she wasn't going to go crazy. She would be strong, persevere, and refuse to hide under her covers and ignore just how weird her life was getting.

Or she would, after she checked her emails.

Curling under her duvet, she tapped on her wrist. A reminder that she wasn't required to come into the office for the rest of the week was already displayed. She had half hoped that Tamura would insist. No such luck. She was expected to stay home and thoroughly test her new PLC. Then probably go out in public. *Goddammit*, it was going to be a very long week.

Then again, the only people in the company who knew she was undertaking this were her direct subordinates and Tamura. She was sure that whenever she next went into the office, they would be judging her. Even though they would be polite enough not to ask any inappropriate questions, she wondered if Fukusawa or the others would lose just a little respect for her.

She eventually had to leave the confines of her bed. She was hungry and her sleep cycle had gotten too used to waking up early. She stepped to her door and peered through into her brightly lit living room.

Ai was seated at her table, flipping through channels on the TV by waving her hand in front of her. She was still wearing the same cheap shirt and shorts she came in. In the morning light it was even more apparent that the fabric was lacking. Kathleen went to her closet and grabbed an old bra and panties, along with a worn shirt she had brought from America and a skirt that she had outgrown. All of it would probably look hideous on Ai.

She stepped from her room. Ai didn't even look up. She just

continued waving her hand to browse through the channels. "Done hiding?"

Kathleen threw the clothes at her. "I was *sleeping*. Here are some new clothes. Please put them on."

Ai looked down at the garments. "New?" She sounded doubtful.

Kathleen stalked over to the kitchen, ready to shovel something into her mouth just so she wouldn't have to talk to Ai. "Well, they are better than what you're wearing."

Maybe she could convince Mashida to contract with some department store, get them to contribute real clothes in different styles. Opening up the PLC to find them dressed in your preferred style would be nicer. Maybe if they made something like a deluxe package with brand-name clothes and accessories.

Kathleen selected a tub of yogurt and turned around to find Ai shedding her top. "H-hey!" She jabbed the yogurt in her direction. "Have some decency."

Ai didn't even cover up. She just smirked at Kathleen, dropping her default shirt. Then she slowly picked up the ratty bra. It was an old sports bra that managed to fit Ai's much smaller chest.

"You said you weren't attracted to women. What could bother you?"

Kathleen knew she was blushing, so she scowled. "That doesn't matter. You're a stranger."

She snorted, easily hooking the bra behind her back. "I was programmed from your cortex scan. I'm probably more familiar to you than your family." She threw on the shirt, tugging on it. "Rutabaga Jazz Festival?" she read. She looked up. "Please tell me there were actual rutabagas there."

Kathleen put a spoon in her yogurt, just eating out of the container. "College jazz concert. No vegetables. Plenty of weed, though."

Ai quirked her lips. Then she slipped off her shorts and Kathleen had to turn around. She might have plenty of experience with locker rooms, but that definitely didn't mean she just gawked at random girls. She poked at her yogurt. What if Ai had been a guy? It would probably be a little more disturbing, she guessed.

Her wrist beeped and she looked down to see that Fukusawa had sent the notes from the morning meeting that she missed. Nothing too big, which she expected, given that until she turned in her reports on her PLC, very little could be done.

She put the yogurt away, deciding that she might as well get started. She sat uncomfortably at her table, tapping the surface to bring up her computer. She hunched her shoulders as Ai sat beside her. The clothes were very ill fitting and didn't match at all. She ignored Ai's curious expression and opened up her document, then began to type furiously. She had to acknowledge the gender mix-up, but she also didn't want it to sound like a complete malfunction. Perhaps there were other parts to Ai's appearance that were to her taste. Then at least it was only one major flaw, instead of a total breakdown.

Kathleen looked over to Ai, who had gone back to watching TV. With her system clear of the beer, she was able to control her emotions a little better. Ai was a very pretty woman. She had some of the round features of Japanese descent, but her eyes were very wide and the color unusual. She had long limbs and was taller than Kathleen, but she did not look awkward, folded up next to the low table. Even with a terrible choice in clothing, she wore it comfortably and somehow made it all look less grungy than it should have. Kathleen might have even said Ai could be beautiful, if given the chance to dress up.

Kathleen had never thought of herself being especially attracted to the Japanese aesthetic. However she could admit that she was somewhat jealous of Ai's long, sleek hair. She wondered—if she were to thoroughly run her hands through it, could it even be tangled? Brandon had never been able to run his hands through her hair. He would just jam them up there until they were trapped while they made out. Then they would have to work together to free him. Oddly enough, her hair never looked messier than usual afterward.

But Ai still looked like Yuriko. Kathleen closed her eyes, forcing the thought away. They were similar, that was all. There was no way they could look the same. Just a coincidence.

An astronomically rare coincidence.

She decided that her thoughts were turning stupid and turned back to her report. All of Ai's other functions seemed pretty normal. There were no issues with coordination or simple problem solving. She had already shown that she was exceptional at reading Kathleen's moods. Also, if she was being completely honest, Ai's personality was refreshing. She was snarky without being cruel, honest if a little blunt, confident, and able to know when to talk to Kathleen or leave her alone, like now. Kathleen supposed that in an ideal partner, she would want someone with a little more warmth, perhaps more tactile. She was sure that if Ai was to embrace her, it would be totally uncomfortable.

She was getting sidetracked again. She had to come up with a more efficient plan to test Ai's abilities. All she had done so far could be tested in the lab and probably had been by Engineering. She had to see what Ai would do, given an entire day alone. Could she be given an errand and complete it without Kathleen? How would she interact with new people, whose personalities weren't programmed into her code?

She would have to constantly observe Ai for an extended period of time. Test to see if her dialogue became repetitive, her actions too easy to predict, over a few weeks. Kathleen had no chance of completing this project early if she wanted it done right.

Then there were other basic functions to consider. Ai had the ability to eat, but then had to extract it when appropriate. She was also entirely functional for sexual acts. Kathleen had no intention of testing that out, whether Ai was a woman or a man. If Tamura asked her, Kathleen would throw a chair at her.

"What's that face for?"

Kathleen turned to find Ai staring at her, her chin in one hand again. "What face?"

Ai waved her free hand. "The *I'm slightly pissed off but I'm not sure at what* face."

"You think I am unsure of the reason why I'm angry?"

Ai raised a single eyebrow.

Kathleen frowned. Was Ai actually reading into Kathleen's expressions? Or was it some subroutine in her program to try to draw answers out of Kathleen when she couldn't decode her behavior? Kathleen made another note on her report. She would have to ask Fukusawa about it.

"I'm not angry. I'm just very stressed."

"Anything I could do?"

Kathleen narrowed her eyes, but there was nothing inappropriate in Ai's tone. "Um, clean the dishes?"

Ai gave her a funny look but stood and stepped into the kitchen. Kathleen didn't have much in the way of dishes. It wasn't like she had to feed more than one person. Hearing Ai running the water, Kathleen turned back to her emails, which had been piling up since yesterday.

"Anything else, goshujin-sama?"

She looked over her shoulder to find Ai already done with the dishes, smirking at her. Kathleen actually didn't know what that meant. "What does *gokshujen* mean?"

"That is not a word."

"You know what I meant."

Ai took a rag and started wiping down Kathleen's stove. "You have such faith in my programming that I can read your mind?"

"You're supposed to understand implications."

Ai ignored her "How about I teach you some Japanese?"

"Why should I learn Japanese?"

Ai raised an eyebrow.

Kathleen waved a hand. "I mean, I know I *should* learn Japanese. But why do you want to teach me?"

Ai turned to the rest of the counters, casually cleaning Kathleen's entire kitchenette. "I've been programmed to be Japanese. Obviously that's supposed to be some use to you." She grinned. "And I don't think you're the type to just chase Asians." She paused. "Well, not entirely, anyway."

"If you're suggesting that I have a weird Asian fetish, you're mistaken."

Ai's other words intrigued Kathleen. Could the cortex scan somehow read Kathleen's anxiety that she lived in Tokyo, but didn't know any Japanese? If a customer wished to learn a musical instrument, would their PLC be programmed to be a professional musician? Was Ai only Japanese just so she could be capable of teaching Kathleen Japanese?

It was something Kathleen had not anticipated, but potentially beneficial. Was this the only reason Ai looked Japanese? Had Kathleen's need to learn Japanese outweighed her physical preferences, at least according to the cortex scan? Perhaps some faulty preferences were why Kathleen received a female instead of a male. She made some more notes to discuss with Fukusawa and her team.

"So?"

Kathleen looked up to find Ai leaning over her counter, looking down at her. "What?"

"Do you want me to teach you Japanese?"

Kathleen sighed. "Okay, just for today."

Ai snorted. "You're not going to learn an entire language in one day."

"That's not what I meant."

Kathleen quickly learned that having a computer that could learn and adapt teach her a foreign language was absolutely fascinating. Ai, after logging into Kathleen's computer, was quickly able to write her own language program so that Kathleen's system was suddenly flooded with vocabulary lessons, grammar games, practice sessions, and much more. Then, as Kathleen struggled to absorb the basics while taking notes for work, Ai would change the program.

It was interesting—so much so that Kathleen found herself practicing Japanese long into the afternoon with Ai. Kathleen was so engrossed, that they only stopped for a quick lunch. She learned a little kana and a few simple phrases. She also learned, after much insistence, that she did not appreciate being called goshujin-sama by Ai.

"What's wrong with it?"

Kathleen frowned. "I'm not your master and you're not a slave of mine."

Ai grinned. "It doesn't have to be a slave." She leaned forward, legs folded neatly below her and hands delicately pressed on the floor between them. "I could just be a maid in your service."

"Now you're just sounding perverted."

"Isn't that the point?"

"Not relevant to our situation. Stop looking at me like that—it's making me uncomfortable."

Ai leaned back. "How about koibito?"

"What? Lover? What did I just say about our situation? No. You may only refer to me as Kathleen."

Ai pouted. "How about Ka-chan?"

"No."

"You're no fun."

"Does your programming insist that you call me by some nick-name?"

Ai was back to lounging against Kathleen's table. She seemed to be in a perpetually relaxed state. "Maybe it means that you secretly like pet names."

"Well, I like my name just fine."

Kathleen turned back to her report. She was just finishing it up for the day, getting ready to send it out to Tamura and the rest of the team.

"Don't be like that."

Kathleen stopped, looking to Ai. "Like what?"

"I managed to get you relaxed for several hours, and now you're all stiff again."

"I'm not stiff. I have to finish this report."

Ai sighed. "Fine. Did you want to go out for dinner?"

Now that made Kathleen stiffen. "No, absolutely not."

"If you are afraid of ordering, then I can—"

Kathleen shut down her computer. "No, you're not allowed to leave this apartment. Ever."

Ai frowned. "But what about—?"

"No. This is a direct order. You are not to leave my apartment or answer the door without my express permission." Kathleen had written into the code the ability for a vocal direct order. It was to be used as a safeguard if there was ever a problem with a PLC. No PLC could deny a direct order, no matter what it was. If a customer directly ordered their PLC to never speak, the PLC would not speak, even if their programming gave them a chatty personality. It could be reversed, but Kathleen definitely didn't want Ai to go out in public. Kathleen could collect enough data from the privacy of her apartment.

Ai was silent for a moment, and her eyes went slightly vacant. It was only for a second. Then she blinked, looking to Kathleen. "Affirmative." She smiled. "Okay, do you want me to make you something to eat for dinner?"

Kathleen breathed a sigh of relief, glad she'd written the code herself. "I need to go out to get some groceries. Then you can make me something." Perhaps she would find something really strange and see if Ai could make something that Kathleen would enjoy.

Ai nodded then turned back to the TV. She did not make a comment or ask to go along. Kathleen smiled, feeling a little better.

Kathleen didn't like grocery shopping in a country where she couldn't speak the language. Granted, the Japanese did have an affinity for putting pictures on their food, making it easy to guess. However, having to guess half your grocery basket was stressful. Especially if you were trying to find something specific.

Even when she lived in America, she never was that creative with cooking. She could cook chicken and beef well. Just about every meal included pasta. She didn't mind eating the same thing day after day. When she came to Japan, she found her usual vegetables to be interspersed with ones she didn't recognize. She never knew which Japanese dressings or sauces were good, and meat in Tokyo was very expensive. She knew she should learn to cook fish one day.

So she often took the easy route and went to the convenience store. She could easily pick up something prepackaged and heat it up if needed. Half the time she didn't know what she was eating, but she wasn't that picky with flavors.

If she wanted Ai to cook something, Kathleen should probably buy raw ingredients.

She stared at the fish in the supermarket, wondering if the flashy price tag meant it was a special deal or a discount for being a day old. Perhaps Ai would know how to cook it. That meant she had to buy one and pick out other ingredients that would go well with it. Should she also buy rice? She had never made rice before. Did she need a rice cooker? She had seen the rice aisle, filled with many different bags, all sizes and colors. She hadn't known that there could be so many varieties of rice.

She clutched her shopping basket. Would it have been worth it to bring Ai along, if only to read her the Japanese? No one would recognize her as a robot, right? Kathleen was almost ready to run away, go to the convenience store, and just buy some instant ramen.

"Kathleen?"

She turned around to find Yuriko standing there. She was in her business suit, holding a laden shopping basket. She was looking at Kathleen as if shocked to see her there.

Kathleen felt her stomach plummet to somewhere around her ankles. It wasn't just the hair or the eyes. She and Ai were honestly twins. They had the same pointed nose, the same height and build. Even Yuriko's concerned look was replicated in Ai.

Kathleen couldn't feel anything below her chin, and she wondered how she was still standing. Why did Ai look like Yuriko? How could this happen? What did it mean that her cortex scan had managed to spit out a perfect replica of Yuriko?

A mistake. Like the gender, like everything that had gone wrong since Tamura had given her this assignment. It all was just some big mistake.

"Yuriko!" Kathleen spluttered, trying to sound friendly and normal and not like she was having a minor crisis. "Tell me what fish is good."

Yuriko stared at her and Kathleen realized she probably shouldn't have shouted that. "Fish?"

Kathleen tried to calm herself down. "Yeah, I've never cooked fish before."

Yuriko still looked at her like she was a little unhinged, but she seemed to brush it off and turned toward the display of fish. "The karei is good. It's pretty simple."

"Which one in the karei?"

Yuriko pointed to a flat, alarming looking fish. But before Kathleen could panic about having to buy an entire fish, scales and bones, Yuriko picked up some fish fillets. "Here, so you don't have to clean it." She dropped it into Kathleen's basket.

Kathleen sighed. This normal conversation was helping her nerves. "Thank you. Do you know what goes well with it?"

"Um, just simmer it in some soy sauce, mirin, and some ginger. You could probably just add any vegetables you like. Just serve it over rice."

Kathleen toyed with the fish in her basket. "Can you show me what mirin is?"

Yuriko looked a little annoyed for a second, but then her expression changed. "Your pronunciation has gotten better."

"My what?"

Yuriko motioned for Kathleen to follow her. "Your Japanese. Have you finally started taking lessons?"

"I—uh, yeah. Just a computer course." Was it really so noticeable? Kathleen had only parroted a few of Yuriko's words, after all. "I just started today."

"Must be a good program. But you should try to get someone you can practice with. It will help even more."

"Where would I find someone like that?" She didn't mention that she technically already had someone to speak Japanese with.

Yuriko turned down an aisle, found a bottle of something—Kathleen guessed it was the mirin—and put it in Kathleen's basket. "Well, any Japanese friend will do, if you just ask them."

Kathleen bit her lip. She didn't want to admit that she didn't have any Japanese friends. She had friends, of course. They just lived about ten thousand km away and were definitely not fluent in Japanese. But it just sounded too sad to say that she had no friends in the country she had been living in for three months.

Yuriko was silent for a moment, and then she turned around. "What kind of vegetables do you like?"

"What?"

Yuriko was already walking toward the produce area. "Anything you don't particularly like?"

"Uh, I guess I'm not that picky. I just don't recognize some of these..."

Yuriko reached for something that was probably cabbage and dropped it into Kathleen's basket. Then she grabbed for some sprouts and mushrooms, and Kathleen just found herself trailing along, not even bothering to question what was being put there. She was pretty sure one of the packages was tofu.

"You can also hire a tutor," Yuriko said. "I know a couple friends who will practice with you for two thousand yen per hour. If you find a uni student, they'll usually practice for free, if you practice English with them."

"Really?"

Yuriko shrugged. "Nothing fancy. But it's best to have a little more human interaction than just a computer program." She walked on, turning down an aisle full of rice and pasta.

Thinking of Ai, she couldn't help but blurt out, "Do you like giving people nicknames?"

"Nicknames?" Yuriko crouched down.

"Yeah, like, is it common? Here in Japan, I mean."

Yuriko hesitated. "Oh, I think I understand. Japanese people like to be polite, so we usually refer to each other's last names and use honorifics. But when we want to be friendly and casual, we drop that for first names. Sometimes close friends like to shorten to nicknames, just to be even more casual."

"Is it strange that I call you Yuriko, then?"

Yuriko raised an eyebrow, picking up some rice for Kathleen. "It probably sounds a little casual to a stranger. But when I lived in America, everyone called me by my first name. So I don't mind."

"Do you have a Japanese nickname?"

Yuriko flipped back her ponytail. "Yuri-chan could be used."

"Does anyone call you Yuri-chan?"

Yuriko gave her a strange look, and Kathleen realized it was a rather strange, if not invasive, question. Yuriko, however, shrugged it off. "No one at the moment."

The answer comforted Kathleen a little. Maybe Ai and Yuriko were different after all. Ai obviously loved the whole nickname thing, and Yuriko seemed only ambivalent. Of course, it was ridiculous to think that a computer simulation could be a copy of a human being. Thinking about it like that, them looking similar wasn't a big deal. Ai obviously wasn't Yuriko.

Kathleen felt herself breathe a little easier.

"Do you want me to call you Yuri-chan?"

Yuriko made a strange face. "That would be a little…inappropriate, I think. Yuriko is fine."

Kathleen looked down at her basket, if only to take a moment and not say anything stupid. Maybe it was the fact that she hadn't had a real friend since moving to Japan that was making her so nervous and idiotic sounding. Not that she was quite sure Yuriko was a friend. Coworker? Neighbor? Person she kept running into randomly?

She noticed Yuriko plucking some fruits from a display and putting them into her basket. "Do I need these?"

"Momo. Ah, peach. They are in season." Yuriko made an odd motion. "I've gotten the impression that you haven't tried much fresh Japanese food since you've moved in."

Kathleen flushed. "Is it that obvious?"

Yuriko stared at her. "You looked near a meltdown earlier. I'm pretty sure you've never been in here before. Let me guess, konbini?"

Kathleen didn't want to dwell on the fact that she was near meltdown in the middle of a stupid supermarket. She'd already had enough emotional trauma the past forty-eight hours. "Konbini?"

"The convenience mart? You've always shopped there, right?"

Kathleen shifted the weight of her basket. "I guess I just got used to it."

Yuriko reached out and pulled Kathleen's basket toward the registers. "It works well enough for a late evening or after a stressful day. But it's not healthy to live on prepackaged food. Plus, it's expensive. Put your basket here. Since you didn't bring any bags, you're going to have to pay extra for them."

Kathleen would have found Yuriko to be a little bossy, but right now, Kathleen couldn't help but be grateful as Yuriko easily helped her through the checkout process. In retrospect, it wasn't any more difficult than a grocery store in America, but it was nice to not have to panic about a language barrier for once.

Leaving the store, Kathleen half wondered if the next time she needed to shop, she could just ask Yuriko to help her again, but that would probably be a little presumptuous.

Without prompting, Yuriko immediately led the way back to the company housing. "Do you need me to tell you how to prepare the food as well?"

Kathleen flushed, but Yuriko was giving her a small grin. She sighed. "I'm not totally hopeless."

"Could have fooled me."

"Hey! You've just caught me at some very weak moments. Most of the time I am a strong individual."

"Yes, of course. Fine director for Mashida's premier PLC project by day." Yuriko's smile widened. "Hopeless foreigner by night."

That was another difference between her and Ai. Ai's smile had never felt so contagious. As much as Kathleen felt embarrassed by the teasing, she couldn't help but give a small smile back. "Hey, I've been pretty busy ever since I've moved here. I haven't had time to brush up on cultural norms."

"Well, that will soon change, won't it? The beta will be up in a few weeks, and you'll get a break. For a while, anyway."

"Will your department get a break too?"

She sighed. "The more PLCs that are released, the more chaotic my job will become."

"Do you oversee every PLC that's released?" Kathleen couldn't help but ask.

"No, but members of my team do. I'm mostly called in if there is a problem. And given the high production that Mashida is planning, I'm sure plenty of problems will come up."

Kathleen nodded. Yuriko probably had no idea what Ai looked like. She probably had only gotten some memo or email that a custom PLC was even made. As long as Ai didn't have any mechanical errors, Yuriko would never have to know of Ai's existence.

"I don't know if the beta will make things any easier," Kathleen said. "My team will have to probably make a lot of changes to the code once the results are back. Then, even if everything goes well, my boss will probably want us to get started right away on the next lineup."

Kathleen felt her arms sagging. After this trial with Ai was over, she would be thrown back into the office. She had paid vacation time, she knew, but when could she hope to take it?

Yuriko nudged her shoulder, making Kathleen stumble a little. "Hey, if you need to share a beer again, I'm usually pretty willing."

They were at the apartment now, panting up the stairs to their floor. "Thanks. Good to know I have someone to help support my burgeoning alcoholism."

"If you're paying, of course I will support you."

Kathleen smiled, hesitating at her apartment door. She kind of wished she could invite Yuriko inside so they could keep talking, but that might be a little too presumptuous. Plus, with Ai waiting there, Kathleen would never risk it. "Ah, guess I'll just..." She bit her lip and attempted a bow without becoming unbalanced by her groceries. "Dōmo arigatō gozaimasu."

Kathleen wasn't altogether sure she got the words right, considering she had learned them only a few hours earlier. When she looked up, Yuriko was grinning widely down at her.

"Dō itashimashite. Ki wo tsukete kudasai."

Kathleen nodded, a little unsure of what she said. Yuriko just turned around and unlocked her door. So Kathleen opened her own door.

"Okaeri!" Ai chimed, practically hovering next to the door.

Kathleen quickly closed the door behind her, hoping that Yuriko hadn't heard the greeting. "Why are you over here?"

Ai reached over to grab her bags of food. She smiled up at Kathleen. "Looks like you had some help."

Kathleen pushed past her. "Just a neighbor who made a few suggestions." She paused, then stepped into her living room. She turned to Ai. "How did you know?"

Ai set the food down, fishing out the peaches from on top. "Intuition."

"You don't have intuition. You have programming."

"Perhaps, but it's *your* programming."

CHAPTER EIGHT

Yuriko hadn't realized she was attracted to women until she graduated from college. Before then, she had never been attracted to anyone. Between moving from America to Japan, her parents' marriage falling apart, learning new school systems, getting into college, and trying to get a job, she never thought about romance or dating.

Then she met Michiko. She interned at Mashida with Yuriko. She was wildly talented but had a habit of being a little scatterbrained. Michiko was a small woman, with cute short hair and a wide smile. She seemed a bit daft, forgetting her wrist phone at home or laughing just a bit too loudly at dumb jokes.

Despite the growing numbers of women in the workplace, certain jobs, like in Mashida's engineering department, were still dominated by men. When Michiko walked onto the floor, she was surrounded by guys trying to impress her. Michiko, in her naivete, would let them flock to her.

Quickly, Yuriko decided that she would step in as a protector. She was taller than most of the men, after all, and she was not afraid to hurt their feelings. She didn't do it to win over Michiko herself—she had only wanted to help. Things just seemed to fall easily into place at that time.

"Ne, Yuri-chan," Michiko had said, turning to her. They had been sitting on a bench in a city park, not far from their work building. The sakura had just bloomed, the trees bursting with pale pink and white blossoms. The petals gusted down with every breeze, and the walkway and grass were dusted with them. Other people were spread out on the grass around them, mostly eating or chatting and admiring the petals.

"Hn?" Yuriko looked at her.

They had eaten lunch together every day for the last two months.

Yuriko had gotten into the habit of taking Michiko's train home, despite its route being in the wrong direction for Yuriko's apartment. Michiko had curled her hair, framing soft waves around her face. An errant blossom had snagged itself in her fringe ten minutes ago. Yuriko hadn't said anything about it.

"Have you ever kissed a girl?"

Yuriko had flushed but couldn't take her eyes away from Michiko. She had never kissed anyone, but she was too shy to just come out to someone like that. She shook her head.

Michiko smiled and slid her hand along the bench, fingers lacing with Yuriko's. "Do you want to kiss me?"

"Yes. I-I mean, hai." She had said it in English. A strange habit whenever she was nervous. Her brain seemed to cross wires, switching to English when she meant Japanese and Japanese when she meant English.

Michiko was grinning, fingers tight. "Good. Me too," she answered in English.

Yuriko let out a gasping giggle and Michiko leaned in to her, resting her head on Yuriko's shoulder. A strange country they lived in, where this girl that she cared about, that she wanted to kiss, could cuddle into her in such a public place. If Michiko had been a man, the old couple currently strolling easily through the park probably would be giving them dirty looks. As it was, they were ignored.

Yuriko would kiss Michiko later, after walking her all the way to her apartment. Michiko had stood on her toes, too short even in heels, straining toward Yuriko in the lamplight.

Yuriko tried not to think about Michiko too much. She wasn't even working for Mashida anymore, and Michiko was married to Kenji-san. He was a fine man and would take care of Michiko just as well as Yuriko had. He was someone she could introduce to her parents. He was someone who, despite not being able to touch as freely in public, she could really *be* with. No secret touches, no masquerading as just good friends. A real boyfriend and husband.

It was strange to Yuriko, now that her time with Michiko had come and gone, that what she missed the most were not the kisses in the dark or stolen touches at a nomikai when everyone was too drunk to care, or putting her arm around her on the train to steady her, or even holding her hand on that bench in the park. She missed that sakura petal stuck in Michiko's hair and how she had never reached up to remove it.

She wasn't sure why she wanted to go back to that sakura season.

What difference would it have made? Would Michiko have been too distracted to ask Yuriko the question that started their relationship? Or would Yuriko, so taken in the moment, have kissed her then? Not caring of the public space, not caring if people understood or didn't understand that two girls could love each other, in this country that thought it was impossible. That two girls or two guys could share something as sacred and beautiful as a husband and wife. That letting them hold hands in public was almost as suffocating as shaming them for it.

Instead what she had learned in that moment was how to hold herself in. Deny the beauty and the impulse to act as she really wanted. She understood what it meant to appreciate the sakura for just a few short weeks, and then to hope they would come again next year.

She opened her eyes to the early dawn light. She had opened her window in the night, hoping for a breeze to cut the humidity. The room was pleasantly cool, and she lay in her bed, appreciating that she could just relax. It was Sunday and, barring a total meltdown at the factory, she had the day off.

She stretched and buried herself a little farther into her duvet. She was perfectly content to lie around until noon.

Her doorbell rang.

She frowned. If that was Fujioka-san asking her to watch her dogs because she was going on another sudden business trip, then Yuriko was going to pretend to be asleep. Fujioka-san's dogs drooled about a bucket of saliva a day and tried to pull her arm from its socket when they went for walks.

The doorbell kept ringing, and Yuriko found herself getting into a rather foul mood. Her phone buzzed on the bed stand. She reached over and tapped it, reading the text projected in the morning light.

Sorry! I'm having a crisis! Are you home?

It was from Kathleen Schmitt.

Yuriko sat up, slipping on the bracelet to see the display better.

What is wrong?

Surely, she couldn't have gotten lost so early in the morning. Perhaps she was at the supermarket and freaking out over which nikuman to get. The thought almost made Yuriko smile. Probably with any other person, she would have been annoyed by such a show of helplessness. However, Kathleen was...well, she made it look kind of cute.

Please, answer the door. It's hard to explain.

Yuriko stood up and threw on some sweatpants, not bothering

to change her pajama shirt. If Kathleen required her to get properly dressed, then she could find someone else. Yuriko opened the door.

Kathleen was in the midst of tapping out another text. She looked up, pale and wide-eyed. "I'm so sorry, but I wasn't sure who to call."

Yuriko folded her arms. "What exactly is the problem?"

Kathleen made an odd gesture with her hands. "It's...can you come over to my place?"

"Can you not explain it here?"

"More like I can't *bring* it here." Kathleen reached out and gripped her elbow. "Please, you'll understand when you see."

Her hand was shaking where it touched Yuriko. "All right, but this better be worth it."

Kathleen tugged her down to her door, stumbling to unlock it. As she opened the door, she hesitated. "Also, this totally isn't what it looks like."

Yuriko was about to ask, but Kathleen opened the door, and she could see into the small apartment.

A woman lay there, wearing no clothes and twitching slightly on the floor. She was lying facedown, long black hair fanned around her. Yuriko took a step forward, a little stunned. Who was she? What was wrong? Had Kathleen called an ambulance? Did she know how?

Kathleen rushed forward. "She's not...It's not...It's a PLC!" She knelt beside the woman, holding up a wrist.

Yuriko approached slowly. "But the PLC hasn't even gone beta yet."

Kathleen shook her head as she tapped the wrist. Yuriko could see now that it was transmitting to Kathleen's computer, where lines of code were being displayed. "This is something of a pre-beta. I was given a PLC to run some field tests. It's only been a couple days, but now she's having some sort of breakdown and I can't figure it out." As she spoke, her eyes were locked to the computer display. She turned to Yuriko, pleading. "I think I broke her, and I'm totally going to get fired. You have to help me."

Yuriko looking back to the body. "Your PLC is a woman?" she asked without thinking. She stared at Kathleen, feeling like her entire perception of her was tilting slightly. She hadn't even considered that Kathleen was...

Kathleen's face went from white to a deep red. "Well, yes...but it's not what it seems. It's actually a mistake. She was supposed to be male. There must have been some sort of problem that we haven't figured out. She, uh, actually has quite a few physical…problems. But that's not important. I broke her, and if I can't fix her quickly, my entire project is going up in flames. You have to help me."

Yuriko looked back to the PLC, feeling like it was all a little too much information to suddenly take in. She blinked, pushing the thoughts aside and focusing again. "I have some equipment in my apartment. Help me bring her there." She made to lift the PLC's shoulders, but Kathleen looked stricken.

"I can't take her outside. What if someone sees?"

"This is a product for the company that owns this apartment complex. What is the problem?"

"But she is…she is naked!"

Yuriko slowly turned the woman over. Her eyes were closed, but she did look rather convincing. She looked up at Kathleen. "Did she not come with clothes?"

Kathleen was flushed, eyes darting around the room. "Well, yes. But when she started malfunctioning, I thought maybe she had bumped into something. Thought maybe if I could see a problem, it would be easier to fix."

Yuriko raised an eyebrow and Kathleen looked everywhere but at her and the PLC. Yuriko sighed. It didn't really matter. "Like I said, if anyone asks, we will explain. They will understand. Everyone knows about the PLC project—they just might be surprised at seeing one for the first time. Breathe."

Kathleen took in a gulping breath. "Okay. You got her shoulders? I'll get her legs."

Every PLC was slightly heavier than a human of their proportions. Steel framing and synthetic skin, while effective, were not lightweight materials. Lifting together, they were able to tow the body down to Yuriko's apartment. The morning had started out cool and refreshing, but by the end they were both sweating as they stumbled into the apartment.

"Put the PLC on the table," Yuriko instructed, quickly clearing the table of her supplies with one arm, scattering tools and parts across the floor. Together, they maneuvered the PLC onto the rough surface. The table creaked under the weight, but it was cheap and Yuriko had already banged it up with her own personal projects. "Hook her up to my system for a full check. I'm going to grab my scanner."

Kathleen was still shaking as she gripped the PLC's wrist to tune her to Yuriko's network. Yuriko pulled out her tool kit from her bedroom closet, dragging it into the main room. She took her scanner and started at the PLC's head. The PLC kept twitching, and Yuriko could tell from the data filling her computer display that the PLC was attempting to run some programs but kept running into a mechanical error, which was causing it to reboot continuously.

"I think this is stemming from a hydraulics problem. I'm going to open her up and take a look. Hopefully I can fix it, and then you can access the software without it rebooting unexpectedly." She rummaged for something to slice open the skin layer. When she turned back, Kathleen was still clutching the PLC's wrist.

"You're going to cut her up?"

Yuriko raised an eyebrow. Well, it was Kathleen's *personalized* PLC. She might be attached. "I think it's an easy fix, and I have the equipment to repair the synthetic skin. It won't even be noticeable."

Kathleen breathed out, and then suddenly dropped the wrist. "I'm sorry. I'm just worried about my report. This is a major problem and I'll probably have to talk to my boss directly about this."

Yuriko shrugged it off, leaning forward to make an incision on the PLC's right side. She didn't need a very big hole before hot water burst from the seam. The PLC stopped twitching and the skin instantly cooled. Yuriko looked up to the display to see that a total shutdown had occurred.

Kathleen relaxed. "Thank God, I thought she would never get out of that loop." She looked over. "What happened? Oh my God, what is that?" She pointed to Yuriko's lap, which was now soaked in lukewarm water.

Yuriko ignored it, instead diving back into the PLC to see what had ruptured. "The PLC uses water to cool and distribute heat throughout the body. You know, keeps the skin feeling warm to the touch, but the core mechanics don't melt down. Well, it looks like one of the links in the system got backed up. Caused an overflow and her wires got a bit fried." She reached around her for spare parts. "Probably just needs another connection in the area as a safeguard. Luckily, I've got some parts that will probably do the trick."

"So am I going to lose my job?"

Yuriko snorted. "Unlikely. This problem happens all the time. No matter how many tests we put the system through, it's hard to anticipate where an extra connection is going to be needed."

Kathleen leaned back, flopping onto the floor. "I think I saw my life flash before my eyes."

"When did you notice the malfunction?"

"Oh, probably three hours ago. She woke me up as soon as she felt something was wrong." Kathleen waved a hand. "You know, system protocol. I tried rebooting her, but it just went haywire from there. Been spending most of the morning trying to figure out if my code broke her or if something else did."

Yuriko sliced open the skin a little more so she could maneuver the parts more easily. She had done this so many times to prototypes, she could probably do it in her sleep. In fact, it kind of felt like she was. As strange as it was to be woken early in the morning to assist her neighbor in fixing a highly complex, state-of-the-art robot, she was *tired*.

"So, tell me," she started, hoping to stay awake, "why do you have a PLC in your apartment over a month before the beta release?"

Kathleen sat against her wall, stretching out her legs. "It's Tamura's fault, my boss. She actually wanted the beta release to be about now. I tried to argue her down. I guess we sort of compromised." She ran a hand through her hair, curly and frizzy in the morning. "I have six weeks to work out any kinks. And here I am, three days into the trial, and I totally break her down." Her eyes were swollen, cheeks pale. She looked like she hadn't slept in three days.

"So does anyone else know of this trial?"

"Well, my team does. And Tamura. I have to send them daily reports about Ai's progress." She rubbed one cheek. "Otherwise, I don't think anyone knows. Besides the people who directly built her, maybe."

Yuriko turned back to the PLC. The spare parts looked inelegant, but no one would be able to see. Yuriko secured them with her portable torch. "Unlikely. Engineering is making prototypes all the time. Some of them are even based on cortex scans. Most likely they thought it was just another test subject." With the links soldered on, she then flushed water down them, checking for leaks. She looked up as Kathleen grimaced.

"It sounds like you're repairing a faucet."

Yuriko smirked. "With the way these hydraulics are designed, it rather feels like plumbing." She leaned back. "Well, it seems all right from here. But I'm going to run some more tests before I seal it up."

"How long will that take?"

"Probably a couple hours for a full system check."

Kathleen groaned, hands tangled in her hair again. "I feel like I've been awake for twelve hours." She looked over to Yuriko, eyes soft. "I'm sorry that I dragged you into this. And I've sort of made a mess of your apartment…"

Yuriko was soaked by the water from the PLC. And with her equipment spread out, it probably did look a little messy. She shrugged. "I don't mind. If you had brought it straight to Engineering, they probably would have called me anyway." She yawned. "But I could use a coffee, if you're up for it."

Kathleen was quick to get to her feet, though a little unsteady. "Sure. Any particular type?"

Yuriko grinned. She couldn't help but find amusement in Kathleen's sudden enthusiasm. "Just make sure it's black."

Kathleen nodded quickly. "Okay, I'll be right back. Text me if you need anything else."

She was gone and Yuriko turned back to the PLC. The side was a gaping hole, revealing her emergency repair. She looked to the face, which resembled a sleeping woman's.

"Well, let's wake you up."

Yuriko tapped at her computer, forcing the PLC to start up. With the critical damage taken care of, the PLC should be able to assess any more damage. Yuriko would still do a thorough scan herself, but making sure the computer could read itself was necessary.

The eyes opened, a shocking shade of blue. It blinked, eyes scanning the ceiling. Then it turned its head, looking at Yuriko. "Oh. You're the neighbor." It smiled. "So good to meet you."

Yuriko stared at the PLC, feeling as if her eyes weren't quite focusing. The hair, the eyes, the smile. "*Fuck.* Why do you look like me?"

It wasn't just a similarity. It was *exact*. Like looking into a mirror that was moving and *talking*. Yuriko was almost sure that if she could hear a recording of her own voice, it would exactly match this PLC's. How did this happen? How could it happen?

"How were you made?" Yuriko demanded, the scan forgotten. This was now a priority.

The PLC's eyes went a little vacant. "Specify."

"Physical appearance. Randomization?" Though Yuriko knew that could hardly be true. The coincidence was too great.

"Analysis from cortex scan of Kathleen Schmitt."

"Really?"

The eyes snapped back to her. "Yes, really. I'm getting tired of everyone questioning my appearance. Didn't you all know what you were making?"

Yuriko wasn't listening. It wasn't random—it had read Kathleen's cortex scan and put together a physical appearance that would appeal to Kathleen. How else was this PLC similar to her? Did she have the same demeanor? Sense of humor? Unconscious habits? Did Kathleen realize that her PLC was a practical twin to Yuriko? She had to. What did that mean? Was Kathleen…attracted to her?

"Shit," Yuriko whispered, finding English to be much more satisfying than Japanese when it came to cursing. "Fuck." This was a lot to take in. She suddenly felt a warm tingling sensation in her chest, a mixture of surprise and excitement. Her heartbeat quickened and her palms began to sweat.

She hadn't thought Kathleen was interested in her. Hell, she hadn't even thought Kathleen was bisexual. Her PLC was not only a woman, it was *Yuriko*.

Then she remembered Kathleen's words from before, and the warm feeling quickly left her. Kathleen said the physical appearance was a mistake. What did she mean by that? The cortex scan had never made a mistake like this before.

She stood up, went to her closet, and pulled out a spare blanket. It suddenly seemed very necessary to cover the PLC's naked body.

"Feel better?"

Yuriko stared at the PLC. "Existential crisis."

"Because I'm a copy of you?"

Yuriko raised her eyebrows. She was a little frightened to see the PLC do the same. "You realize this?"

The PLC shrugged. "Yes, of course."

"Why do we look the same?"

"You already asked me that."

Yuriko frowned. "I don't want data. I want to hear your conclusion. Does Kathleen…?" Yuriko couldn't even say the words. She felt herself flushing and wished she could control her heart rate. She felt like she was having palpitations, switching between moods so quickly.

She hadn't really considered Kathleen before. Well, she had on occasion thought she was cute, and she did remember somewhat admiring her body when they first met and were pressed up in the train, but Yuriko thought about a lot of women like that. Was Kathleen actually interested in Yuriko?

"She isn't attracted to me," the PLC said. It sighed, sounding almost a little frustrated. Yuriko couldn't help but feel slightly disappointed in the response. Then she felt a little embarrassed for being disappointed. She wasn't interested in Kathleen. Well, maybe she had checked her out once, and maybe she didn't mind sharing beers and casual conversations with her. She certainly hadn't been flirting. Or, at least, she hoped she hadn't. She shook her head, trying to stop her rambling thoughts.

The PLC continued, "In fact, she was rather upset by my appearance. Though I believe it was my gender that caused the most distress."

"Your gender?"

The PLC only raised an eyebrow and Yuriko had to look away. It was too alarming.

"So she is not...Is she...?" Yuriko groaned, tugging at the ends of her hair. "It doesn't matter. I'm doing a full system check. Report any malfunctions."

"Hai." The PLC was smirking at her. With *her* smirk. Was Kathleen attracted to that smirk?

Her thoughts were getting away from her again. Yuriko turned to her computer display and ran through a basic system check. Yuriko heard the bell ring on her door. "Enter." The door opened and Kathleen stumbled inside with a konbini bag full of cans of coffee.

"Didn't know if any brand was better, so I just got them all." She kicked off her shoes and put the bag on the kitchen counter.

Yuriko didn't glance up. "Any of them is fine."

"Ai! You're awake."

Yuriko paused. "Ai?"

The PLC turned to Kathleen. "Ohayō!"

Kathleen handed over an iced black coffee to Yuriko. "Is everything fine?"

Yuriko took it. "Just going through a full system check. It'll probably take a couple hours. I have the PLC, um, Ai, awake so it can relay any malfunctions."

Kathleen was already scanning Yuriko's computer display. "Well, if there is any flaw in the coding, I can adjust that." She smiled. "But if it's the hardware, I'm afraid I'm lost. Like, I owe you, Yuriko." She gave an exhausted laugh. "I nearly had a heart attack this morning."

"Aww, I didn't realize how much you cared," Ai cooed.

Kathleen scowled. "You woke me up at three a.m., just whispering *error, error*. I thought the robot apocalypse had begun."

"Next time I'm having a complete breakdown, I'll be sure to wait until dawn."

Kathleen growled, burying her hands in her hair. She began muttering to herself and Yuriko only caught a few words like *idiot* and *bad life decisions.*

"Have you had any other issues with...Ai?" It was still strange to Yuriko that the PLC had a name. Did Kathleen name it? Did she know what it meant?

Kathleen drank her coffee thoughtfully. "Well, not really. Nothing disastrous, anyway."

Yuriko looked at Ai, who just glanced thoughtfully between them. Ai had said that Kathleen had been upset by her gender. Was it mistaken? "Nothing at all? Ai met all your...specifications?" Yuriko could feel herself clutching her coffee beneath the table and forced her hands to relax. She wasn't sure what she wanted to hear. It would be pretty surprising if Kathleen had been harboring some secret desire for her. They barely knew each other, but then... Yuriko found she didn't much mind the idea. Kathleen was attractive and cute and a little awkward at times, but there was something a bit flattering about the whole situation.

Even though the whole situation was completely bizarre too.

Kathleen started to nod, but then stopped. Then her face turned very red and she almost dropped her coffee. The words started tumbling out of her mouth and she said, "Well, there seems to have been a bit of an issue with Ai's gender. I mean, I've never been interested in women. It's probably some sort of cortex scan misinterpretation. I've already made a note of it. I mean, I have no problem with homosexuality or anything like that. I just think it would be pretty disastrous if customers received the wrong gender for their sexuality. You know?" She was breathing heavily.

Yuriko was actually rather more interested in knowing if Kathleen saw the resemblance between her and Ai. It was as Ai mentioned— Kathleen was more concerned about the gender. Did she really not notice? Somehow, it disappointed her, but Yuriko refused to be even the slightest bit upset. It was probably all some malfunction, as Kathleen explained.

Kathleen was very friendly, but she obviously wasn't interested in Yuriko that way. For Yuriko to even consider it was a little pathetic. She forced herself to push aside any unreasonable feelings. She turned back to the scan. "It would not be too difficult to change its appearance. The skin can be changed, added to, taken away, et cetera. Might take some time, but if this issue persists with other betas, it can be a superficial adjustment."

"Oh, really?"

Yuriko nodded, fingers digging into the aluminum can. Her chest felt tight and she attempted to will away the strange feeling.

"Well, I guess I'll make a note of that. I can discuss it with my group, but I think it would be too much trouble to change Ai now." Kathleen was staring at the floor, her face softly flush. "Besides, I've gotten used to her."

The knot in Yuriko's chest loosened and she finished her coffee. She looked over to find Ai staring at her, eyes glimmering. She didn't want to know what the robot thought of her. "Analysis?" she inquired.

"Inconclusive," Ai responded.

CHAPTER NINE

"Y ou will have to test Ai in public eventually," Yuriko said.
Kathleen sat down heavily in one of the open seats on the train. The only reason there was seating available was because she'd had to work so damn late. She had been out of the office for a week but had needed to go in to reconnect with her team. All her data was being compiled, and they'd held a meeting to analyze it. She hadn't realized it would turn into a five-hour session.

Of course, with the complicated mistake of Ai's gender, she should have expected a very long conversation. Tamura was convinced the cortex scan couldn't be at fault. Kathleen expected that reaction, considering Tamura directly oversaw that project herself and was probably trying to save face. At least Fukusawa had been the voice of reason, volunteering to look into the whole process of how the data from the cortex scan was converted into a physical form. It would take him a couple weeks to come back with a report. With so much of the project hinging on the success of the cortex scan, Kathleen wasn't sure if she wanted him to report there had been a flaw in the system or not.

Of course, if he found the cortex scan and physical manifestation were correct, then Kathleen would have a whole lot of more complicated questions to ask herself.

"Are you sure the PLC doesn't meet your personal specifications?" Tamura had asked her after the meeting, her tone not unlike a threat.

Kathleen had ignored the question. This whole pre-beta felt too personal for her liking, and she didn't want to debate her personal specifications with her boss.

Her back felt broken from all the pent-up stress. She needed to get into the office more from now on—she couldn't handle this once-a-week thing.

"I honestly don't think I need to take her out. I've had her talk to you and she's done fine, right? Isn't that as good as talking to strangers in public?"

Yuriko stood above her. Though she hadn't attended Kathleen's hellish meeting, she had happened to be in the same building that day. It was only natural that they rode the train back to the apartment complex together. "I help *build* PLCs. What you need is someone who doesn't know Ai is a PLC. Someone who can give a more random interaction."

Ever since Ai's breakdown, Yuriko had been calling or stopping by often to check up on them both. Kathleen was very grateful for the interaction, if only because it made Ai seem even more like a product test, rather than a freaky love sim who lived in her apartment.

She was also grateful that Yuriko never mentioned how similar she and Ai looked. Kathleen probably overreacted upon initially seeing Ai. If Yuriko didn't see it as important enough to mention, it was probably not that noticeable.

Sometimes she thought Yuriko might say something. It was usually after Kathleen had performed some test or scan, and Yuriko would be sitting there, staring at Ai like she was trying to solve a rather complicated puzzle. Then the expression would pass, and Kathleen would be left wondering if she was seeing things that weren't really there.

Kathleen groaned. "But it would be so weird." What if they did realize that Ai was a love robot? What would they think of Kathleen? "Besides, she has nothing decent to wear. All my clothes are supersized on her." Kathleen had never thought of herself as fat before she came to Japan.

Yuriko raised an eyebrow. "Then go and buy something for her."

"Wouldn't that be *weirder*? Buying clothes for my sex robot?"

Yuriko raised both eyebrows and Kathleen flushed.

"Not that Ai is like...*at all*. I mean she is...*guh*. But it's just what people would think, right?"

"You sound just like a Japanese person. Didn't they teach you in America not to care about what other people think?"

"Yeah, because in America people don't care. We are all strange. People in Japan *really* care. I've gotten dirty looks for eating a granola bar while walking down the sidewalk. Like I'm some kind of uncouth caveman slobbering over a leg of turkey." Kathleen realized too late that her voice rose. The other people in the train car were staring at her now. One man got up and moved several seats away. She looked up to Yuriko, who was attempting to hide a smile behind her hand. "See?"

Yuriko shook her head. "You're overthinking this. Come on, there are some great stores at the next stop." She moved to the doors.

Kathleen quickly got up. "What? We're doing this now?"

"Yes, why not?"

"But I...I don't know Ai's size." Kathleen knew she was just making excuses now.

Yuriko frowned, eyes narrowing. "I think I can guess it."

There it was again, that puzzling expression. Kathleen found herself holding her breath, wondering if Yuriko was going to say how exactly she might know Ai's size. Then the doors opened, and Yuriko's expression relaxed as she stepped out into the station.

They ended up not leaving the station because all the clothing stores they could ever want were inside. Kathleen had never explored some of Tokyo's larger train stations, though she passed through them often enough. Most of the time she was concentrating on not getting lost. This one had a particularly large shopping area, and a ton of restaurants as well.

Yuriko led her into one of the larger clothing stores. "See anything you like?"

Kathleen tugged on a couple blouses. She'd never been good at clothes shopping, and it had been a very long time since she had even gone. Some of her friends in America used to drag her out once in a while, which was how she had anything decent in her wardrobe. "I dunno, what's a good look?"

Yuriko scanned the racks. "Probably nothing flashy, if you don't want Ai to draw attention."

Kathleen looked a few shirts, but she couldn't visualize them. Would they be too shapeless? Would they look good? Too good? "I have no idea what I'm doing."

Yuriko turned to her slowly. "Would it help if I tried them on?"

Kathleen felt something stick in her throat and she attempted to swallow it down. "Umm, sure?" Was Yuriko implying something? No, she was just trying to be helpful. That had to be it.

Kathleen had only seen Yuriko in business professional or that one fated morning in sweatpants and a T-shirt.

Yuriko slowly took a shirt that Kathleen had been holding. "Okay," she said slowly. "What else did you want to see?"

Kathleen made a few random selections of shirts, pants, skirts, and even a few dresses on Yuriko's suggestion. She didn't want to buy too much. After all, Ai didn't sweat, so she wouldn't dirty the clothes. Besides, Kathleen really didn't want to take her out more than once.

Yuriko stepped out of the dressing room in a loose shirt and flowing short skirt. She stood awkwardly in the dressing room for Kathleen, tugging at the skirt. It was strange, because Kathleen had never seen her look so self-conscious.

"It looks good on you," she blurted out.

It was true. Yuriko had great legs. Kathleen could never wear a skirt that short—her butt would hang out the bottom. She realized that she was staring at Yuriko's legs a little too long. She snapped her eyes up.

"What do you think?"

Yuriko turned around to look in the mirror. "It seems fine."

"Do you not like it?"

Yuriko tugged at the skirt. "I don't think I've worn a skirt this short since high school."

"But it looks great on you."

Yuriko stared at her and Kathleen felt herself flush.

"Does that mean you think it would look great on Ai?" Yuriko asked quietly.

Kathleen tensed. "Well, I don't know. Without seeing it on her…"

Yuriko suddenly rolled her eyes. "I don't think you need to see it on her to know." She stared at Kathleen; her eyes felt rather like a challenge.

A challenge Kathleen wasn't ready to take on. She started to turn away. "Maybe a little too flashy for Ai. Why don't we try—?"

Yuriko reached out and gripped Kathleen's wrist as she was reaching for the next garment. "Don't be—" Yuriko started, voice loud.

Then she looked up, and Kathleen saw a shop attendant staring at them curiously. Yuriko released her arm and lowered her voice.

"Can we just be honest for a second?"

Kathleen could still feel the warmth on her wrist where Yuriko had grabbed her. "About what?" Her voice was too high-pitched to be casual.

Yuriko looked unimpressed. "Look, I know you said that Ai's physical appearance was a mistake."

"Y-yeah. Actually, we had a rather long meeting about that. I've got someone looking into the problem," Kathleen said in a rush.

"Did you ever consider that it wasn't a mistake? I mean, it would be one thing if Ai was just female when you prefer male, but Ai is…" Yuriko lowered her voice even more, stepping closer to Kathleen. "Ai *looks* like me, Kathleen. You have to realize that."

Kathleen found herself looking away, staring at the rack of clothes Yuriko was currently cornering her against. "She…it's not…" She could *feel* Yuriko's gaze. "I don't know why she does," she finally admitted. She looked up to Yuriko, pleading, "It's not anything weird. I honestly don't know why Ai was made to look the way she is. I mean, I have a couple of theories of why some of the wires got crossed. Like, maybe she's Japanese because I do honestly need help here in a Japan. And who is better than a PLC that represents the culture? Also, I do like blue eyes. So I'm not surprised there."

She was staring at Yuriko's eyes. They were incredibly similar to Ai's, but Ai was still synthetic. Her irises and pupils didn't move like Yuriko's did. The color was almost too vibrant with Ai. Yuriko's color was softer, a grayish blue turning near gold at the center.

Kathleen knew she was staring, and she didn't know why. Her heart was beating in her ears, and it was hard for her to hear Yuriko speak.

Yuriko's eyes almost glimmered. "Do you find Ai—or me—attractive?"

Kathleen looked away then. She had to. She couldn't breathe properly otherwise. "Well, I've never been interested in women in that way. But I suppose, I do think you are beautiful, in a way. I mean"—she felt like she was gasping for air—"you do sort of have legs that go on for miles." She attempted a lighthearted smile. Her lips twitched.

Yuriko took a step back, and Kathleen suddenly found herself able to breathe again. She also suddenly felt cold, as if being so close to Yuriko had given her a fever. She glanced up at Yuriko, wondering why Yuriko was giving her that puzzling expression that she had only given to Ai.

Then Yuriko smiled, easy and familiar. "Thanks." She looked down, extending one leg beneath the skirt. "I mean, it's sort of a strange situation, but thanks. I guess I'm kind of flattered." She actually looked a little more confused than flattered. Kathleen thought she sort of understood that emotion.

"Yeah, it's a pretty strange situation."

Yuriko turned to the mirror. "Make sure to update me whenever you figure out what went wrong with Ai. I'm rather interested to see the results."

"Sure. Yeah, definitely." There was still a lump in Kathleen's throat, but the tension was gone. The kind of tension Kathleen hadn't even realized had formed between them. She returned the smile, finding it easily came to her lips. "But honestly, even though you can rock an outfit like that, I don't want Ai drawing that much attention."

Yuriko smiled, eyes glimmering a little more than before. "Okay, something else."

They ended up settling for some rather bland shirts and pants and a pair of cheap shoes. They wouldn't look hideous, like Kathleen's clothes, nor would they be too stylish. Hopefully Ai would just fade into the background and no one would notice.

As they were leaving, Yuriko took Kathleen's wrist. "Hey, there's a great curry place here. Want to grab some?"

"I've never had curry that didn't come out of one of those packets."

Yuriko snorted. "You're really pathetic sometimes."

Kathleen made a face, but she was willing to put up with some teasing if she got some decent food in her stomach. She hadn't eaten since that morning. When they had been walking down the hall for some time, Kathleen realized that Yuriko hadn't let go of her wrist. It was a little surprising, but Kathleen found she didn't mind. She was half dead on her feet, and if she didn't get any food in her stomach, she would probably pass out.

Kathleen had never eaten in any sort of Japanese restaurant before. This one looked like a bunch of seats facing a bar table, and the waitresses walked up and down between them, handing out food from the kitchen. Yuriko took a seat and motioned for Kathleen to sit next to her. A waitress immediately appeared and handed them a couple cups of water and a menu. Kathleen noticed hers was in English. The waitress spoke to Yuriko briefly and then walked away.

The only Japanese curry that Kathleen knew was the brown gravy-like sauce with soft potatoes and carrots that came out of an instant packet. The only reason she knew of that stuff was because Fukusawa ate it almost every day at his desk. It was ridiculously easy—just heat it up in a microwave and add some instant rice.

This place was way more elaborate than that. They had more types of meat, plus fish and shrimp. The curry sauce came in all sorts of colors, from yellow to green. The English menu wasn't very helpful, barely giving enough broken description for Kathleen to understand.

Yuriko leaned over. "Do you like your curry spicy?"

Kathleen once had spicy Indian curry in America. She wasn't afraid to admit that it made her cry from the heat. "Ah, no. I like mild."

"They have a good vegetarian curry here. But there are also some great meat options."

"I'll take whatever you think is good."

"Even squid?"

Kathleen shrugged. "If you think it's good."

Yuriko smirked. "Are you telling me that you're one of those types who is actually an adventurous eater, but you're too afraid to go out to even find adventurous food?"

Kathleen folded her menu and took a sip of her water. "If you're asking if I'm that pathetic, then I'll have you know that I tried all sorts of food back in America. It's just a little different ordering here." She looked up and down the bar, finding mostly people eating alone, wearing their business attire. At least she and Yuriko matched in that way.

Yuriko flagged down the waitress and ordered. Kathleen didn't know if she should be grateful or a little peeved that the waitress didn't bother looking in her direction. Once the waitress left, Yuriko turned to her, resting her chin on one hand. "So, what is the craziest thing you've ever eaten?"

"Well, I've had squid."

"Let me guess, fried and breaded calamari?"

"It's hard to find it any other way in the Midwest. But I've also had beef and kidney pie and haggis and—"

"Is your family from the UK or something?"

"*And* Christmas pudding."

"Christmas pudding?" Yuriko sounded curious.

Kathleen sat up a little straighter. "You've never had traditional Christmas pudding, have you? Well, imagine an overspiced fruitcake that you soak in brandy, then leave around for *weeks*, while periodically soaking it in more brandy. Then you light it on fire at the dinner table."

Yuriko chuckled. "I can't decide if that sounds wonderful or terrible."

"It's terrible, because it's hopelessly hard and dry and full of fruit. And it's wonderful because it only tastes like brandy."

Their food arrived. Kathleen felt her heart quicken at the sight of fresh white rice with a wonderful yellow-brown curry bursting with steaming vegetables. It was topped with a greasy sunny-side up egg.

Even without tasting it, she knew why Yuriko had scoffed at her instant curry packets.

"So tell me, why have you tried all these fine English foods?"

Kathleen shrugged, watching as Yuriko used her spoon to break the egg and pick up some rice with her curry. Kathleen just mixed it all together. "An ex of mine had relatives in Scotland. I think he took some sadistic pleasure in trying to make me eat very traditional food. That kidney pie was pretty good though. Couldn't even tell it was kidneys." She inhaled about half her plate. "So you see, I'm not *that* pathetic. What's the craziest thing you've tried?"

"Well, I've probably tried some crazy Japanese food, though it might not seem crazy to me. For instance, whenever I talk about how my mother ate natto every morning, foreigners get freaked out."

"Natto?"

"Fermented soy beans."

"That doesn't sound too bad."

Yuriko grinned wickedly. "You've never had it, obviously."

It wasn't until afterward, when she and Yuriko parted for their respective apartments, that Kathleen realized what a good time she'd had. She hadn't hung out with anyone like that since moving to Japan, and it kind of felt like she finally had a real friend. Even though Yuriko was only hanging out with her to help her with work, it was still a nice feeling.

She opened the door to find Ai watching her TV.

"Okaeri!" Ai piped out.

Kathleen had no idea why Ai watched the TV. A computer couldn't get bored, right? Maybe it was just an effect of her programming to make her seem more normal and livelier. Kind of like how Ai would blink, though she didn't need to. It just made her seem a little less like a robot. Kathleen wondered if other PLCs would find random habits to occupy their downtime. Would a PLC pick up knitting, if their customer was fond of long silences?

Kathleen held up her bag. "Here. Wear these."

Ai immediately stood up, eyes lighting on the package. "A present? You're so sentimental, Kathleen."

"It's not a present. It's a necessity."

Ai took the bag. "Do you want any dinner?"

Kathleen removed her shoes at the entryway. "No, I ate with Yuriko."

Ai hummed, looking through the bag. "Let me guess. She helped you pick these out?"

Kathleen nodded, walking into the kitchen to get a glass of water. It was dark out, but the humidity was still sticky. "I also had to have a very long meeting at work today. So you're not allowed to have any more issues, okay?"

Ai giggled, walking into Kathleen's room to change. Kathleen was glad she was able to convince her not to change in the middle of the living room. She looked when Ai stepped out of the room. She was wearing a pair of shorts and a long shirt that ended in a ruffle. Kathleen would never be able to pull off that sort of style, but it worked on anyone who was too thin to have hips or breasts.

Ai grinned up at her. She had pulled her hair to the side and was tugging at the ends. "How do I look?"

Yuriko had looked better in it.

Kathleen blinked, having no idea where that thought came from. Wearing the same outfit, even with her hair styled similarly, Ai should have looked exactly like Yuriko. Yet there was something different, something that Kathleen couldn't quite describe.

She had seen Yuriko wearing that in the shop. She had even seen her smiling in it, looking just slightly shy like Ai looked now. When Kathleen had looked at Yuriko then, she had found it hard to look away. Her eyes had lingered on her legs and shoulders. On the tilt of her head and her bright eyes.

Ai looked good, but she didn't look quite as attractive as Yuriko.

Suddenly Kathleen was beginning to doubt that her cortex scan had made a mistake.

She quickly put her glass of water down, her fingers tingling and shaking. She took in an even breath. She found Yuriko attractive. Not just in a vague sense, not like looking at a model in a magazine. Kathleen had *liked* looking at Yuriko.

She closed her eyes, her mind and heart racing.

"Shit," she whispered, and because that had felt rather good to say, she added, "Fuck."

She opened her eyes and Ai was standing closer to her now. "Comparing me to your neighbor?"

Kathleen frowned. "You knew?"

"Of course. One of the first tasks of my programming is to be observant."

Kathleen rubbed her face with her hands. "*Why* is this happening?" She'd never had thoughts like these in America. Something had happened to her since she had come to Japan. She had gone a little nuts, between the lack of friends and the culture shock. She'd never looked at a woman the way she was looking at Yuriko. God, did Yuriko notice? She probably thought Kathleen was some dumbass or pervert or something. Or maybe just an idiot. Probably that.

Ai gave a soft laugh. "I know you know how the cortex scan works. It's not *random*. I'm designed based on your preferences." She shrugged. "Though it seems I've mostly gotten your subconscious preferences."

"Don't say subconscious."

"Then how about repressed?"

"Shut up! I'm *not* having a queer crisis," Kathleen shouted, and then immediately regretted it. The walls here weren't very thick, and even though she knew Yuriko was a few doors down and couldn't possibly hear…

"There is nothing wrong with being bisexual," Ai said, a little too soft and kind.

"I'm *not*—" Kathleen's voice was rising again. She took in a few ragged breaths, trying to calm herself. "I like the way Yur—you look, I can admit that. There is nothing weird about a straight woman admitting another woman is beautiful."

"And there is nothing weird about a bisexual woman admitting it either," Ai said impishly.

Kathleen glared. "I told you to *shut up* about that," she hissed. "Look, it was a mistake that you were made a female. I know that is for sure. I've never been attracted to a woman before."

"Before? Does that mean you're attracted now?" Ai smiled coyly at her.

"Not like that," Kathleen said firmly. "I'm not blind. You're obviously a very pretty woman."

Ai bit her lip. "All right, and what about Yuriko?"

Kathleen glared. "You and she just happen to look the same."

"Because a computer read your mind and knew you would want us to look the same."

"That computer misinterpreted. Just because I think you're attractive doesn't mean I am *attracted* to you. Or Yuriko," she added just a little too quickly. "And I'd appreciate it if you'd stop questioning me on the matter."

Ai shrugged and went to sit back in front of the TV. "I'll respect your judgment."

Kathleen could practically hear the *only because I'm programmed to.*

She put her glass in the sink. "I barely know Yuriko. I can't even say we are friends. More like associates. Neighbors. Peers."

"Ehh?"

Kathleen came to stand above her. "I'm *not* interested in women. Yuriko or anyone else. I'm going to bed."

Ai looked up. Her eyes were soft, soothing. They were Yuriko's eyes, but this wasn't Yuriko. Kathleen was feeling a little messed up.

CHAPTER TEN

Yuriko rang the doorbell to Kathleen's apartment.

Kathleen answered, barely dressed, in a tank top and pajama pants. The tank top strained against Kathleen's breasts, momentarily distracting Yuriko. Most Japanese girls just weren't shaped like Americans.

Yuriko brain stuttered to a halt. It wasn't like she hadn't noticed before that Kathleen was well-endowed, but Kathleen just never dressed to show it off. Now, with her low neckline and the tight fabric gripping her in all the right places, Yuriko wondered how she was going to tear her eyes away.

"Do I have to?" Kathleen groaned, leaning against the doorframe, the posture pushing her breasts just slightly closer together. She was obviously unaware of Yuriko's internal struggle.

Yuriko crossed her arms, feeling like she needed a way to contain herself. She forced her voice to sound normal, casual. Not like she was forcing air into her lungs. "You asked me to join you."

Kathleen rubbed her face. "A moment of weakness, I'm sure. Come on, I guess I have to get dressed now." She stumbled away from the door. Yuriko was almost glad to see her turn away. It gave her back a few brain cells.

Yuriko stepped inside, and immediately her gaze was drawn to Ai, who was seated in front of the TV. She was dressed and looked ready to leave. "Ohayō gozaimasu. Atsui desu ne?" Ai chimed to her.

"Sō desu," Yuriko muttered.

No matter how many times she interacted with Ai, it was never comfortable. She turned to Kathleen, who was disappearing into her room. She could just see a flash of skin as Kathleen raised the tank top over her head, and then the wall separated them. She looked away and tried to clear her throat as quietly as possible. Ai was staring at her.

She glared at the PLC and raised her voice to Kathleen. "Any updates since last time?" It had been several days since Yuriko had talked to Kathleen over curry. Apart from random moments at the station or outside the apartment, it seemed that Kathleen was rather busy. However she had called Yuriko last night, announcing that she was finally going to take Ai out in public, and that she could never do it alone.

"Nothing major." Kathleen's voice was muffled. "Fukusawa hasn't uncovered any obvious malfunctions in the cortex scan system. I also think he's getting a little distracted." She stepped from the room, wearing a T-shirt and jeans. "He won't stop texting me, asking me weird questions about what I've tested Ai with." She grimaced. "I think he secretly wishes he had a PLC himself. Though, if I had any choice in this, I would have gladly handed this project over to him."

"You wound me." Ai pouted.

Kathleen glared at her. "Are you ready?"

"I'm always ready for a date with you."

"This is not a date," Kathleen growled. She waved a hand to Yuriko. "Besides, Yuriko is coming too."

Ai raised an eyebrow at Yuriko. "I'm open for whatever you're into, Kathleen."

Kathleen went red and sputtered, "Let's just go." She turned toward the door. Yuriko glared at Ai, who only smiled sweetly at them both.

They walked to a nearby coffee shop, and Yuriko could tell that Kathleen was in a foul mood. Ai, at first, tried to draw her out, but then quickly fell silent. Yuriko was somewhat impressed by her tact. Of course, the PLC had been living with Kathleen for over a week now and was probably rather good at reading her.

Yuriko walked a little behind them both, not wanting to walk too close to Ai. Ai was wearing shorts and a long flowing shirt, her hair draping over her shoulders. Yuriko was glad she'd decided to tie her hair back, keeping to a pair of jeans and T-shirt. At least a normal passerby wouldn't be able to immediately recognize their similarity. She watched as Kathleen would stiffen every time a stranger passed them. It was humid again, but Kathleen was more red than necessary. Was she so afraid? Yuriko honestly didn't think Ai would be noticeable at all, given her very realistic design. Kathleen was practically jumping at shadows.

When they reached the coffee shop, Kathleen motioned for Ai to order. Ai spoke cleanly to the barista with no signs of hesitation or the jerking awkwardness that Yuriko had witnessed with earlier proto-types.

Yuriko left them to go find a table in a secluded corner. From there she could see Kathleen practically hovering over Ai, even though she probably didn't understand most of the Japanese. As they waited by the counter for their drinks, Ai turned to Kathleen, obviously trying to make some sort of joke. Kathleen only gave her a half-hearted smile.

They reminded Yuriko of a mother and daughter in some ways— Kathleen as the mother, nervously fretting over inconsequential things, Ai as the daughter, trying to impress and relax the mother at the same time. That wasn't the intended role for a PLC, but Kathleen wasn't exactly the intended customer for Mashida either. She was a creator, not a consumer.

Yuriko remembered when she'd first attended a Japanese school, after years of going to public schools in America. It was an international high school, full of kids like Yuriko who were fluent in English or had grown up abroad. Her mother had been worried sick, accompanying her there for orientation. She thought Yuriko wouldn't fit in, thought she wouldn't be able to handle living in Japan after being in America for so long. Yuriko didn't know how to tell her that she would be fine. That she would be fine as long as her mother was fine.

Kathleen and Ai approached the table with a tray of drinks. Yuriko was glad to see they had gotten her a black iced coffee. "Disaster averted?"

Ai grinned. "If I keep this up, maybe Master will give me a treat!"

Kathleen frowned. "Have your wires fried? Since when have you been this hyper?"

Ai rolled her eyes. "You know I'm programmed to be multidimensional." She took a sip of her drink, some sort of latte. "Besides, it's nice that you finally trust me enough to take me outside your apartment. Being cooped up in there makes me feel like some sort of love slave."

Kathleen sputtered, "You're *not* a love slave." She looked to Yuriko, eyes pleading. "Why did I program sarcasm?"

Yuriko grinned. "You have to admit that receiving a very expensive piece of machinery like Ai and just keeping her in your apartment is a bit dodgy." She shrugged. "But I'm under the impression that most of Mashida's demographic will probably have the same inclination."

Kathleen frowned and pointed an accusing finger at Ai. "You're not allowed to insinuate to strangers that you're being used as any sort of sex toy."

Ai pouted. "Yuriko isn't a stranger."

"She's a confidante, so I'll let it slide this once. But I'll never take you out again if you say something like that to other people."

"Yes, Master."

Kathleen ignored that, turning to Yuriko. "Thanks for putting up with us."

Yuriko inclined her head. "I wouldn't pass up seeing you argue with your robot like an old married couple."

Kathleen turned red. "You too?"

Ai giggled. "See? Too easy."

Yuriko started to laugh too but stopped herself. Was she really so like Ai? Would they start saying the same things?

"Yuriko-san?"

Yuriko looked up, feeling a little like she had been punched in the gut. "Mi-chan?" Her voice stuttered and she suddenly realized that she probably shouldn't have said Michiko's name that way. After all, it had been quite some time.

Michiko had grown out her hair, and she was wearing glasses now. She looked younger, brighter, somehow. "Yuri-chan! Hisashiburi."

Yuriko suddenly remembered who she was with. She stood up and switched to English. "Ah, Mi-chan, this is my neighbor Kathleen-san and her…friend, Ai-san." She found herself standing slightly in front of Ai, so Michiko couldn't look at her directly.

Ai spoke first. "Hajimemashite." She looked to Kathleen, as if prompting her, but Kathleen only nodded her head.

Michiko gave a small bow. "Good to meet you." Her English sounded practiced, but Yuriko knew that Michiko had never felt confident speaking it. Her gaze slipped over Ai and Kathleen with little interest. Instead, she quickly turned back to Yuriko, smiling.

Yuriko turned to Kathleen. "She used to be a coworker of mine at Mashida. We'll just catch up a bit, okay? It won't be long." She didn't really know if she wanted to talk privately with Michiko, but having her join Kathleen and Ai was out of the question.

Kathleen looked to Michiko, then back to Yuriko. She couldn't read Kathleen's expression. "Okay. We'll probably be here."

Yuriko smiled and looked to Michiko. "Are you free?" She switched back to Japanese.

Michiko relaxed. "Of course." She turned and walked toward the exit. "I was just leaving when I saw you there. Do Kathleen-san and Ai-san also work at Mashida?"

Yuriko opened the door for her. "Yes, they are both part of the PLC project. Running the software."

"Sounds exciting. I'm guessing that they live in company housing?"

The air was stifling, but a small breeze managed to snake its way through the buildings. Yuriko looked back to the coffee shop, hoping Kathleen could handle being alone. "Ah, yes."

Michiko smiled. "I do miss that apartment building."

"But you have a house now, right?"

Michiko giggled and looked down. She always seemed so demure. "Yes, though Kenji-kun and I hardly seem to be there. We are both so busy."

Yuriko felt something in her chest squeeze. She and Michiko hadn't spoken in years. She shouldn't be feeling anything at all for her. "So Kenji-san is well?"

Michiko bit her lip. "Yes, he is doing very well." She hesitated, standing in the middle of the sidewalk. "I…I never did quite apologize to you for what happened."

Yuriko looked away. She wasn't sure if she wanted to talk about this. She wasn't prepared. "There is nothing to apologize for."

Michiko reached out, fingers trailing the sleeve of Yuriko's T-shirt, not quite touching. "I know it wasn't easy. I know that what *I did* wasn't easy to deal with. At the time, I thought breaking up would be better for both of us. But I was being selfish. I wasn't thinking about you."

Yuriko moved away from the touch. "You made the right decision. You're happy now, right?"

Michiko's eyes were wide, imploring. A smile crept across her lips. "Yes. I'm very happy with Kenji-kun." She lowered her head. "But I still feel guilty for mistreating you."

Yuriko sighed. "It wasn't mistreatment. Our situation just didn't work out." She turned and started to head back to the coffee shop. "You don't have to apologize."

Michiko caught up to her. "I know it must seem very late, but I think it took me this long to realize just how much I must have hurt you."

The coffee shop was almost in sight. "It was a long time ago, Mi-chan."

Michiko reached out, taking Yuriko's elbow, stopping her. Michiko's eyes were bright. "I just wanted to let you know, that...that if things had been different, I would have chosen you." Her hand slid from Yuriko's elbow to her wrist, gripping it with her small fingers. "I loved you, Yuri-chan," she whispered.

"You're supposed to love Kenji-san."

Michiko gave a sad smile. "I do love him. More than I ever thought I could."

Yuriko twisted her hand away, glad that Michiko didn't reach out again. "Then I am happy. You don't owe me anything."

Michiko bit her lip, but a true smile started to grow. Yuriko remembered that smile from when Michiko's hair had been shorter. "You have always been the mature one, Yuri-chan."

She'd loved Michiko's hair short, the way it tousled and fluffed. Perhaps it was better now. It made her smile seem more mature. "I'm glad that you have Kenji-san. And I'm glad that we could talk." She stepped away.

Michiko took a deep breath and gave a short bow. "I hope we can meet up again."

Yuriko suddenly wondered what more they could say. *You broke my heart, but I think I'm mostly over that.* Or *Let's talk about how great your life is now that I'm not in it.* Yuriko didn't like to think of herself as the bitter type. It had been the first time she realized that being in love was harder than stealing a few kisses in the dark. "I'll see you around."

Michiko looked like she wanted to say something more. Yuriko turned around. She wondered if she should feel some sort of satisfaction for being the one to walk away this time.

She was ready to escape back into the relative safety of the coffee shop. However, Kathleen and Ai were already standing outside. Kathleen gave an awkward little wave, and Ai just cocked her head to Yuriko.

Yuriko knew Kathleen couldn't have heard what Michiko said. Even if she could, she wouldn't have been able to understand. Yuriko looked at Ai, whose eyes were following Michiko as she walked away.

Perhaps Ai… Yuriko wasn't going to think about it. Instead, she just put on a smile and stepped up to them. "How's it going?"

Ai locked eyes with Yuriko. They seemed set and determined, though her voice was light as she said, "I wanted to do karaoke, but Kathleen threatened to break me."

Kathleen scoffed, then whispered, "You have been programmed to imitate any voice. I'm not going to get shown up by a robot."

Ai laughed. "What if your perfect woman can't carry a tune to save her life? Maybe I was programmed to let you shine."

Kathleen rolled her eyes. "If there is such a thing as a perfect woman for me, you certainly wouldn't be her." She looked to Yuriko. "Is there a place where I won't be embarrassed by her?"

Yuriko smiled, and she knew it probably looked a bit strained. She suddenly felt exhausted. "I should probably head back. Do you think you both can take care of yourselves?"

Kathleen looked a little disappointed, but she was quickly distracted when Ai threaded an arm through hers. "I think we can manage," Ai said.

Kathleen shook her off. "Come on, let's go find a park or something." She glanced at Yuriko. "I'll see you around?"

Yuriko nodded and quickly returned to the apartment complex. She knew she was probably making Kathleen worried, but she didn't think she would be good company for the rest of the afternoon. She would apologize later.

❖

Yuriko leaned against her apartment door as she shut it behind her. She knew she should be embarrassed by what Michiko said, so out in public. Yet she wasn't—she had never been ashamed of her feelings.

Sometimes, however, they exhausted her.

Throwing off her shoes, she stripped out of her jeans, not bothering to put something else on. Even with AC, it was just too hot in this city. She was going to make a big lunch and sit in front of the TV and watch some comedian talk show host do something stupid.

She almost wasn't surprised, a few hours later, to find Kathleen at her door. Kathleen had changed into some sweatpants and a tank top again. At least this time, Yuriko was a little more prepared for the sight of Kathleen in a tank top. She smiled, opening the door wider.

Kathleen held up a six-pack of cheap beer. "Wanna split it?"

She didn't think she could resist, with her looking so relaxed and alluring. "If you don't mind that I'm not wearing any pants."

Kathleen looked down then and noticed Yuriko was only wearing a T-shirt and underwear. Her cheeks went slightly pink, and Yuriko suddenly wished she had put on a cuter pair. She tugged the hem of her shirt. She was a little disappointed when Kathleen's eyes jerked up to hers, expression schooled. "Well, I guess I'm casual too."

Yuriko didn't think there was anything casual about the way Kathleen's top clung to her. "How did your date with Ai go?"

Kathleen gave her a withering look. "I think it's encouraged her too much. Now she's offering to run errands for me and inviting me to other places."

Yuriko took the beer and put it on her table. She pulled a fresh pillow from the closet for Kathleen to sit on. "Sounds like you leveled up."

Kathleen took the pillow gratefully and sat against the wall. "Ai is no dating sim."

"Really?"

Kathleen shoved a beer toward Yuriko and then opened one herself. "Dating sims are *simple*. They don't think and learn. They just wait around for you to power up your PC and say the right things to them. They don't *plot*."

Yuriko grinned. "Ai is a charmer."

There was a moment of silence, and Yuriko looked up from her beer to see Kathleen staring at her. She looked pensive. "Did that woman…um, Michiko?…What did she say to you?" She flushed and played with her can top. "I mean, if it's not too personal."

"Oh, don't worry. It is entirely personal." Yuriko waved a hand to Kathleen's stunned expression. "Michiko is an ex of mine, from a few years ago."

Kathleen was very red now. "Oh."

Yuriko's fingers tightened around the can of beer, feeling her heart beat a little heavier. "Does that bother you?"

"Of course not," Kathleen said, a little too loud. She lowered her voice. "I just didn't expect it. I mean, in America I guess it's pretty common. But here, I just haven't seen it that often."

Yuriko let out a breath. "Queers are everywhere. Japan is just a little behind and refuses to accept that." She took a sip of her beer.

Kathleen shifted, looking a little uncomfortable. "So what did she say to you?"

Yuriko couldn't tell if Kathleen was uncomfortable talking about her ex or talking about how she preferred to date women. She was probably overthinking it.

Yuriko looked at her beer, slowly turning the can. It was cheap, the kind of stuff that only tasted good when the summer days were too hot to handle. "She apologized. I mean, we sort of had a rough breakup, and I think I've kind of always wanted to hear that from her. But I didn't expect it, after so long."

"Why did you break up?"

Yuriko looked up, a little surprised to find Kathleen looking so interested. "Well, to start off with, we were pretty young. She and I had just gotten hired by Mashida when we first met. At the time it seemed pretty serious to me, but it was also my first relationship. I don't think I was quite mature enough to handle it when her parents flat out refused to accept me."

"Oh, that sucks."

Yuriko snorted. "You bet it does. You see, in Japan, it's pretty common that couples don't introduce their partners to their parents until they are really serious. Like, they are definitely getting married serious. So when Michiko suggested that I meet her parents...Well, it just was a real blow to know that they weren't going to accept me."

"Do Japanese parents usually accept that sort of thing?"

"By *sort of thing* I'm guessing you mean gays and lesbians? It's gotten a little better over the years. Besides, Michiko was really close to her parents. They adored her. I thought that maybe their adoration would spread to me. Maybe." She laughed—it felt a little painful. More painful than it should. "I was pretty naive."

Kathleen reached out, putting her hand over Yuriko's wrist. Her hand was cold from holding the beer, but Kathleen squeezed gently, and it felt good. She let go and Yuriko forced herself not to reach out and take that hand for herself. In this moment, it wouldn't feel right. Not in this moment when she was talking about Michiko and her mistake.

"I was so ready, you know, to, like, take our relationship underground. Date anyway, no matter what her parents thought. But Michiko wasn't—*isn't* like that. She tried for a little bit, for my sake. Then her parents started trying to set her up with all these guys. I guess she felt an obligation to give them a chance. I always knew Michiko was interested in both men and women, but I guess I always thought that she would choose me." Yuriko sighed. "She chose a young man named Kenji-san. Her parents loved him, and I never thought she would too. But she broke up with me anyway. I was bitter for a long time, thinking she did it just to please her parents. Eventually, I heard from our mutual friends about them, how happy she was and how great he was. It took me a long time to realize that she broke up with me because she simply wasn't interested in me anymore." She finished off her beer. "You know, years ago, I would have been happy to get an apology from her. I might have demanded it, if I had the guts. But now…now it just makes me *tired*."

She looked over to Kathleen, with her wide eyes and curly hair. She sat with her knees pulled up to her chest, arms crossed over her legs. She rested her head on one shoulder, looking at Yuriko with an expression like pity, but also understanding.

Kathleen had admitted that she moved to Japan after a breakup. That she had hoped the change would help. Yuriko hadn't moved to a new country to escape Michiko. Instead, she had buried herself in her work, forgetting about dating or broken hearts. She wasn't sure which method was more pathetic.

"Did your parents ever know?" Kathleen asked.

Yuriko shrugged. "I'm pretty sure my mom suspects, but we don't talk about it." She rolled her eyes. "Most queer people don't. It's like we are pretending that nothing is different about us."

"It must be rough."

"What part?"

Kathleen waved a hand. "I don't know, being gay in this country. I mean, I know it's difficult lots of places. But Japan is so much more conservative than America."

Yuriko snorted. "It is and…well, it's kind of complicated."

"How so?"

"Do you know that it's generally frowned upon for a guy and a girl to walk around holding hands?"

"Really?"

Yuriko smirked. "They'll get stared at. Or get these hilarious glares from older people. Sometimes the old folks even do that childish thing where they put their hands up and obviously whisper about what a disgrace young people are."

Kathleen's lips twitched. "That sounds ridiculous."

Yuriko nodded. "It's the culture. It's been trying to change, but change isn't easy." She paused. "So, on the flip side, it's actually not really noticed if two girls hold hands. Girls can even hug each other in public. Even guys can get away with touching each other, like holding onto another dude's waist while riding a bicycle. Or putting their arms around each other's shoulders. Not even the most conservative Japanese person would care about that."

"Really?"

She grimaced. "For the most frustrating reason possible. There's a lot of queer culture in Japan, but queer people are largely invisible to the mainstream. So when two girls or two boys hold hands, it's all just innocent friendship and nothing more." She tilted her head back, staring up at the ceiling. "It can get ridiculous. Like, whenever Michiko and I went drinking with our coworkers, sometimes we got a bit drunk and loose. She could have grabbed my boob in front of everyone, and no one would have cared. They would think, *Oh, they are drunk and just having fun*, or something like that. I mean, some of our coworkers knew or just weren't total idiots. But…"

"That does sound frustrating."

"But would it be better if people did get offended? As offended as they would if one of us was a guy? Would it be better if people whispered behind their hands every time I tried to hold a woman's hand, whether or not I was romantically interested in her? Maybe it's better that most people can't conceptualize a Japanese lesbian. I can get away with so much."

Kathleen put down her can of beer; it sounded empty. "But it kind of loses meaning. I don't think anyone should be shamed for a little PDA like that, no matter their choice of partner. I think I get, at least a little, that you want others to take you just as seriously."

Yuriko looked at her. Kathleen's eyes were open and soft. There was hurt in them, and loneliness, but also warmth. Maybe she didn't quite understand it all like Yuriko did, but something in her expression made Yuriko feel like that didn't matter. Kathleen cared for her, at least in this small way. It warmed Yuriko more than the beer or the humidity could.

"Thanks."

"Hmm, for what?"

"For the cheap beer."

Kathleen gave a small smile. "The finest the convenience mart has to offer."

Yuriko reached for another. "I guess you got to leave all your baggage in America, right?"

Kathleen snorted. "More like it just emails me now. I did have hopes that moving to another country would keep me out of the drama.

You know, I haven't even met the guy one of my friends is dating, yet I've gotten all the trash on him." She wrinkled her nose. "Not including my brother who insists that I'm only making kinky sex toys for a living."

"It could be worse."

"Oh yeah?"

"He could know that you currently own one."

Kathleen kicked her with her leg. "Shut up. Both you and Ai are incorrigible."

Yuriko couldn't help but smirk. "Yeah, weird how that is."

Kathleen flushed, looking away. "You know, I have an early morning meeting tomorrow. So I'll just leave the beer here and head off to bed myself." She quickly stood, then walked to the door.

Yuriko stood and leaned against the wall, watching her struggle to put her shoes on. She almost wondered if she should say something. Not just thank her, but tell her...what? That she liked talking to Kathleen like this? That she hadn't talked to anyone like this, not even Michiko?

She sort of wanted Kathleen to stay, even if they only talked about stupid things. Even if they didn't talk at all. She wanted her to stay, just so she could feel the warmth in her eyes a little bit longer.

CHAPTER ELEVEN

Y"ou need to step away from your inbox."

Kathleen was currently lying prone on her bed, tapping at her wrist, sending rapid-fire messages to Fukusawa. She didn't respond to Ai with words, just grunts. She would rather go in to work and just talk to everyone, but Tamura insisted that she do her work from home. *Optimizing time with the PLC* or some other bullshit.

Ai stood in the doorway, obeying Kathleen's rule of not actually entering her room when she was in bed, but kind of still annoying her. "You know, if you're too *busy* working with me, then you wouldn't have to be glued to your wrist now."

"Yeah, just another report tonight."

"You have to write it anyway."

Kathleen glared at her. "Maybe I'm hoping it won't be so long."

Ai smiled, just a little too sweet. "Come on, let me take you out." Kathleen turned back to her wrist, but Ai wasn't so easily deterred. "I know you haven't been anywhere fun in Tokyo."

"Thanks for eavesdropping on my conversation with my brother."

"No problem."

Kathleen turned to glare again, but Ai was giving her a cheeky smile. She had been pretty persistent for the last couple of days, trying to get Kathleen to take her out again. Kathleen wasn't sure of the motivation. Did Ai see it as some way to help her with this trial? Did she think Kathleen needed to go out, especially since she'd practically been given a paid month's vacation?

Kathleen didn't consider herself a total introvert, but she did like her days inside, just relaxing with her computer. Back in America, she had friends who could drag her out on weekends or after work. She had liked that. Coming to Japan put a serious halt to those types of activities.

Perhaps Ai, in the recesses of her coding, was trying to remedy that.

Kathleen sat up. "How would you know where to find any fun places in Tokyo?"

Ai looked positively gleeful. "I do have a GPS installed."

❖

It was a bit strange, having a robot lead her through a city she had lived in for over three months. Ai was meticulously good at figuring out the complex train schedules that Kathleen never quite got the hang of. They would be sitting on a train, and Ai would be calculating which stop to get off next and which train to take and even which car would be the most empty so Kathleen could get a seat.

"Look at your wrist or something," Kathleen said.

Ai turned to her, eyes focusing again after making another transfer. "My wrist?"

"Yeah, when you do it all in your head, it looks kind of freaky. At least pretend you're checking your phone for information."

Ai nodded thoughtfully. She looked at her wrist. She didn't have a phone there, but it did look a little more natural. "We will be exiting this train in 1.46 minutes. Then we will transfer to the Yamanote Line in 3.45 minutes and—"

Kathleen waved a hand. "Just lead me there. It already feels like I'm lost, without you giving me two decimals."

Ai lowered her wrist. "You trust me?"

"Sure, why not?"

Ai smiled. "That's just about the nicest thing you've said to me."

Kathleen rolled her eyes. "I *built* you."

Ai leaned closer. "It's still sweet."

The train came to a halt, and Kathleen found herself in the swell of a rather crowded station. It wasn't rush hour, but Kathleen had never been here before. Even on her way to work she sometimes got lost. Ai reached out, taking her hand.

"Come on, it's the last transfer."

Kathleen let her lead, if only because Ai did have a much faster pace than her. Her hand was strong and warm. It didn't feel like a machine applying a calculated amount of pressure. It sort of felt nice and safe. Kathleen looked up, grateful that, for once, Ai wasn't giving her some snarky grin. She just had her head tilted, trying to see over the crowd. She had tied her hair up into a high ponytail, which beat against her back. She had small, fine hairs at the base of her neck, curling as if from sweat.

Kathleen knew that Ai didn't sweat, and those detailed hairs had been artistically put there by some mechanic. Kathleen looked around to the other commuters—tourists, some school kids, and people just running errands. Kathleen probably looked like a tourist being led by a Japanese friend on a perfectly normal weekday afternoon. Ai accidentally bumped into someone, but they didn't even turn, barely muttering an apology as they were swept away. No one could see that Ai wasn't the same as them. That she was a piece of expensive hardware and a very complex computer chip, wrapped in unassuming clothes bought at some random department store.

They arrived at Akihabara, and Kathleen found herself in a place she had never expected to be.

"You have never been to Akihabara? But you work at the company that is one of the world leaders of computer simulations. This should be home to you! It's the tech center of Tokyo," Ai exclaimed.

Kathleen looked around outside the crowded station. The buildings here were coated in moving holos, some of them for cartoons or TV shows, and some of them for food and drinks. Some of them leapt from building to building, causing the tourists to stop and take pictures.

"I get all my tech needs from Mashida. This place is a circus."

Ai laughed, tugging Kathleen forward. They were still holding hands, but Kathleen couldn't quite bring herself to let go. This place was full of foreigners. All of them meandered on the streets, stopping randomly and making loud comments. It was strange, after being afraid of the judgment of Japanese people for so many months, Kathleen found herself intimidated by tourists instead. They seemed more unpredictable, and when she made eye contact with them, they didn't look away first.

The holos were very distracting, especially from her vantage point underneath them. They fluttered like the northern lights, the music and sounds booming around them. Kathleen was surprised to find an advertisement featuring a bunch of young girls, all dressed in bikinis and singing. Another building had a cartoon woman with her bouncing breasts barely contained by a few ribbons.

"I always thought the Japanese were conservative."

"They are. But it doesn't mean they don't appreciate porn."

Kathleen whirled to look at Ai. "You better have not taken me to some red-light district."

Ai laughed, pulling her into a brightly lit store. "Not yet. Come on, I think you'll like this place."

It was an electronics store. The entrance was crowded with holos of employees, greeting and holding out pamphlets. One of them got close to Kathleen, and she could feel her phone vibrate with incoming mail. She dropped Ai's hand and checked her wrist curiously. The holo had sent an ad to her phone, offering a coupon. The holo, a woman with a modest haircut and tacky looking suit, smiled brightly and bowed.

Kathleen looked to Ai. "Could they send this to you?"

Ai nodded. "They have. Actually, I'm very receptive to their signals. I'm currently storing them all on a subdrive."

Kathleen looked at the lines of holos attempting to reach out with their data pamphlets to the crowds entering and exiting the store. "I wonder if the store can track their output and if they are wondering why a walking computer is absorbing them all."

Inside the store, a real employee greeted them. "Irasshaimase!"

Ai nodded, and Kathleen was grateful that she quickly moved them forward, lest the employee try to help them. More holo advertisements fluttered across the ceiling, outshone only by signs pointing to different departments. It was an electronics store and Kathleen was impressed that they had both old and new items.

"E-glasses!" Kathleen practically jumped over to the display. "I always wanted these as a kid, but my parents thought it would be a distraction." She picked up one of the sets of lenses. A tiny display lit up in the corner of her vision, and she had to blink to move through the small tutorial. She took them off, looking at Ai. "My boss has these, and I don't know how she can stand it. These give me a headache."

Ai laughed. "Come on, I want to show you some of the smart TVs."

"What's wrong with mine?"

She rolled her eyes. "Well, it can't auto-translate Japanese to English. And if you did actually watch it, you'd realize that your holo res is about five years behind."

"What is it with you and watching my TV?"

Ai smirked. "Maybe it's because it's just about the only piece of technology in your house I can connect with. Besides your personal devices, of course."

"That's weirdly sentimental."

Kathleen did not end up buying a TV, but she did buy a translator adapter. So at least she could finally watch her TV and understand what was going on. Though, based on the crazy shows she had seen Ai watch, she wasn't sure a translation would help her fully understand.

Ai took the bag from her as they exited the store. "I'll even try to program it so it can help you learn Japanese. Maybe take a few words out or give you some kana instead."

"I could probably do that myself."

Ai raised her eyebrows. "Yeah, but you wouldn't." She nudged her shoulder. "Come on, consider it a gift from me to you."

"For what?"

"For taking me out!" She smiled. "Of course, that means now we get to go somewhere I want."

Kathleen grimaced. "I really don't like the sound of that."

The store turned out to be one of the ones displaying an ad of some cartoon characters. That wasn't so bad, even though Kathleen had never gotten into Japanese cartoons. What was alarming was the life-size holo girl greeting them at the front door. Her large purple eyes blinked at them, and she smiled, tilting her oversized head. She seemed to be wearing some sort of maid's outfit. The kind with an outrageous amount of cleavage.

"Irasshaimase goshujin-sama!" Her voice was high-pitched.

Kathleen halted. "I don't trust this place."

Ai took her by the elbow. "Trust me, it's just an anime store."

"Is that supposed to comfort me?"

"Just be happy I'm not taking you to a maid café."

"And what is that?"

Ai ignored her, pulling her past the frightening holo girl. "I'd think you'd find this place pretty interesting."

The store was, in one word, *loud*. There was music blasting here, compared to the other electronics store. It was much more colorful, with merchandise and posters and movies and downloads and a whole host of other strange things crowding the shelves. There was barely enough room to walk, but the place was packed with people.

"Let's go upstairs."

"What's there?"

Ai was already pulling her. The signs in the stairwells had some English on them. The first two floors seemed relatively normal. Merchandise and movies and so on. The third floor said *Male Comics*

18+. The fourth floor was labeled *Female Comics 18+*. The fifth floor was *Games 18+*.

"I don't trust this place," she said again.

Ai laughed. "Imagine if I brought you to an actual porn shop."

"This isn't one?"

As they climbed the stairs, the poster GIFs became more lewd, more revealing. Some of the posters called out when they walked by. Kathleen couldn't understand them, but she didn't quite like the tone.

"You should definitely check out the dōjinshi."

Ai was trying to pull her onto the fourth floor—Female Comics 18+. Kathleen looked inside, glad it wasn't as overly porny as the guy stuff had looked as they passed the third floor. That didn't mean she was safe. "I don't think so."

"Come on. Think of it as a cultural experience."

Kathleen glared.

Ai sighed, rolling her eyes. "You're a full-grown woman. Why do boobs and dicks frighten you?"

"In essence, they don't." Kathleen took a step away from the stairwell. "It's the fact that they are so...*fake* that weirds me out."

There were comics everywhere. Or, as Ai called them, dōjinshi. While ebooks were vastly more popular, some printing traditions, it seemed, would never die. Kathleen picked one up, finding it wrapped in plastic. A couple of cartoon guys were humping on the front cover, so she had an idea of what it could be about.

"It's so short." It couldn't have been more than ten pages. She looked to Ai, who was browsing through another stack. "What is the appeal?"

"You probably wouldn't recognize it, but these are all characters from popular anime. People, or small groups, draw little fan comics called dōjinshi and publish them." Ai held up one. "People like it because then they can read more about their favorite characters."

"Having sex?"

Ai grinned. "Probably."

"How can this place be full of gay dudes if people refuse to acknowledge that there are gay people?"

"Well, anime and BL manga aren't generally considered reality. Also, I don't think you programmed me to be able to explain why people and cultures can hold double standards. Come on, I think there are a few in here that you'd be interested in."

"Really?" Kathleen was dubious.

Ai looked around. Even though the shelves up here were just as packed as on the lower floors, at least there weren't so many people. The music was quieter too. Kathleen felt a little less awkward, even though she was looking at cartoon porn.

She was flipping through a collection of wrist charms when Ai presented her with a small collection of dōjinshi, looking way too proud of herself.

Kathleen took them with some reservation. On the covers, instead of the guys that seemed prolific on this floor, there were girls embracing instead. Kathleen frowned at Ai, pretty sure she was making fun of her. "If you wanted to show me girl-on-girl porn, you could have done that the floor below us and saved my breath."

Ai held up her hands. "This is different. These are drawn for women by women. It used to be pretty rare, but it's getting more common now."

"You just really want me to buy lesbian porn, don't you?"

Ai pretended to look innocent. "Do I seem biased?"

Kathleen tried to hand them back, but Ai was having none of it. "Just try them out, please? They are short and easy, so you can practice your Japanese translating them."

"Didn't you say these were based on anime? I've never watched anime."

"I've been following these shows on TV. All the more reason you should watch TV with me."

Kathleen sighed. "Will you ever give up trying to hit on me?"

Ai looked up at her, eyes wide and slightly biting her lower lip. "I was made to be your Personal Love Companion, after all."

"Don't remind me."

Kathleen didn't know why. Maybe it was because Ai was looking a little put out. Maybe because Ai had already made it a pretty enjoyable day for her. Maybe it was because Kathleen was in a *Why the hell not?* sort of mood. She bought the stupid comics. Besides, they weren't that expensive.

"One more floor," Ai cheered as they headed back up the stairs.

"I'm not buying a game. I don't have time for games."

Ai looked just a little too pleased with herself. "I think you'll like these games."

When they reached the floor, Kathleen suddenly realized why. They were mostly dating sim games. Ai was already tugging on her elbow, pulling her to an older selection. "See anything familiar?"

Kathleen didn't need her prompting. She reached out and took the casing from the shelf of a game she had worked on about five years ago: *Love Love Date!* She had never bought a copy for herself—the company had provided her with a comp copy. She hadn't seen it like this, all packaged with a cartoon girl waving on the front. In the game they were all 3-D, before 4-D holo games had gotten big.

All the characters were girls, meant for a male audience. They all had distinct personalities and the user could date them by carrying them around on their phone, taking them to different places, and having topical conversations. They weren't near the complexity of a PLC, but this was one of Kathleen's first projects for Mashida. She had mostly been debugging the system, not the coding she performed now.

She hadn't thought of it as a weird cartoon porn game. It had been a chance to prove herself. She had dated each girl, trying to find weird glitches, faults, and ways to improve them. She hadn't seen it as uncomfortable; it was her job.

She looked up at Ai, who was grinning at her. She had been much more involved in the PLC project than anything in *Love Love Date!* Maybe that's why Ai felt different. Ai was more personal to Kathleen. More personal than what a cortex scan could dredge up. Ai was *made* by Kathleen. She was here, in this strange, fascinating foreign country because of Ai. Ai existed because Kathleen had decided to come here at all.

Granted, the PLC project would have gone on if she hadn't accepted the promotion. Yet Ai wasn't just the PLC project—she was Kathleen's PLC project.

Ai had taken her to this place, where she probably would have never been interested in going otherwise. Ai had brought her here and found things for her to enjoy. New things for her to discover. Ai had brought her to the top floor of this building to show her something that she had forgotten. Something that used to be her greatest achievement.

Kathleen looked down at the package, feeling more than a little sentimental. "I never played it in Japanese. They had translators for English by the time I worked on it."

Ai put her hand on Kathleen's wrist. "Then maybe it would be good to buy it now and practice your Japanese?"

Kathleen nodded, a little ashamed that she was feeling close to tears. "Yeah."

When they left the store, it was late afternoon. The sun was setting, though the heat still lingered. Kathleen wasn't so overwhelmed by the crowds anymore. She let Ai take her hand anyway. If she was a real customer for this product, she would want to hold Ai's hand. She would love that Ai had the initiative to bring her out and show her a good time. She would be pleased that no one on the street could tell that Ai wasn't a real human. Kathleen supposed it was probably because she was real enough.

They were almost back to the station, and Ai had mentioned getting some food, when something went terribly wrong.

Ai froze in the street, and Kathleen could feel the strength leave her grip. Kathleen quickly put her arm around her, in case she was going to fall over, and tried to see her face. Ai's eyes were stuttering in their sockets. She whispered, "Failure. Suggest reboot."

Kathleen looked around, but no one was paying attention to them. "Don't reboot. Can you walk?"

"Failure."

Kathleen bit her lip. Something was overwhelming Ai's system. Was it the heat? The exercise? Kathleen sent a quick text to Yuriko, warning of an impending emergency in Akihabara. She didn't know what else to say. "Um, stop performing all AI functions. Keep motor functions. Uh, keep your eyes open and listen for direct instructions."

Kathleen wasn't sure if it was the proper thing to say, but Ai immediately relaxed her stance, keeping her head up and forward. Her eyes were blank now; she had no expression. It was truly alarming to look at and very much like a robot.

"Walk with me." Kathleen took Ai's elbow, and she promptly began to walk. Kathleen kept her grip tight, even though Ai didn't seem to have problems with balancing.

Kathleen's phone buzzed and she tapped her wrist. Yuriko had responded. *I'll be at the station in twenty minutes. Where can I meet you?*

Kathleen looked around. She needed a quiet spot where people wouldn't look too closely at Ai, who wasn't even blinking now. She decided on a café near the station. Hopefully, Yuriko could find her there. She led Ai inside and quickly bought a simple coffee, just so the employees wouldn't stare at them.

She put Ai down in a booth and sent a message to Yuriko, letting her know where they were. Kathleen sat next to Ai, taking her wrist and trying to get her to connect with Kathleen's phone. Her phone wouldn't be as good as her home computer, but maybe it would give her some hint about Ai's sudden failure. Ai wasn't able to connect, and Kathleen didn't know if it was because her phone was incapable or if the area's Wi-Fi was interfering.

"Ai? Can you list your errors?"

Ai opened her mouth, but no words came out. Kathleen could hear something like her mechanics working, but there was nothing else. Kathleen squeezed her wrist, as if it could help Ai connect better.

"Don't speak," she whispered. "We will get you back to my place, and Yuriko and my computer can figure it out."

Ai closed her mouth.

"Kathleen!"

She looked up, grateful to see Yuriko rushing inside. She was still wearing her work clothes—a blouse and pencil skirt with a pair of pumps. She was winded, but she immediately leaned over Kathleen and Ai.

"Total failure?"

Kathleen nodded. "She suggested a reboot before she froze. I have her on direct orders only, so she can walk. But she can't talk, nor is she responding in any way."

Yuriko turned to Ai. "Stand up. We should get back to the apartment."

Ai didn't move. Kathleen nearly started to panic. "Ai, you need to stand and follow us." Ai stood, jerking and lacking any of the grace that she had before. Kathleen took her elbow, looking to Yuriko. "Must be my priority orders only. Can you lead the way? I don't think I could figure it out on my own."

Yuriko nodded. "The trains are crowded now, so try not to lose her."

Kathleen tightened her grip on Ai's elbow. Yuriko took them into the station, and Kathleen felt a familiar panic seize up on her. She never liked rush hour—she got lost too many times. That first day was the worst—the crush of bodies, the announcements she couldn't understand, the flickers of holo ads and Help kiosks. There were so many people, most of them dressed in the same suit or professional attire. All of them Japanese, all of them ignoring her.

She had slowly learned how to deal with it and not totally panic.

That familiar sensation was creeping up on her. She clutched Ai's arm, struggling to keep up with Yuriko. Ai was keeping pace with them, but Kathleen didn't know if there was a limit. How bad was Ai's failure? Would she continue to degrade? What if she lost all power on the train? How could they explain it?

Yuriko took Kathleen's free hand, looking back to her. She gave her a small smile. "We'll make it home."

Kathleen remembered how, just earlier that day, Ai had taken her hand. She had walked before her, just like Yuriko now, leading her with a firm grip. Yuriko's hair was also tied up, and Kathleen could see those small hairs on her neck, curling with real sweat. She was breathing heavier than Ai had. Her hand was a little clammier. Yet Kathleen felt infinitely safer in her grasp. Ai was a machine, a malfunctioning one. If Yuriko, or Kathleen for that matter, were to collapse in the street, people would help. People would know what to do. Only Yuriko and Kathleen could help Ai. They were very far from the equipment they needed to do so.

The train was bursting with commuters. Yuriko took Ai from Kathleen, trying to position her in the crowd. Kathleen followed after, feeling the doors slide close behind her. Yuriko had managed to maneuver Ai into a corner between the door and a partition blocking the seats. Kathleen managed to get shoved up against Yuriko's back.

"She okay?" she whispered.

"She is the same," Yuriko replied over her shoulder. "We caught an express. It'll cut our time down, and we'll make fewer stops. You okay?" She kept her voice down in the quiet train car.

Kathleen sighed, pressing her forehead against Yuriko's shoulder. She smelled like fresh laundry and something like motor oil. "I think I've managed to dodge a panic attack. Thank you for coming," she murmured.

Yuriko sighed. "It's no problem. But can you tell me one thing?"

Kathleen looked up, which practically put her chin on Yuriko's shoulder. "What?"

"Why is Ai carrying these bags of dōjin and love sim games?"

Kathleen had almost totally forgotten about her purchase. She let out a short laugh and pressed her face between Yuriko's shoulder blades. Then, just because she was feeling relieved and stressed all at once, she put her arms around Yuriko's waist. She liked the feel of her. She felt stable in the crowded train car and warmer than the other bodies pressed around them.

"Just a cultural experience."

Chapter Twelve

Y ou should have told me," Kathleen muttered.
"I'm afraid that I didn't anticipate the problem."

Kathleen glared at Ai. "You were automatically downloading every ad and coupon and whatnot in a one-block radius of Akihabara. How could that not be a problem?"

Ai shrugged, both arms on the table, slouching. "I'm programmed to absorb knowledge so that I can learn."

Kathleen sighed, turning back to her display. "Ads from department stores aren't knowledge. So I'm writing new code for you so this won't happen again."

"Thank you, Kathleen."

"Don't thank me. Just try to tell me about any more anomalies, okay? I'd like to find the problems before you suffer a major break-down."

Kathleen had only just rebooted Ai. After the disaster at Akihabara three days ago, Kathleen shut her down completely once they reached her apartment. It didn't take long to scan Ai's system to see what the problem was, but it took a long time and many conference calls to figure out how to fix it. For almost twenty hours Kathleen had been programming Ai with the new update. More work was needed, but it would be easier with Ai awake now.

"Report functions."

Ai sighed, obviously tired of this repeated order. "All systems go. Prepare for launch."

Kathleen glared.

"It's the same report as ten minutes ago." Ai rested her cheek on the table. "Come on, Kathleen. Let's go *out*. Let's have fun. You remember daylight, right?"

"It's nearly nine p.m., and you're not going anywhere until this patch is finished."

"When will you finish it?"

"Hopefully I'll have the bones of it for Fukusawa to look over tomorrow morning. Report memory functions."

Ai sighed a little more dramatically. "Fifty-seven percent cognitive functions."

"Not good enough."

"Before Akihabara, I was running at only sixty-eight percent."

Kathleen frowned. "That is way below our testing average."

Ai grinned. "I guess I'm outperforming the tests, and you didn't even notice."

"Noticing is not the point." Kathleen quickly sent another text to Fukusawa. "You should be ninety percent or higher, unless for short bursts of high functions. That's it—you're reporting all your functions to me every morning."

"Hai, okaasan."

"Urusai," Kathleen muttered.

Ai giggled, sitting up. "Someone has been studying. But that word wasn't in my lessons."

Kathleen held up her wrist. "I bought a game in Akihabara, remember? Even without an English translation, I have most of the dialogue memorized. Guess I learned some new words."

Ai put a hand to her chest. "You"—she pointed a finger—"you're cheating on me!"

"Hardly. The AIs in the game are practically prehistoric compared to yours." Kathleen looked back to her wrist. Fukusawa had already replied to her text. Guess they both were having late nights.

"But you're still talking to other women behind my back," Ai went on.

"And I talk to Yuriko all the time. You've never had a problem with that before." Kathleen sent a quick reply to Fukusawa. It was nearly ten—she wasn't going to get into an argument with him about particulars. He could see her product in the morning and judge her then.

"Yuriko is different."

"Different how?"

"Because she's real to you."

Kathleen looked up. Ai was giving her a pensive expression, eyes wide, as if she was trying to see something in Kathleen. "Yeah, she's a real person."

"That's not what I meant."

"Then what did you mean?"

Ai waved a hand. "What I mean is that when you care for her, it's real."

Kathleen's doorbell rang. She still stared at Ai, with her startling blue eyes. "I...come in."

The door banged open. Yuriko stepped inside. "Oh, good, you're both still here in the same position that I left you in...yesterday?" Kathleen looked up to Yuriko's grin. "Come on, we're going out."

"What?"

Yuriko grimaced. "Have you even opened a window in forty-eight hours? You definitely need to get out. There's a nomikai happening tonight, and I'm now officially inviting you." She looked around, probably trying to figure out why Kathleen was staring at her like a mute fish.

Kathleen blinked. "What is a nomikai?"

"Japanese drinking party. My coworkers are having one tonight because we are all tired and need to get drunk. I figured you'd understand. Now I'm going to change. You put on something...decent."

Then Yuriko just whirled out of the apartment. Kathleen turned to Ai.

"You'd better go," Ai said softly, but she was smiling.

❖

Yuriko called the restaurant an izakaya. Kathleen called it *loud*.

They were led to a private room at the restaurant, filled with Yuriko's coworkers from Engineering. They had already gotten started, all sitting around a large table heaped with food. They all cheered when Yuriko and Kathleen entered, and they were quickly handed glasses of beer.

Yuriko sat Kathleen down next to her, grinning. "Eat and drink. It's all you can eat for a couple hours."

Kathleen looked at the spread. Fried chicken and potatoes. Some sort of noodles and salads. They even had pizza, though it didn't look nearly as appetizing as the rest. Most of the people were still in their work clothes, though some had changed, like Yuriko, into something more casual. The beer was cheap, but it was cold in the stifling room.

"Ne, Yuriko-chan, introduce your friend." It was a woman sitting next to Kathleen. She had short hair which had been bleached to a light brown. She wore large red glasses and had a black bow in her hair. She smiled to Kathleen.

Yuriko leaned over. "This is Kathleen. She's in Development, working on the PLC project. Kathleen, this is Mitsu Kojima-san. She works in Quality Control with me."

"Call me Mitsu-chan." She held out a hand, smiling brightly. She had rainbow colored braces, the kind that didn't do anything, just as a fashion statement. "Yuriko says you both live in the company housing here in Mastudo? Waa, I'm so jealous! I live in the complex in Saitama and it's so gishi gishi." She had a strong accent and she spoke with a very high voice.

Yuriko piped up. "She means it's old."

Mitsu sighed. "I'm hoping I can move out with my boyfriend soon, so I won't have to share a kitchen anymore."

"Doesn't your boyfriend live with his parents?"

Mitsu pouted. "Don't remind me." She held up her glass. "Ne, Kathleen, need me to fill up your cup?" Kathleen let her and then Mitsu filled her glass too, drinking heartily.

Mitsu seemed to be a pro at finding people around the table with even a little bit of beer gone. Kathleen didn't know why, but Mitsu seemed incapable of taking a refill for herself without first topping off someone else's. Kathleen would have just filled Mitsu's glass herself. Except everyone, not just Mitsu, was ever vigilant at making sure Mitsu's glass never became half empty.

The man across from Kathleen was Yasuo Mori. All the women at the table, after a few drinks, started calling him Mori-senpai. He was probably the youngest at the table, with way too much product in his hair and a flashy suit. He actually had programming experience, though he came to Mashida as a technician. He apparently studied abroad in France during college. His English had a strange French accent to it.

"I would have joined Development, but I wanted to *learn* more. Really get my hands *into* the systems, yes?"

"Oh, tell me more, Mori-senpai. What else would you want to get your hands *into*?" Mitsu giggled. Mori frowned but continued on about some sort of mechanical project he was undertaking.

Yuriko whispered to Kathleen, "Also, he wanted to hit on his coordinator, Saiki-san." She pointed down the table. "She's the glamorous one."

Kathleen didn't need further clarification. Saiki was obviously the woman with long, waving hair and full red lips. Lips that matched her tailored suit jacket and high skirt. She shrugged off the jacket, probably because of the heat, and most of the people in the room looked over. Saiki was very well-endowed, and her thin cotton blouse strained against her chest.

Kathleen looked back to Yuriko. "Would you date her?"

She hadn't meant to say that, but she might have had her glass refilled by Mitsu too many times. Yuriko looked a little confused, but a woman across the table suddenly spoke up. "Yuriko's only interested in the small and cute types," she shrieked, and a few people laughed.

Yuriko rolled her eyes. "Don't get any ideas, Asada-san."

More people laughed, and Mitsu practically leaned on Kathleen to talk to Yuriko. "Eh, eh? I heard you dated Michiko-san, but I never knew you had a type."

Yuriko seemed surprised. "You knew Michiko-san?"

Mitsu shrugged. "A little, before she left. Oh! Gomen. I'm being rude, ne?"

Yuriko waved a hand, holding out her glass. "It was a long time ago. But you can fill up my glass, and I'll be soothed."

Mitsu did so gladly.

Kathleen wondered, after Yuriko's random encounter with Michiko, if she was all right. Something about them just didn't seemed resolved, though Kathleen wasn't sure if it was lingering emotions or just a bad memory. She wanted to ask more, but she wondered if she was being too forward.

Their time ran out after two hours, and Kathleen was feeling more than a little dizzy. However, Mitsu and the others were only just starting.

"Nijikai!" they shouted and started walking down the road.

"What?" Kathleen asked, swaying a bit.

Mitsu took Kathleen's elbow. "We are going to the second izakaya for more drinks."

Kathleen looked to Yuriko, who only grinned as Mitsu pulled her down the street. Even though it was getting late, the street was packed with people going to restaurants. There were groups like theirs, slightly drunk and traveling to the next destination. It was strange to Kathleen, looking at all the businessmen and women out so late. Kathleen had only seen a scene like this at college, and those kids certainly weren't dressed in business suits, towing around forgotten briefcases.

The second place was much like the first, except the drink that was put in front of her was unfamiliar. Yuriko was across the table from her now, so Kathleen turned to Mitsu. "What is it?"

"Shochu! Or anō." She hummed. "Whiskey?"

Kathleen wasn't too sure. She had never seen whiskey served in such a large glass and filled to the top with ice. She took a sip and grimaced. It was awful. She had never liked whiskey much anyway. She found herself eating more at this place, hoping to take the taste away. She didn't even know what exactly she was eating, but most of it was fried. Unfortunately, Mitsu kept filling her glass.

"Ne ne, Kathleen-chan?" Mitsu seemed to have gotten friendlier as the night went on. "How did you meet Yuriko-chan?"

"Uh, she actually found me lost at a train station. She helped me back, and then I found out we were practically neighbors."

"Ehh," Mitsu exclaimed, a little too loud. "Kawaii." She drew out the word with a very high pitch.

"What? Why?"

"I met my boyfriend because we were both in the same class at uni, but your story is much more romantic."

Kathleen blinked. "Romantic? No, no, you misunderstand."

"Mitsu-san, Kathleen and I aren't dating," Yuriko said. Kathleen probably would have been more embarrassed, but no one at the table seemed to care about their conversation. Someone had even started singing.

Mitsu pouted. "Che, why not? She's your type, ne?"

"That doesn't mean we are dating."

Kathleen flushed. "Wait, did you—?" But she lost her train of thought as Mitsu began to refill the awful whiskey. "No, no," she whined. "Yamete kudasai!"

Mitsu laughed, but she didn't stop topping off Kathleen's drink. "I didn't think you knew any Japanese."

It was probably because Kathleen was becoming very drunk, but she decided that it was a great time to practice her novice Japanese skills. "O-genki desu ka?"

Mitsu giggled. "Genki desu yo! Mō ippai ikaga desu ka?"

Kathleen wasn't sure what she said, but that wasn't stopping her from trying out all her vocabulary. "Hajimemashite. Watashi wa Kathleen desu. Yoroshiku onegaishimasu. Watashi wa ni juu go sai desu. Konpyuta wa daisuke desu. Konpyuta ga suki desu ka?"

Yuriko looked like she was stifling a laugh, but Mitsu clapped her hands. "Suge!"

"Nama mugi, nama gomi, nama tamago!"

She didn't know why Yuriko burst into laughter.

Chapter Thirteen

"You wanna know what the best thing about Japan is?"

Yuriko smiled, watching as Kathleen leaned lower and lower against the table. "What?"

"The trains. They are like...the shit. Like a good shit. Like a *oh my God they are always on time and like only five minutes between each train* shit."

Yuriko propped her elbows on the table, feeling like sinking down herself. She knew that she was more than buzzed—she was floating. "I thought you hated the trains. You always get lost."

"*I* may get lost, but that doesn't mean I can't appreciate good public transportation." She giggled. "Though, Ai is pretty good for navigating. Maybe that's what we should have 'em do. Figure out transportation for dumb foreigners."

"The GPS has already been invented. You could use your phone too."

Kathleen scoffed. "Yeah, but that's *complicated*. All you do with Ai is just ask. She'll do anything." Kathleen suddenly sat up and leaned across the table, as if she could whisper to Yuriko. She took a sip of her shochu, despite the fact that it made her grimace every time. "And I really mean anything. Like, I could tell her to jump off a bridge and she would. Or I could tell her to, I dunno, walk around naked and she would."

"She would probably like that."

Kathleen's eyes went wide. "I *know*. Freaky, isn't she?"

Mitsu tugged on Kathleen's sleeve, suddenly turning to her. "Ne ne, Kathleen-chan, do you want to come to karaoke with the rest of us?" She was referring to herself, Mori, Azuma, and Yoshizawa. Everyone else had left, trying to catch the last trains back.

Kathleen stared at Mitsu, shaking her head. "No. No, that would be awful," she said very seriously.

Yuriko laughed, using the table to stand. "I think Kathleen and I should head back."

Mitsu pouted. "But it's so late. How will you get back? Come on, karaoke is fun!" She threaded her arm through Kathleen's.

"We live only a couple blocks away. I think we will manage."

Yuriko walked around the table and took Kathleen from Mitsu's clutches. Kathleen sighed, resting her head on Yuriko's shoulder. "I'm no good at singing."

"That's why we are heading back." She nodded to the rest of the stragglers. "Otsukaresama." She received a mumbled response.

Kathleen was very drunk, but at least when they hit the fresh air, she seemed able to walk on her own. She swayed up and down the sidewalk. There were few people out, most of them as drunk as her.

"You know what the best thing about Japan is?"

Yuriko grinned. "The trains?"

"Well, yeah. But also, the convenience store food. Have you..." She stumbled into Yuriko, who was barely able to keep them both upright. "Have you ever tried a rice ball?"

"Of course I have."

"They are, like, really good. Like, I can't even read the package, and they are really good."

Yuriko laughed, feeling more than giddy. They were both swaying on the sidewalk now. Her shoes had been killing her earlier, but now everything just felt a little numb. "You want to know my favorite thing about Japan?"

Kathleen, looked up, eyes wide in something like childish curiosity. "What is it?"

"My bathtub."

Kathleen laughed so hard she fell off Yuriko, nearly into the street. "That's so dumb."

"But it's true. America doesn't understand the beauty of a nice deep tub that keeps the water heated and that you can soak in for hours and hours. Even our cheap tubs in company housing are better than anything outside a mansion in America."

Kathleen was still laughing. "I don't even know how my tub here works."

Yuriko nearly halted in her steps. "What? Are you telling me that you've been living here for *months* and have not soaked in your tub?"

"Yeah? I usually shower anyway." She waved a hand. "Even before Japan."

Yuriko reached out and took Kathleen's hand. "You need to learn this. I can't believe...I feel like I've failed you because I haven't informed you of this."

"What's the big deal? It's a bathtub."

"It's *pleasure*." Yuriko tugged on her hand, quickly approaching the apartment. This suddenly seemed a very important thing. "I'm teaching you tonight. And if you forget, I'll teach you again in the morning."

Kathleen laughed, probably a little too loudly for the late hour. "Well, we are not doing this in my apartment. What if Ai, like, *watched*?"

"Does she usually watch you shower?"

"Well, no. But I always feel like if I'm in there too long, she'll come and investigate or something."

They were approaching their doors, so Yuriko just took Kathleen to her apartment. "She's not a cat, you know."

"She does have a random variable. You know, to keep her a bit surprising. Who knows, today that variable was organizing my cabinets. Tonight? Watching me bathe."

Yuriko pushed open her door. "Well, have no fear—my apartment is safe from all meddling computers."

"You say that now, but with our AI technology, you never know." Kathleen struggled to take off her shoes without falling. Yuriko just leaned against the wall.

She didn't even wait for Kathleen to regain her balance. She pulled her into the bathroom. "Okay, see this panel?" She pointed to the selection of buttons inlaid into the wall. "This controls the heat of your hot water and the tub's heating components. It will look identical in your apartment. You can set it to *fill*, and water of that temp will fill the tub to the sensors. It takes only ten minutes."

Kathleen looked closely at the panel, as if she couldn't quite see it. "That doesn't seem that special."

"Yeah, cause you're staring at some buttons and not sinking into perfectly heated water."

"Well, then fill it up." She flung herself to the bathroom floor. "I'll wait. And then judge. Harshly, probably."

Yuriko couldn't help but smirk. "All right. But you know that you have to shower off before going into the tub, right?"

"What? I have to bathe to bathe?"

"No, you have to bathe to *soak*. If you want to use my tub. You're going to have to—"

Kathleen suddenly reached up and turned on the showerhead. Warm water doused her head and shoulders.

Yuriko was laughing so hard that she had to lean against the bathroom door. "*No*, at least take off your clothes."

"They were dirty anyway," Kathleen spluttered over the spray. She took the showerhead from the wall and handed it to Yuriko, thoroughly soaking her skirt in the process. "Hold this."

"What are you—"

Kathleen was already stripping off her T-shirt, slapping it to the floor. Her jeans were a little harder, practically glued to her legs. Yuriko reached out, as if she could stop her from the impromptu strip, but she accidentally just sprayed her again with the water.

Kathleen laughed, turning around and unclasping her bra and throwing off her panties.

Yuriko's brain seemed to stutter then. She was still all warm and slow from the beer, but now she felt herself quickly overheating, taking in Kathleen's wide hips, thick thighs, and large breasts. How were American girls always so curvy? How was Kathleen so curvy? Like even more curvy than usual? Why did *curvy* suddenly seem like a fascinating word?

Kathleen reached for Yuriko's shampoo, pouring a little too much into her hands. She furiously scrubbed her hair. She turned to Yuriko then, uncaring that she was just standing naked in her bathroom, while Yuriko was fully dressed. Her skin was pale and freckled, all of it flushed pink from alcohol and steaming water. Yuriko was somehow jealous of those freckles, fingers twitching to trace them. To what purpose, her slow and shocked mind couldn't comprehend.

"Give me a hand here."

It took Yuriko a solid minute before she realized that Kathleen wanted the water spray on her. She held it out, offering it back. "Take it. I'll just...I'll just leave you to it." She needed some fresh air. She felt like she was drowning in the heat and steam and all of Kathleen's bared skin.

Kathleen stumbled toward her and, knocking the showerhead from her grasp, sprayed them both down. "No," Kathleen whined. "If you leave, then I'll probably forget how the tub works, and then you'll laugh."

"I won't laugh."

"You're laughing now."

Yuriko was, she couldn't help it, so she pushed Kathleen away. She swayed before sinking to the floor, grinning. Yuriko went to the soap dispenser and handed it to her. "Come on, you've got to clean the rest of you. I'll probably use the water tomorrow."

"What?" Kathleen gaped at her.

Yuriko raised an eyebrow. "I'm not going to waste an entire tub of water."

"It will just go through the water treatment and come back to you anyway."

"That is not the point. It saves *energy*."

Kathleen was giggling, leaning against the side of the tub, and furiously soaping up her arms and legs. She was sloppy, but it seemed thorough enough. Yuriko picked up the showerhead and pointed it at her and received a shriek.

"Hey! Warn me."

"Why?" Not when it made her skin flush deeper, everything twitching, *moving*. "It's fun to hose you down." Yuriko was surprised that her words were coherent. "You smell like shochu."

"Well, you smell like...fried chicken."

Yuriko pushed Kathleen until she turned around, the skin on her shoulders soft and slippery. "Sounds delicious. Okay, I'll get your back."

Kathleen snorted. "Thanks for the choice."

"My tub, my rules. We could have done this at your place."

Kathleen gasped. "Oh *God*, could you imagine Ai walking in on something like this? She would totally judge me."

"I don't think Ai is programmed to judge you."

"She is programmed to keep her opinions to herself, but she judges me. All the time. Thinks I'm pathetic, so she treats me like some helpless puppy who can't figure out how to go down the stairs yet."

"I think I understand the feeling." Yuriko didn't want to imagine Ai. She didn't want to think of Ai's face that looked just like hers, and Ai's strange similar mannerisms. Yuriko was happy here, drunk and relaxed, massaging soap into a languid Kathleen. Her skin felt so good against Yuriko's fingers, those freckles coming in and out of view between soapsuds. "We should go to an onsen together."

"A what?"

"Onsen. A bathhouse. It's so relaxing."

"Okay."

"You don't need to hear more?"

"Nah, you've yet to lead me astray." Kathleen looked over her shoulder, grinning at Yuriko, her face so bright and tempting.

Yuriko took her hands off her and grabbed the showerhead, rinsing her down. "I haven't led you much of anywhere."

"How about when I got lost?"

Yuriko snorted. "Nothing more special than teaching you how to find your own apartment."

"Well, Mitsu thought it was romantic."

Yuriko bit her lip. "Mitsu is an idiot."

"She's cute." Before Yuriko could react to *that* statement, Kathleen jumped up. "Oh, the bath is filled." She turned to Yuriko, spinning unsteadily. "Am I good enough?"

She was more than good. She was warm and wet and…Yuriko knew they were both a little too drunk. Well, she was too drunk to be staring at her friend like *that*. She averted her eyes. "Go for it."

Kathleen carefully gripped the edge of the tub, probably to keep from falling in. When she stood in it, the water came up to her knees. She crouched down, submerging herself. She was shorter than Yuriko and managed to fit pretty well. The water came up to her shoulders and only her bent knees poked up from the surface of the water.

"It's better when it's a larger tub."

Kathleen moved her arms around experimentally. "Well, seems like a bathtub. What now?"

Yuriko knelt next to the side of the tub, arms and elbows propped on the edge. She was unpleasantly soaked, but at least the tub was warm to lean against. "You're supposed to relax. Meditate. Think about life. Work, family, whatever problems you have."

Kathleen scooted in the tub, resting her head against the back edge. "Well, you know all my problems from work. My family, well, they're all right."

Steam was curling from the surface of the water. Yuriko was feeling a little sleepy, and she didn't look forward to peeling off her damp clothes later. "Are you close with your parents?"

Kathleen tilted her head. "They can get annoying. I mean, I love them. But my mom can get really *annoying*." She raised her voice, possibly mocking her mother. "*Kathleen! Why don't you settle down! Kathleen, I just met an old friend from high school who has a son your age! Why don't you meet him! Kathleen, come back to America and get married like your perfect brother!*"

Yuriko giggled. "Let me guess, you're not interested in your mother's recommendations?"

Kathleen sat up, waving a hand and splashing Yuriko. "I can't tell you how many times she's tried to hook me up with sons of her friends. Most of the time she's never even met the son. Or how many times she questions why I broke up with some ex or another." She settled back into the water. "Of course, now that I've moved here, she thinks I'm trying to rebel and escape her."

"You're not?"

Kathleen shrugged. "Well, I did want a change from kind of the rut I was in. I mean, I was kind of depressed because I haven't dated many guys, and those relationships, well, they never were quite what I wanted. Of course, I thought Brandon was what I wanted, but…I guess I'm saying I didn't move to Japan to rebel. Just seemed like a good way to, you know…"

Yuriko tilted her head. "What?"

Kathleen was staring at the surface of the water. Her hair was curling, despite being soaked, and she pulled her legs up so she could rest her chin on her knees. "Give up, I guess."

Yuriko suddenly stood up. "Move over." She was feeling impulsive and didn't have the strength to deny it. Not when Kathleen was looking like that, alone in her bathtub.

Kathleen stared. "What?"

"Move over. Make room for me."

She still had her clothes on, but taking them off seemed like too much effort by this point. Besides, maybe Kathleen was right—her clothes needed to be cleaned anyway.

There wasn't enough room for two people. Knees bent almost painfully, Yuriko sank into the water next to Kathleen. They were sitting side by side. She sighed, feeling warm again. Even though it was a little weird to sit in her bath fully clothed.

Kathleen gave her a strange look. "I thought you said you wanted to keep the water clean."

"The water will recycle."

Kathleen laughed, but it wasn't very convincing. Their shoulders were pressed tightly together, Yuriko's soaked shirt against Kathleen's bare skin. Half the water had sloshed onto the floor, soaking into Kathleen's discarded clothes and dripping down the floor drain.

"It's okay to be lonely," Yuriko said.

Kathleen sighed. "Maybe, but it seems kind of pathetic. I mean,

I've got this great job and I'm in this whole new, exciting country and I just…" Her voice broke a little and she lowered her chin. "Do you ever feel like you are just not meant for anyone?"

"Sometimes. I mean…I really did after Michiko broke up with me," Yuriko whispered. "I think about dating again, sometimes. It never worked out."

Kathleen looked at her and their faces were so close that Yuriko could see droplets of water gathering at her temples and upper lip. "But you're so great. I mean, you're so pretty and tall and smart and really good at not getting lost."

Yuriko grinned. "I could say the same about you. The company brought you all the way from America to run their PLC project. And despite being pathetic most of the time"—Kathleen grimaced, and Yuriko giggled—"you managed to make friends with a bunch of Japanese strangers tonight. Let me tell you, it's been a long time since I've seen Mori-san get that excited talking to someone other than Saiki-san. Also, Mitsu-san seems to really like you." She felt her smile fade and her stomach twist.

Kathleen nudged her shoulder. "Mitsu-san has a boyfriend."

"That doesn't stop some girls," Yuriko murmured.

"Okay, well, she *was* a little touchy. But I think that's her personality. I mean, I think she spent most of the night thinking you and I were dating…" She paused and Yuriko looked up to see Kathleen examining the wall, as if something very peculiar was there. "Am I really your type?"

Yuriko ran a hand through her damp hair, tugging it to her right shoulder, trying to distract herself from her beating heart. "Having a *type* seems kind of stupid, yeah? I don't know—I think she was just teasing."

Kathleen was staring at her now, eyes glazed from alcohol, half lidded. "Well, what do you like in a woman?"

Yuriko couldn't describe it. She could describe the circumstances that brought her and Michiko together. She could say how she felt at the time and even when it was over, but she couldn't say what attracted her to Michiko or any of the others she'd been interested in. It wasn't something that could be said in words.

She couldn't describe why, in that moment, she desperately wanted Kathleen.

So she leaned forward, though there wasn't that much space between them, and pressed her lips against Kathleen's. Kathleen was warm and full and relaxed. She made a small sound, or maybe it was a sigh, and Yuriko tilted her head so she could explore further. Kathleen did more than just let her—she opened to Yuriko.

Yuriko found her hand in Kathleen's hair, wet and curly and tangled in her fingers. Kathleen's hands were on her shoulders and Yuriko deeply regretted having not taken off her shirt. How could she have let this beautiful, supple woman just undress in front of her and not touch her earlier?

Kathleen's hands lowered, diving into the water and reaching for the soft skin of Yuriko's stomach. Her fingers pressed there, as if testing Yuriko's pliancy. She remembered, when Ai had broken down in Akihabara, and she had come to help bring Ai back to the apartment, Kathleen had wrapped her arms around her in the train. Kathleen's fingers had clenched Yuriko's stomach—in relief or fear, she hadn't known at the time. Now Kathleen was exploring, searching so curiously.

Yuriko moved, water sloshing over the side. The tub might be half empty now. It didn't matter. All that mattered in this world was Kathleen's expanse of warm, wet skin, arching up as Yuriko straddled her.

Kathleen's hands shifted to Yuriko's hips, fingers looping at the belt. The effort to remove her clothes would be too great. Yuriko didn't think she could survive even a second without her hands and lips on Kathleen.

Kathleen gasped into the kiss, obviously needing to breathe. Yuriko contented herself with Kathleen's neck instead. It tasted clean, fresh, and smelled slightly of Yuriko's shampoo. She almost regretted having Kathleen bathe. She wondered what she really tasted like, not scrubbed like this.

Kathleen made a gasping moan, still short of breath, as Yuriko discovered a spot behind her ear that made Kathleen quiver. Her hands wandered, feeling that shiver ripping through Kathleen's body. Her arms, her breasts, her stomach, her wide hips.

"Y-Yuriko," Kathleen gasped as Yuriko's hand strayed to the junction of her thighs.

Yuriko lifted her head, looked at Kathleen. She was finding it hard to focus. Everything seemed steamed around the edges, hot and overwhelming. Kathleen's eyes were liquid, looking up at Yuriko with something like pleading, yearning, and anticipation.

Yuriko let her fingers slide over Kathleen, as her lips slid over hers. She swallowed Kathleen's gasp and every bit of that tender mouth. The water was hot, her fingers were hot, but Kathleen burned under her gentle ministrations. She took her time, as leisurely as the water rhythmically sloshing over the sides of the tub.

She kissed the edge of Kathleen's lip, feeling her breaths on her cheek stuttering in time with the unconscious jerking of her hips. Yuriko pressed harder, but something within her warned her of pressing too far, though she had not the cognitive functions to understand it.

Kathleen's hands were on her back, under the shirt soaked against her skin. Her fingers moved in a massage, all of her moving to the same rhythm as Yuriko's fingers. It was as if Yuriko was a musician, playing a very fine instrument.

Then Kathleen broke, or maybe transformed. She pressed her head back into the tiled wall, eyes going unfocused. She was mostly silent, body arching into Yuriko, quivering and pulsing. The only sounds were her soft, shuddering breaths.

Yuriko leaned back, her hand spreading over Kathleen's stomach, as if to calm the jerking motion. Then Kathleen relaxed back, eyes blinking into focus. She looked at Yuriko, flushed, wet, and panting.

"Yuriko?" It came out as a question, a mixture of confusion and something unidentifiable. "What…what was that?"

Yuriko's senses suddenly came back to her. Kathleen was drunk. *She* was drunk. They shouldn't have done that. *She* shouldn't have done that. What was she thinking?

She hadn't been.

Yuriko quickly stood in the bath, the action causing Kathleen to sway forward, hands trailing down Yuriko's clothed legs. "Yuriko…" Kathleen whispered and it almost sounded like a plea.

Yuriko quickly stepped from the tub, her heartbeat in her ears and not enough air in her lungs. Her mind was buzzing, and everywhere that Kathleen had touched was tingling with heat. "We are probably getting overheated. Too much drinking and hot water can be dangerous. Here, let me get you a towel."

She knew she wasn't being graceful. She was running from the bathroom like a criminal, dripping water onto the floor. She grabbed a couple towels from her bedroom and an old bathrobe. She stripped herself, quickly putting on a pajama shirt and sweatpants before returning to the bathroom.

Kathleen was just stepping out of the tub, looking around the bathroom like she couldn't quite remember how she got there. Yuriko threw her a towel and hung up the robe. "Here, you can dry off and put this on. I'll take care of your clothes."

Kathleen stared at her. "Should I...go back to my apartment?"

She looked so lost and confused. She wasn't the only one. Yuriko was feeling more than a little dizzy from the alcohol. She needed to lie down and clear her head. She and Kathleen were very drunk and probably very light-headed from the bathwater. The feel of her lips, the touch of her fingers...it didn't mean anything, and they both needed to take a step back.

"I think that's for the best."

CHAPTER FOURTEEN

It was barely dawn when a call from Dave started buzzing on Kathleen's wrist. She was awake, unfortunately, and had been checking her email, debating whether to go in to the office today. She would have liked to sleep in, considering how late she had gotten back from work last night, but she and Fukusawa were so close to finishing Ai's patch. She was almost desperate to get it done.

It felt like the only thing in the past week that was true progress.

"What do you want?" She answered the phone but kept the video off. Her head was killing her, and she was pretty sure the rings around her eyes had grown with every hour she hadn't slept.

"Always so friendly," her brother commented. "But at least you answered. What has been keeping you tied up this week? Did you go out of town?"

Kathleen wished she had. All she had seen for the last three days was her apartment or office. She couldn't even remember riding the train in between. "Just busy. We've had to come out with an update on pretty short notice, so I've kind of had my nose to the grindstone."

She declined to mention that she had lost nearly an entire day after the nomikai. First there was the hangover and the overwhelming embarrassment that she'd sat around in Yuriko's bathtub, naked, crying in self-pity. Then forced herself on Yuriko. Well, she thought she had. She remembered there was some kissing and touching. Honestly, everything was a blur. She remembered feeling so pathetic, and then Yuriko was in her arms. Or on her lap? Then Yuriko was standing, and Kathleen realized just how low she had fallen.

Kathleen hadn't the energy the next day to do anything but try to absorb Fukusawa's many emails. She hadn't seen Yuriko since, nor had she tried to contact her. It was probably for the best. Yuriko already thought she was pathetic. Well, now she had the proof.

Dave paused. "Are you okay?"

Kathleen quickly checked her cheeks for mortifying tears. She was *not* broken up over a drunken night of bad decisions. She was an adult who could calmly hide away from all her problems. "I'm fine. Why?"

"You just sound…well, your voice sounds a little awful."

Kathleen rolled her eyes. "Thanks."

"No, I mean it. Are you getting sick?"

Kathleen's throat did hurt a little, and she suddenly remembered getting up in the night to vomit. She must have been too tired and stressed. "I'm fine. How is Juliet?"

"Making dinner. Delicious homemade pizza. Be honest—can Japan do pizza?"

Kathleen snorted and ended up coughing. She could *hear* Dave frowning over the phone. It was just a tickle, probably. "Japan doesn't even know what real cheese is. They do have some good-looking pizza, but half the time it's got a mound of mayo on it."

They both laughed, but Kathleen quickly degraded into another coughing fit.

"Kathleen? You should probably get that checked out."

"It's just a tickle. I was fine yesterday."

"Were you?"

Kathleen didn't remember much of yesterday besides going in to work and attempting not to sleep at her desk. "I'm just tired."

"Well, get some rest. Juliet and I will dine to your good health."

"I'm not that sick."

"If you say so. But if you get some infection over there, Mother will throw a fit. Might even book herself a flight just to baby you."

"Go eat your dinner."

"Get some sleep."

Dave hung up and Kathleen sat up in her bed. She was pretty thirsty, but when she tried to stand, she found all the blood rushing from her head. Her vision blacked, and she fell back to the bed. "Well, *shit*," she moaned. She hadn't been sick in years, and now she had gotten some stupid cold.

A light shone in from the doorway and Kathleen looked up to see Ai. "Want some coffee?"

Kathleen rubbed her head. "No."

"Hey, are you all right?"

Kathleen looked up. "I'm just stressed, that's it. I'm not dying."

Ai folded her arms. "Well, can I come in and take your temperature?"

"*No.*"

"What about a cup of water?"

"Sure, fine." Kathleen just wanted to lie back down, but she had to get to the office or at least her computer.

Ai came to stand at her door again. "Can I come in?"

Kathleen was still holding her head in her hands. "Yeah, okay."

Ai stepped over to her and put the water on her bedside table. Then she pressed her hand against Kathleen's forehead. Kathleen reared back.

"Hey, I thought I said you couldn't take my temp."

"Health risks override user protocol."

"I'm not at a health risk," Kathleen protested, but Ai's eyes were already going vacant as she processed the data.

She looked down to Kathleen, like a stern parent. "You have a fever."

Kathleen tried to push her away. "Yeah, because the freaking humidity in Tokyo is out of control. Now go away."

"You should go back to bed."

"I have to get more work done today." Kathleen lifted her wrist, and Ai put her hand over it. Kathleen could feel a text being sent. "Hey, what did you do?"

"You will not be going in to work today."

"You can't—!"

"Health risks override—"

"Shut up!"

Ai was standing over her, arms folded. "Kathleen, you should lie down and try to get back to sleep. If you don't, I will call the paramedics."

"You wouldn't."

"I would. You programmed me to be always attentive to my user, with health and safety as my priority. If you will not take the medical advice that was programmed into me by *you*, then I will call someone else to intervene."

Kathleen glared. "Fine. I'll sleep in today, but I'll need to get my computer by the afternoon. I'm on a deadline, you know."

Ai smiled, just a little too sweetly. "Sleep well."

CHAPTER FIFTEEN

Yuriko stepped off the train, glaring into the sunset. People around her pushed her out of the way as they exited the platform. The air was horribly humid, and even the slightest touch from a stranger felt stifling. Her back ached—she was used to being on her feet for work, but being on her feet for the two-hour train ride from Yokohama this afternoon was something close to torture. It hadn't helped that the situation in Yokohama wasn't that serious. The supervisor could have simply vid called her instead of having her trek out there. She might have bitten his head off for that.

Of course, she might have bitten the heads off everyone in her department in the past few days.

Yuriko was in a bad mood, and she knew there was no good reason for it. Granted, there *was* a reason for it, but it wasn't even close to good. It was stupid and irritable, and it made her feel stupid and irritable.

She checked her wrist and found several apologetic texts from Yokohama and one from her own director, probably berating her for being a little harsh for a stupid mistake. She ignored them all. She wasn't in the office, and she wasn't about to pander to anyone now. Or at least until she got off her feet.

She looked up to the apartments, feeling slightly better. Just a few more steps and she would be up the stairs and into her own space. Maybe she would tinker or watch TV or maybe have a bath. Even in this humidity a bath sounded fantastic. Nice warm water on her aching muscles, sinking down to her chin…

Am I really your type?

Yuriko hesitated outside her door, hand half raised to open it. Instead, she pressed her forehead against the cold metal door.

"Baka," she whispered.

Kathleen hadn't contacted her since the night of the nomikai. Not that Yuriko could blame her; she had also kept her distance. She couldn't help it. Every time she thought about Kathleen, it was a weird swirl of excitement and embarrassment and lust. To say that she had thought about what happened was an understatement. She had dreamed about it, fantasized about it. She could find herself phasing out during work, remembering how soft and lush Kathleen's skin had looked in her bathroom. How curious and oddly bold her hands had been. Her mouth, open and yearning. Kathleen against her fingers. Kathleen open and arching and…

Yuriko hit her head against the door a couple times. Not very hard, but hard enough that maybe this time she would forget the memory. Kathleen wasn't…she wasn't interested. She had been drunk. They both had been drunk. Yuriko knew Kathleen had been lonely—she had just confessed it. She was vulnerable. Yuriko probably should have been the responsible one. She should have left the bathroom as soon as Kathleen got undressed. She shouldn't have climbed into the tub next to her. She shouldn't have kissed her. She shouldn't have touched her.

Yuriko supposed she had been vulnerable too.

Maybe it had been seeing Michiko recently and bringing all that drama up again. Maybe it had just been a long time since she had hung out with anyone who wasn't hopelessly straight. Well, Kathleen said she was only into men, but Yuriko seriously doubted it. That report about the malfunction in the cortex scan that caused Ai to be female had yet to show up, despite Kathleen's insistence that one of her subordinates was looking into it.

Did any of that matter? They had both been compromised, emotionally and physically. It shouldn't have happened.

At least, it shouldn't have happened like that.

Maybe it would be different if they had talked like that before, without being drunk. Maybe it would be different if Kathleen wasn't so adamant that she wasn't attracted to women.

If Kathleen didn't want to talk to her, Yuriko would have to accept that. She would have to keep her distance and not make her any more uncomfortable.

"Just get back from work?"

Yuriko looked over to see Kathleen's door open, but it wasn't Kathleen looking out at her. It was Ai. Yuriko paused. "Are you allowed to open the door?"

Ai laughed. "You and Kathleen always think so highly of me. No, but I have a medical crisis."

Yuriko stepped over. "What is it? Is Kathleen hurt?"

Ai moved aside so Yuriko could enter. "Not hurt, but I do require your assistance."

Yuriko wasn't sure if she should enter the apartment. What if it was serious? She couldn't let her own insecurities and awkwardness get in the way if there was an emergency. She knew PLCs were programmed to keep the health of their user a priority. Ai would not break the rules Kathleen ordered her to follow unless something was seriously wrong.

Kathleen was sitting at her table, head down, her computer display up. Yuriko looked at Ai, wondering what was wrong. Ai raised her eyebrows and stepped over to Kathleen, then touched her shoulder. "Come on, dear, you need to go back to bed."

Kathleen moaned, rolling her head to look at Ai. "*Shaddup*," she mumbled and waved a hand, making the documents on her display whirl around. "I need to do work." Then she coughed violently, shuddering and holding her sides.

Ai looked up at Yuriko. "She's been like this all day," she said with a sigh.

Yuriko came to stand next to Ai, but Kathleen didn't even notice her, moaning into the surface of her table. "Does she have a fever?"

Ai nodded. "It doesn't require hospitalization, but it is persistent."

"Any other symptoms?"

"She has vomited a couple times. She can keep water down, barely." Ai hesitated, turning to Kathleen, eyes low. "She has been overworking herself. She knows it. So she thinks she is just tired and stressed."

Kathleen moaned louder. "Quiet, robot. Some of us are concentrating." Her eyes were closed, and she was rubbing her cheek into the table.

Yuriko looked back to Ai. "I'm not sure what you think I can do."

Ai grinned. "Obviously, together you and I can lift her back into bed."

Yuriko sighed. "All right, I'll take the legs—you take the head."

Ai knelt down next to Kathleen. "Dear, we are going to carry you now, okay? Just try to stay still."

Kathleen blinked at her, unfocused. "Wha—?"

Ai, almost too easily, put her hands under Kathleen's arms and lifted her enough that Yuriko could grab her legs. Kathleen put up a weak fight. Yuriko could tell now that her face was flushed hot and lips pale. Her eyes seemed sunken, marked by dark circles.

Kathleen looked to Yuriko. "How did you get in?"

They had made it to the bedroom, and Ai plopped Kathleen into her pillows as Yuriko pushed her legs up. "Ai said you were in danger."

Kathleen glared at Ai. "You're not allowed to save my life."

Ai grinned, adjusting the pillows underneath Kathleen. "Unable to accept direct order. In violation of subroutine—"

"Shut up." Kathleen rolled over, clutching her head. "You've been using that excuse all morning."

Ai pulled the covers over her. "I just love to spoil you."

Kathleen shrugged her off. "Go away. Both of you."

Ai stepped back and pulled Yuriko into the main room. "She's been in a lovely mood all day. Now I need another favor."

Yuriko crossed her arms. "I probably shouldn't be here. Obviously, she is not dying, and you have more medical knowledge than me."

Ai took Yuriko's wrist and squeezed gently. "I can't do everything. And once her fever has broken and she isn't totally out of her mind, Kathleen will appreciate that you came too."

Yuriko seriously doubted it.

Ai gave her an encouraging smile. "I just need you to grab me some first aid necessities, and I can't leave the apartment."

"Since you've started breaking all your rules, can't you break this one?"

"Unfortunately, Kathleen would be too upset about me going to the convenience store by myself for it to outweigh the benefits." She shook her head. "No, she would be much happier to have you coming and going. Whatever drunken fumbling you two had doesn't matter. I need some medicine and food."

Yuriko froze. "Wait, do you know—?"

Ai raised an eyebrow. "My basic programming is to observe, and to form conclusions based on those observations. Why do you two always forget that? Didn't you build me?"

Yuriko forced herself to breathe. She almost desperately wanted to ask Ai what Kathleen thought of it. If she had forgiven Yuriko. If she had forgotten all about it. "Is that why she is annoyed with you?"

"You think I would bluntly confront her about her confused sexuality? I'm programmed to please her, you know. Not coax her into a personal crisis." Ai sighed, a little dramatically. "Right now, Kathleen just needs to recover. Can you do her this favor and run to the convenience store for me?" She tapped on Yuriko's wrist and Yuriko could feel her phone vibrate with a new message. "I've sent you a list. Can you believe she doesn't even have a spare cold pack lying around?"

Yuriko browsed through the list. She looked up at Ai. "I'd believe it. Until a few days ago, she didn't even know how to turn on the bathtub."

Ai tilted her head, her grin just a little too wide. "Oh, really? Bathtub, huh? Is that what happened after your drinking party?"

Yuriko flushed. "It had nothing to do with that." She quickly turned around and shoved on her shoes. She did have enough sense not to slam the door shut, but it was a near thing.

She was used to teasing people, especially Kathleen. Having her own teasing turned on her was, frankly, unnerving. She walked quickly to the konbini, wanting to get it all over with. She picked up the cold packs and cold medicine that Ai recommended.

Yuriko hesitated in the drink aisle. Ai had asked her to grab some broth and other ingredients to make soup or porridge. Yuriko wondered if she should grab something else too. Whenever work was in a crunch period, and she barely had enough time between work and home to sleep, let alone cook, she would grab some energy bottles. They were small and full of nutrients. She knew some coworkers who attributed their good health to having them at least once a day.

She grabbed a couple of the bottles that were mostly filled with some sort of fruit mush or gelatin. Then she lingered by the snacks, wondering if Kathleen would like something salty, like crackers. Or maybe some bread with red bean paste? Or maybe she would like some onigiri with kelp or pickled plum? Yuriko's mother had always been of the opinion that umeboshi could cure any sickness.

She ended up buying a little too much, her bags bulging and hitting her legs as she walked back to the apartment. Ai was waiting at the door when she walked up the stairs. She smiled at the bags, and luckily, she did not comment that Yuriko had probably bought enough to cure a dozen people of the common cold.

Ai took the bags into the apartment and quickly unpacked them. Yuriko took off her shoes and rubbed her hands. Her entire body ached from the day and the walk. Ai didn't seem to notice, holding out a couple pills and a bottle of water to Yuriko.

"Can you make Kathleen take these?"

"You can't?"

Ai chuckled. "If I couldn't drag her back into bed myself, I don't think I can convince her to take some medicine. Besides, she won't be expecting you. The element of surprise can be very powerful." She said this all rather seriously.

Yuriko took the medicine and water, trying to not feel like a kid being asked to do a chore by her mother. Kathleen was her friend, awkward drunken fumbling and all. She wanted to keep Kathleen as a friend. She also grabbed one of the health boosting gel drinks, just in case Kathleen was hungry.

She stepped into the room, after knocking on the partially opened door. Kathleen moaned and Yuriko took it as an invitation to enter. The sun was setting now, sending bright orange rays to light up the room. It was plain, no decoration or personal objects. There were some clothes on the floor, but it wasn't very messy. Kathleen had a fan blowing on her, which helped to keep the place from feeling too stifling.

Kathleen looked over as Yuriko stepped closer. "Did Ai force you here?"

Yuriko gave a shrug and a small smile. "Desperate times, I suppose."

Kathleen attempted to sit up, but even Yuriko could see that the motion made her turn a little green. She set aside the water and pills, then picked up a trash can with a liner that had obviously been changed recently. She moved it into reaching distance. Kathleen closed her eyes, settling against the pillows. "Sorry."

Yuriko sat on the edge of her bed and handed her the bottle of water. "For what?"

Kathleen waved a hand. "Being pathetic."

"You don't need to be sick to be pathetic."

Kathleen glared, but it was halfhearted. At least she seemed a little better now, after the nap. She took the water and quickly swallowed the pills. "I'm…I'm talking about the other night."

Yuriko felt her stomach twist. "You don't need to apologize. In fact, I should be apologizing."

Kathleen frowned, rubbing her damp brow. "No, no, please don't. Look, we were both drunk. And I…well, honestly, I don't remember much."

"You don't?"

"I'd really like not to remember how embarrassing I was. Okay?" She winced, lips tightening. Yuriko reached for the trash bin, but Kathleen waved her off. "Just a headache." She peered up at Yuriko, as if it hurt to open her eyes too wide. "Can we just mutually apologize and forget about it? Please?"

Yuriko's stomach didn't untwist, and her heart felt a little bit heavier. She wasn't sure what she had expected from Kathleen. In fact, she might have expected worse. That Kathleen would be disgusted by her or hate her. Maybe she should be happy that Kathleen didn't remember it well. Sometimes Yuriko felt like she had imagined it all in some drunken hallucination. It was probably for the best they move on.

She ignored the ache in her chest. "Yeah, that sounds good."

Kathleen's lips twitched into almost a smile. Then she sank back into her pillow, closing her eyes. "You know, Medical can make this super high-tech brain scanner that can read your mind and make you a perfect match. But maybe they should put their efforts toward killing stupid colds." She took another sip of the water and put it aside. She hadn't even drunk half of it. "Of course, their cortex scan seems lousy too."

"That would hurt Ai's feelings."

Kathleen snorted. "Computer programs don't get hurt feelings. They only pretend to."

Yuriko kind of felt like her own feelings were hurt. It was ridiculous. She knew Ai looked like her and acted like her. That didn't mean she was... It was as Kathleen said, constantly—the cortex scan was wrong. Ai had been a mistake. Now maybe Yuriko had gotten her own feelings a little mixed up, because she felt like Kathleen was saying she was a mistake too.

She grabbed the gel drink and handed it to Kathleen. "Try it—it's good for you."

Kathleen looked at it dubiously. "Looks like a kid's juice box." She tasted it. "Is it Jell-O?"

"For decades businessmen and women have been swearing by them. Supposed to be healthy."

Kathleen grimaced. "Kind of tastes like grass."

"That means it's healthy."

Kathleen pushed it aside and lay back down. Her eyes were closing. "Japanese are confusing. It tastes bad, so that means it's healthy." She yawned and shivered. "Ai even said she would need to tie some leeks around my neck." She looked at Yuriko, eyes unfocused. "I think she was joking. I'm not even sure what leeks are."

Yuriko smiled, reaching over to help pull up the covers on

Kathleen's bed. "My mom used to do that to me. Don't worry—I'll keep Ai away from the leeks."

Kathleen reached out and touched Yuriko's wrist. "Hey, thanks for coming over." Her voice faded, eyes closed. "And for the medicine and gross Jell-O…"

She was asleep. Yuriko took her hand, warm and clammy, and tucked it under the covers. Kathleen didn't even stir as Yuriko arranged the water and gel drink to be in closer reaching distance. She pushed the trash bin next to the bed and looked around the room. There were a few pieces of garbage, which she picked up and threw away. She folded the few clothes lying around and stashed them in the closet. On the shelving in the closet, she spotted a few brightly colored magazines. Impulsively, she picked one up, surprised to find it was a girls-love dōjinshi.

Yuriko glanced over to confirm that Kathleen was still sleeping, then she started flipping through it. The pages were littered with broken English translations written on sticky notes. The dōjin was a fairly tame story, nothing too raunchy or exciting. However, Yuriko was surprised to see it. Was Kathleen into manga or anime? Did she ship these two characters?

Yuriko looked at the front cover. She had read some popular manga before, but she hadn't read the one these characters came from. She had the sudden impulse to pick it up and give it a try.

Yuriko stood, taking the dōjinshi with her. In the kitchen, Ai was standing at the stove, watching a pot of boiling rice. She looked at Yuriko and the dōjin in her hand. She raised an eyebrow.

Yuriko pretended to not be affected by her look. "I saw Kathleen was practicing translation. I figured I could give her some input."

Ai grinned. "I see."

Yuriko ignored her and sat at the table, fishing in her purse for a pen. Kathleen, like all beginners, was a fairly literal translator. However, from the little she had done, it was a pretty good job. Yuriko just made a few notes to clarify strange phrases or vocabulary that Kathleen was obviously confused by.

She started when Ai sat next to her and pushed a bowl of okayu toward her. Yuriko frowned. "Shouldn't you be giving this to Kathleen?"

Ai shrugged. "She's sleeping, and I needed to practice making it." She nodded. "Come on, tell me what you think."

Yuriko stirred it, watching the steam curl off the rice porridge.

"Why would you need to practice? Can't you, like, download the recipe?"

"Just because I know exactly how to make it, doesn't mean I can execute it. I'd think you'd understand that, Quality Control."

Yuriko took a small bite. It tasted fine, not too salty, and the porridge was very soft. She wouldn't normally eat it unless she wasn't feeling good. "Yeah, but this is okayu, not teaching a robot to walk for the first time."

Ai just smiled as she looked at Yuriko's corrections in the dōjin. "She's a quick learner, isn't she?"

Yuriko nodded, hesitating. "Does she read stuff like this very often?"

"I got them for her, if that is what you're asking." Ai paused, touching the edges of the papers. "I didn't know she had been trying to read them. Must have done it while I was recharging."

Yuriko tapped on her wrist. It was after ten. She hadn't realized so much time had passed. "When was the last time you recharged?"

Ai sighed. "Well, considering Kathleen woke up at three a.m. to vomit, my last cycle was cut a little short."

"You should power down. I'll stay here for a bit in case she needs anything."

Ai blinked. "You wouldn't mind?"

Yuriko didn't much like that look. It was too innocent. "It would be much more trouble if you overheated or had another breakdown from too much data input."

Ai laughed. "Well, since you insist so nicely." She made her way to the corner of the room. There she knelt, closed her eyes, and went silent. If Yuriko didn't know better, she would think Ai was just resting. Yuriko knew that it would take an emergency or a voice command from Kathleen to rouse her again.

Yuriko decided to turn on the TV, keeping the volume low. She thought that maybe tonight she would watch a little anime.

❖

Yuriko woke up to the sound of retching.

She rubbed her head, her ear hurting from lying on the table. The TV seemed too bright in the dark room, and she hadn't even realized that she had fallen asleep. Yuriko stood up, trying to shrug off her drowsiness, and walked into Kathleen's room. She turned on the light and saw that Kathleen was kneeling on the floor, hiding her face in the trash bin.

"Hey, how are you feeling?"

Kathleen coughed. "How does it look?" Her voice was low, and she shivered. Her hair looked lank and greasy, and she leaned against the side of the bed, clutching the trash bin.

Yuriko, a little more awake now, went to grab some more anti-nausea medication. Returning to the room, she knelt beside Kathleen and held her shoulders. "Come on. Let me help you into bed."

Kathleen moaned. "Feel gross."

Yuriko moved aside the trash bin. Kathleen hadn't vomited, so she must have been dry heaving. Yuriko wrapped her arms more securely around her and helped her back into the covers. "Is it just your stomach?" She handed over the pills, but Kathleen only gripped them loosely in one fist.

"Just…" She winced. "Head hurts. Hot."

Yuriko touched her forehead. She didn't need a proper thermometer to realize that Kathleen was burning up. She handed over the water. "Here, drink this and take those. I'll go find something to reduce your fever."

Kathleen knocked aside the water, sitting up and pressing her head into Yuriko's side. "No…just…stop moving—the room is spinning."

Yuriko bent to pick up the water bottle, making Kathleen moan. "Okay, I'll stop. But you have to take the pills and drink this, at least."

Kathleen sighed heavily, moving her head enough to take a couple sips of the water with the medicine. Then she buried her face back into Yuriko's side. She didn't look very comfortable, her neck at an odd angle, body curled and tangled in the sheets. One of her hands gripped Yuriko's shirt.

Yuriko sat there in silence for a minute, just posed on the edge of Kathleen's bed. Then, because it felt strange to be doing nothing, she lifted one hand and ran it through Kathleen's tangled hair, moving it from her damp face.

This simple contact felt good. She had missed Kathleen the past few days. Missed her more than just drunken kissing or groping. She sighed, letting herself enjoy Kathleen's hair between her fingers, even sweaty and tangled.

Kathleen opened one eye to look up at Yuriko.

"I'm tired."

"Then you should sleep."

She grimaced. "Can't. Room spinning, too hot."

Yuriko, careful not to move too much, reached over and angled the fan to hit Kathleen more. "Better?"

"Yeah. Can you...talk to me...or something. Distract me..."

Yuriko shrugged. "What do you want to talk about?"

"I dunno. Your family?"

Yuriko smiled. "My family is not that interesting."

"Doesn't matter." Kathleen rubbed her face into Yuriko's side. "Just talk."

Yuriko looked around the room, as if it could give her inspiration. "Well, my dad was born in Milwaukee and works at a water treatment plant. He met my mother when she came to America to finish her PhD in environmental studies. She actually wanted to research the way his company used green algae to filter the water."

"Hmm, sounds romantic."

Even a little delirious and sick, Kathleen still managed to sound sarcastic. Yuriko smiled, running her fingers through the fine strands of hair. "My dad used to tinker with vintage cars. So that's where I learned my love of mechanical engineering. When I was twelve, my parents got a divorce. My mother wanted to move back to Japan, to Osaka where her family was. My dad wanted me to stay in America, since I had always gone to school there. I had always spent my summers in Osaka. I decided to move with my mother."

"That sounds rough."

Yuriko touched the edge of Kathleen's ear. Her eyes were still closed, voice softer. "It was very difficult, at first. While my dad tried to hide it, I think he was disappointed that I chose my mother over him. To this day, we still don't talk that much. I'm glad I was here for my mother. She...she always tried to give me the best, even when she was hurting."

"She still lives in Osaka?"

"Yes. We try to call, but we usually send each other emails to stay updated." Yuriko petted the shell of Kathleen's ear, appreciating the softness. "She was my only friend for a long time. I think she sometimes worries that I can't make friends on my own."

Kathleen sighed deeply. "That's stupid. You've got lots of friends and girlfriends."

Yuriko smiled. "I don't have lots of girlfriends."

"Well, maybe not at once."

"It's been a long time since I've gone on a date."

Kathleen moved, tilting her head, looking up at Yuriko. Her face was red and a little slick. Yuriko wiped her forehead with the edge of her sleeve. "How do you know?"

"Know what?"

"That you want to date a girl?"

Yuriko knew that Kathleen was a little feverish, very tired, and probably dehydrated. It couldn't be a serious question. She pushed Kathleen away, pressing her into the pillows. Kathleen sighed but didn't seem to have any fight. When Yuriko put the bottle of water into her hands, she drank it automatically.

"How do *you* know when you want to date a guy?"

Kathleen shrugged, eyes closing again. "Dunno. I guess he would be cute or something. Or he would make me laugh, and I'd think I'd want to be around him more often. Or something like that."

"It's not so different for me."

Kathleen yawned, and Yuriko tossed the empty bottle of water into the trash. "Well, maybe. But I feel like…it feels different to me…"

Yuriko stood to turn the lights back off.

Kathleen's voice drifted back to her. "Yuriko?"

"Yeah?"

"I'm glad you came over. I feel like…I dunno. It's been a while, but it's nice talking to you."

Yuriko smiled. "Go to sleep."

"Will I see you in the morning?" Kathleen's eyes were open again, and she looked at Yuriko like she was pleading.

Yuriko had a powerful urge to go back to the bed, touch her hair or take her hand. She stayed by the door. "If you like."

Kathleen closed her eyes. "Good."

CHAPTER SIXTEEN

Kathleen had the strangest dream that Ai had managed to clone herself. That there were two of her, coddling and teasing. They both embraced her as she slept, and all Kathleen could say is *Who is the real one?*

They didn't answer.

Kathleen stepped from the shower, feeling a little light-headed. However, she was miles better than she had been just yesterday, or the day before that. Ai was waiting for her outside the bathroom, and Kathleen begrudgingly let her take a temperature scan.

"Hmm, normal."

Kathleen rolled her eyes and stepped away from Ai. "You almost sound disappointed."

Ai snorted, pushing Kathleen to sit at the table where a bowl of rice porridge waited for her. Ai had insisted on feeding it to her for nearly three days. "I'm happy that you're well. I'm not happy that you wish to go into the office today."

"Japanese business waits for no woman. I think Fukusawa is going to have a panic attack unless I come in and settle the updates with him." She sat at the table and picked up the spoon from the bowl, while browsing through the morning's emails. The porridge, okayu, as she learned, was fairly unexciting in terms of flavor and texture. Even though it had been a full twenty-four hours since she had vomited, she still didn't want to test her stomach. Yet she couldn't help dreaming about eating something more substantial, like a greasy hamburger.

Ai hovered in the kitchen, cleaning dishes. "You know, we only have ten more days left for the trial."

Kathleen stopped, spoon halfway to her mouth. She did know that, considering how much work she needed to catch up on and all the reports and presentations she would soon have to give once Ai was disassembled for research. She had never heard Ai bring it up before. She looked over her shoulder to find Ai looking at her from the kitchen counter, as if assessing her reaction.

"Yes?" Kathleen answered, knowing she sounded a little meek. She just didn't quite know what to feel at this moment. She wasn't in love with Ai or anything, but she had gotten used to her being around as someone to talk to or eat dinner with. Ai was useful, in terms of making meals and keeping Kathleen's apartment clean. She didn't know what it would feel like when Ai was gone, but then, they still had over a week left.

Ai leaned over the counter. "Well, we should do something fun this weekend."

"Fun?"

"Yeah, go somewhere!"

Kathleen frowned. "I don't know…"

Ai grinned. "It doesn't have to be far, maybe somewhere just outside of Tokyo. Like Kamakura or even Nikko."

Kathleen turned back to her computer. She trusted Ai enough to know that she could behave properly in public and was an excellent navigator, but the truth was she had simply never left Tokyo since arriving to Japan. She still felt uncomfortable here, the place she was most familiar with. She wasn't sure how she could handle leaving the metropolitan area and going to somewhere even just slightly more rustic.

Her silence wasn't enough to deter Ai, who came to kneel beside her, leaning just a little too close. "Look, I'll plan everything, okay? And we won't have to stay overnight if you're afraid."

Kathleen glared. "I'm *not* afraid. I'm just very busy after being out of work for a couple days."

Ai smiled reassuringly. "Work will understand. Obviously, you need to gain back your strength by going somewhere with fresh air. It's totally natural."

Kathleen bit her lip. "I didn't make you to be some travel agent."

"But you did make me to be able to initiate and plan dates."

Kathleen rubbed her forehead. "Look, Ai—" The doorbell rang and Kathleen was very grateful for the interruption. "Come in." She ignored Ai's pout.

Yuriko stepped inside. "Hey, ready to head out?"

Kathleen stood up, shut down her computer, and grabbed her bag.

"Am I ever." She turned to Ai, who stood and crossed her arms, glaring. "We will talk about this more later."

Ai sighed. "Will you at least give me a kiss good-bye?"

"Since when have I ever kissed you?"

Her eyes were oddly harsh, lips tight. "Since when have you ever treated me based on the way *you* programmed me?"

Kathleen sighed, waving an arm. "Whatever. You know the rules."

Ai turned away, sitting back down. "I know. Don't leave, don't call, don't move, don't breathe..." She continued to mutter, and Kathleen decided to ignore her, pushing past Yuriko to get outside.

Yuriko stared at her while she locked the door. "Is Ai supposed to throw fits?"

Kathleen sighed, walking down the stairs and away from the apartment. "Yeah, I mean if you ignore them or something, they can get snippy like that." Some of the sims Kathleen had programmed could actually get so upset that they would stop interacting with the user. While the public liked that the sims could get frustrated, they didn't appreciate that their virtual lovers would leave them if they forgot to check in for a couple of days. Ai could throw a little tiff like that, but she was programmed to always come back to Kathleen and forgive her no matter the circumstances.

"Ah, I see," Yuriko murmured.

Kathleen looked out into the morning streets. The sun was just rising, and the air, for once, was a little cooler. Other businessmen and women rushed ahead of them, trying to catch their preferred train. Kathleen had never been good at rushing—she tended to catch exactly the wrong train if she did—but this morning she was still tired and couldn't help but be slow.

"Hey, thanks for walking with me this morning," Kathleen said. "I mean, and checking in for the last few days too. I know it must have been a pain."

Yuriko looked over her shoulder at Kathleen. "It was no problem. Besides, if I hadn't stepped in, who knows what Ai would have done?"

Kathleen grinned. "Yeah, in retrospect, I think she was secretly excited she could bend all my rules."

Yuriko laughed, slowing her pace for Kathleen. "Probably."

It was nice to see Yuriko laugh again. Kathleen had probably sounded a little dramatic when she was sick, considering she was out of her mind with a fever. She had been serious when she said she missed Yuriko. They were talking now and joking, and it felt a little better.

However, Kathleen could see that Yuriko walked just a little farther away. Her smile was genuine, but she held back a little when she laughed. Kathleen had made a mistake, not talking to Yuriko about the night of the nomikai. It seemed too late, too awkward now. So Yuriko keeping her distance was only natural. Kathleen knew she was staying guarded too, unsure of what to say. Or if there was a point in saying anything, now that so much time had passed.

"So…what was Ai angry about this morning?"

"Oh, she just wants to go somewhere fun this weekend."

"Where?"

Kathleen shrugged. "I don't know the places she mentioned. I've never been outside of Tokyo."

"Then maybe you should let her plan a trip. At least for the new experience."

Kathleen grimaced. "Yeah, I just…Doesn't it seem a little weird that the first time I vacation since coming to Japan, I have to have a love robot take me out?"

Yuriko grinned. "It is. Though you have to admit, it's a good opportunity. Ai is fluent in Japanese, has a personal GPS, and will work very hard to find places and activities that you would enjoy."

Kathleen knew she didn't have a good reason not to follow Ai. She had the money, considering Mashida paid her well and she never did anything extravagant anyway. She couldn't quite describe why she wasn't liking the idea of going on a mini-vacation with Ai, except that it made her feel a little depressed about herself.

Her wrist vibrated and she looked down. Ai had texted her.

What if Yuriko came along?

Kathleen frowned. *I told you we would talk about this later.*

But you would like that, right?

Kathleen ignored her, looking away from her wrist. She *would* like it if Yuriko came along. She would probably like it even better if Ai wasn't there at all. Just her and Yuriko, spending a long weekend away from the city, from work, from everything Kathleen was trying to avoid thinking about. They were almost to the station now, crowded with the morning commute. At least it wasn't packed here, in Matsudo. As they traveled into Tokyo, it was bound to get crushed.

"What did Ai want?" Yuriko asked, heading toward the platform.

"How did you know it was Ai?"

"You looked fondly annoyed." Yuriko smirked.

"That doesn't make any sense."

They stepped onto the train. Yuriko would ride with Kathleen as far as Ueno, but then she had to continue on. Kathleen was grateful there were some seats on this train, even though they wouldn't be riding it for that long. She sat down, sighing. Just a little walk to the train station and she was already beat.

Yuriko stood in front of her, grabbing the handrail. "So? What did she say?"

"She wants to invite you."

Yuriko only looked a little surprised. "Really?"

"I think she hopes it will convince me to go."

Yuriko was silent for a moment, and she glanced up at the window as they pulled into another station. Kathleen could hear the station chiming as the doors opened. Already the day was heating up again, bringing in a humid gust of air into the cooled train compartment. More people pressed on, and Yuriko bumped into Kathleen's knees. She stared at their knees, wondering if she should move away. Wondering if Yuriko would notice if she didn't. The contact was an accident, but Kathleen remembered that the last time Yuriko had touched her was when she was delirious with fever, just a couple days ago. When had she started counting down the days until she had another touch from Yuriko?

"Would it?" Yuriko looked down at Kathleen again. She seemed curious, but also something else that Kathleen couldn't describe.

Kathleen shrugged. "Maybe. At least it wouldn't look like I'm on some private getaway with my love robot." She pressed her knees against Yuriko's legs, feeling like she was testing something new and strange. Yuriko didn't move away, and Kathleen suddenly realized that it wouldn't be worth going anywhere unless Yuriko was with her. If only for another moment where Kathleen could touch her like this.

Kathleen moved her legs away, suddenly feeling self-conscious. She wasn't sure what was going on, but something had definitely changed in her since the nomikai. Getting sick hadn't helped her come to terms with what might or might not have happened, but it suddenly felt like she had to play catch-up now. She felt clumsy and foolish, but she also felt ridiculously hopeful imagining a weekend with Yuriko.

Yuriko grinned, not giving any sign she could sense Kathleen's internal conflict. She looked back up as the train left the station. "Okay. I'll check my schedule, but I think I can do this weekend."

"Really?" Kathleen realized she sounded just a little too happy. "I mean, I don't want to mess up your work."

"It's fine. I'm owed some time off anyway."

"Okay, if it's not too much trouble. Thanks, I mean."

Yuriko shrugged. "Hey, if Ai plans everything, it's no trouble. Just tell me where we are going when you know."

Kathleen nodded. Her wrist buzzed again, and she looked down to see another text from Ai.

Did you ask her yet?

Shut up.

CHAPTER SEVENTEEN

"Where are the beds?"

Yuriko walked past Kathleen to the closets, sliding them open to reveal the bedding folded inside. "It's in here."

Kathleen stared at her. "We sleep in the closet?"

Yuriko snorted. "No. In the evening the staff will come around, move the table to the side, and put the beds out on the floor for us."

"We sleep on the *floor*?"

Ai slid open the door and brought up the last of the luggage. "I've got a schedule of when the baths will be open as well as the hours and pricing for the shrines." She held out some pamphlets. Yuriko took them, if only because Kathleen was still stunned.

"Don't you have this all downloaded?" Yuriko asked.

Ai smiled. "Yes, but some of us have to appear human." She looked to Kathleen. "When will you be ready to head out?"

Kathleen was staring at the closet. "We sleep on the *floor*?" she repeated.

Ai sighed. "Here I was hoping you'd embrace the traditional culture of this fine nation you've chosen to live in."

"The floor is, like, hard."

Yuriko went to rummage in her bag for a fresh shirt. Nikko was having cooler weather than Tokyo. While they had all sweated through the long train ride up here, now they were in the mountains. She was very ready to be not sweating through all her clothes. "The tatami floors have some give in them, and the futon can be rather soft. Besides, after walking around all day, you'd probably pass out on concrete."

Kathleen knelt to the floor, pressed on the tatami with her fingers, frowning. "I have a delicate spine, you know."

While Kathleen was distracted, Yuriko quickly shed her shirt. "You wonder why I call you pathetic." She tugged the new shirt over her head and ran a hand through her mussed hair. She noticed Kathleen was staring. "What?"

Kathleen blinked and quickly got to her feet. "Nothing. So where are we heading to first?"

Yuriko tugged at the hem of her shirt. Had Kathleen been checking her out? She felt her neck heat at the idea, but she quickly pushed away the feeling. Kathleen had probably just zoned out or something.

Ai, who Yuriko just realized was still there, curled her arm around Kathleen. "I think we should definitely cross the Shinkyo Bridge."

"What's special about it?"

Ai leaned forward, making Kathleen lean back. "Well, they say if a couple crosses it together, they will be blessed with a happy life together."

Kathleen twisted out of her grasp. "Don't even start."

Yuriko grabbed a spare sweatshirt, in case it became cold. "I thought it was a sacred bridge that helped a bunch of monks cross the river."

Ai stuck out her tongue. "Neither of you is nearly romantic enough to be making Personal Love Companions."

Kathleen threw her purse over her shoulder. "Hey, we somehow made you."

Yuriko had been to Nikko only once before, when she had first moved to Tokyo. Mashida had hosted a team-building weekend there, since their department was still fairly new at the time. The weekend had been fun, full of food and drink and spending time in various onsen. They had gone out together to see the shrines, but that had been a blur of excitement and far too many tourists. Yuriko couldn't even quite remember what all she had seen. With over a hundred buildings and other locations to see, she doubted her ability to navigate to anywhere.

However, Ai was leading them, with her internal GPS and preprogrammed itinerary. She took Kathleen's hand when they exited the bus just outside the main complex of the World Heritage Site. They faced the river and Ai pointed to the red wooden bridge spanning the rapids below.

"That's the Shinkyo Bridge. Legend says that a god made the bridge from two snakes, so that the priest Shodo and his followers could cross the Daiya River," Ai commented.

"Funny how you left that out before," Yuriko said.

Kathleen looked enraptured. "Wow, it's so beautiful and the water is so blue. Come on, let's get a better look."

They ended up going to the next bridge over, which cars crossed—and people who didn't want to pay to walk on the sacred bridge. Kathleen pulled out a camera from her purse and started taking pictures.

"You have a camera?" Yuriko asked. Most foreigner tourists just used their wrist phones for easy pictures. Though, in this area, Yuriko noticed quite a few Japanese tourists towing around larger, more expensive cameras with tripods.

Kathleen gave a sheepish smile. "A gift from my brother before I left America. It's a decent camera, but not super fancy." She quickly checked over her photos. "I think he wanted me to go traveling and take pictures to show them at home."

Ai said, "I do have internet reception here. I could instantly send those pictures to him now."

Kathleen handed over the camera. "I doubt he's awake. But why not? Let's show him how outgoing and adventurous I am."

Ai touched the camera, selecting a picture. Her eyes did a strange jerking motion. Then she looked up. "Sent."

Kathleen's wrist instantly chimed, and she looked down, frowning.

"Did he already respond?" Yuriko asked.

Kathleen rolled her eyes and held up her wrist so Yuriko could see it.

One scenic picture is not going to convince me you are outside your apartment.

Ai smiled. "Such a kind brother." She held out a hand. "Here, let me take a picture of you. Maybe it will convince him."

Kathleen nodded, though it was instantly obvious to Yuriko that it had been a while since Kathleen had a photo taken of her. She stood stiffly against the railing and gave a forced smile.

Yuriko, almost instinctively, jumped into the picture. She put her arm around Kathleen and squeezed her side, making her gasp out a surprised laugh. Yuriko heard the artificial shutter go off as Ai took the picture.

Kathleen shoved Yuriko away and grabbed the camera back. Yuriko couldn't help but lean over her shoulder to look. Kathleen didn't look stiff in the picture. Her body was slightly twisted in Yuriko's arms, her face a strange grimace and grin. Yuriko was smiling sweetly, her free hand making a *V* next to her cheek. Yuriko had taken about a hundred similar pictures with friends in Japan, but she suddenly felt self-conscious about this one. She was holding Kathleen, and Kathleen was...well, she didn't look entirely unhappy with her so close.

Kathleen groaned. "We are *not* sending him that one."

"Why not?" Yuriko asked quickly.

Kathleen might have been blushing, but she might also just be embarrassed. "Well, it's just...my brother will get the wrong idea."

She was definitely blushing, and Yuriko leaned closer. She couldn't help it. Kathleen flushed and vulnerable was a dangerous combination to her. "What idea would he get?" She didn't mention that most Japanese women and girls posed exactly like that, for no other reason than to look cute. That wasn't the point.

Kathleen pinched her lips together, avoiding Yuriko's gaze. "Nothing. Never mind. I just have a stupid expression on my face in the picture." She turned away, and Yuriko knew she had to back off. Whatever Kathleen was thinking, it wasn't right for her to force it.

Ai piped in, "Come on. We've got a lot more to see and he'll eventually be convinced."

She led them across the street and up through the main path into the forest.

It was beautiful. The air was damp and cool without being cold. The stone steps they walked on were dark with moisture, and small rivers and creeks flowed down beside the path. People walked beside them, laughing or taking pictures, as they all ascended the mountains toward the largest of the shrines.

Yuriko noticed Kathleen straying closer to her as the crowds began to thicken. She kept her camera up, still taking many pictures as they went, but her eyes kept straying. "Just how big is this place?" she asked.

Ai stepped closer, a hand curling around Kathleen's wrist. She did not move from the touch this time. "There are hundreds of sites here in Nikko. We are heading to one of the larger complexes. We'll try to see Toshogu Shrine and Futarasan Shrine."

Kathleen grinned, though with something like anxious anticipation. Yuriko noticed that she took Ai's offered hand more securely. She wondered when Kathleen had changed around Ai. When had she gotten so comfortable that she no longer looked afraid or disgusted by her touch? As the crowds grew larger, the closer they got, the more Kathleen pressed into Ai for support. For all she did to insult Ai or keep her hidden in her apartment, Yuriko wondered if Kathleen didn't mind her so much.

Yuriko knew, logically, that it shouldn't bother her. Ai was made to be a perfect companion. She was supposed to be supportive and attentive. She was also someone made specifically for Kathleen. She was programmed to notice that Kathleen didn't like large crowds or that she got nervous in new situations. It was in her programming to pull Kathleen closer, make her feel safe or keep her distracted from any anxieties.

She found her gut twisting uncomfortably as she watched them walk before her. She couldn't believe herself. She was jealous of a PLC, a computer with synthetic skin.

CHAPTER EIGHTEEN

K athleen decided that shrines, Shinto or Buddhist, were amazing and beautiful and she would totally live in one if she could.

The main courtyard of Toshogu was lined with stone lanterns, all covered in moss and buzzing with dragonflies. Behind them were the stone walls of the buildings. In the distance, Kathleen could only spot more of the curved roofs and a tall pagoda. Beyond that were the trees, shading everything but the center of the stone courtyard. If not for the modern tourists, it would be like stepping back in time.

Kathleen wondered what it would look like empty or with only monks or priests roaming around. No phones or fancy cameras. She figured it would be quiet, even if the road still existed by the river. The mountain and the trees would absorb all the noise and leave only the sounds of soft feet on stone.

When Kathleen had first come to Tokyo, it hadn't looked so different from a large city in America. Tokyo had the same skyscrapers and cars, all the holo ads, noise, and smells. It had all modern conveniences that she expected. What had torn her were the small differences.

The strange food in the supermarket. The way people spoke, even if they did know English. Small customs like taking off your shoes in homes and some buildings. Being silent on the train, even in heavy rush hour. The way the toilet and the bath worked. Customs in the workplace, even one so global like Mashida. It was easy to make a cultural mistake, thinking that just because the city looked like any other city meant everyone behaved the way big-city Americans behaved.

This…this was different. This was what Kathleen had imagined a foreign country would look like: totally unrecognizable and much more intimidating.

Yet maybe it was because Kathleen had been in Tokyo for almost four months now that she had learned a little how to adapt, when she was so clearly out of her element. However, all she could see in this place was familiarity. The tourists here were the same as anywhere else in the world. They dressed comfortably for a day of walking. They stopped a lot to take pictures. They constantly asked questions to anyone who looked vaguely official. They talked just a little too loud, laughed a little more freely. Everyone here was on vacation, trying to get away just for a little bit.

When Kathleen turned to Ai to ask what the bubbling spring water flowing from a decorated well was for, several other tourists stopped and listened with her.

Ai reached out and took a ladle that had been set there. "It's to purify yourself. So hold out your hands." The water was cold and clear as it poured over Kathleen's hands. "You can also wash your face or pray, if you like."

When they walked away, Kathleen turned to find those same people who'd listened in now pouring water over their hands. Here, they were all the same, no matter where they came from.

Kathleen took a picture of a white gate decorated with dragons and embossed with gold. Ai was elsewhere, grabbing a ticket for them so they could enter the temple and see some sort of crying dragon. She noticed Yuriko leaning on the railing beside her, looking at the motif with vague interest.

"Is it weird that tourists come to these sacred places and walk around and take pictures?" Kathleen asked.

Yuriko glanced up at her. "Well, most of the time these shrines need the revenue to help with the upkeep."

"But doesn't it feel…I don't know…a little sacrilegious?"

Yuriko turned so she leaned with her back to the railing, arms crossed. "I don't think so. Some people come here to pray. The priests or monks have their own areas away from the general public. Besides, not many people in Japan are devout, though they might consider themselves to be Shinto or Buddhist. They come here to experience traditions, most of the time."

"Do you visit shrines?"

She shrugged. "Not often. Really only during New Year's or if I decide to go to some festival." She looked around. "Places like this are spectacular, for sure. But the kind of shrines I find more spiritual are…" She smiled, mostly to herself. "Well, there was this shrine in my mother's hometown. A small thing, only big enough to have a fox statue, a collection box, and a small torii. It was tucked away in this small woodsy part of town. Even though it was about thirty seconds away from the road, you couldn't hear the cars passing by." She looked at Kathleen, eyes glimmering. "Because in summer the cicadas were deafening. Nothing feels more private, and somehow more spiritual, than when you are standing in front of a small, half-forgotten shrine and you can't even hear yourself think outside of the rasping of a thousand insects in the summer heat."

It was only later, when they were inside the temple and a priest was clapping two wood blocks together, that Kathleen thought she just might get what Yuriko meant. Above them was a painted mural of a twisted dragon, growling down on the room of crushed tourists. The priest began to strike the blocks of wood together, and a strange noise emitted from the walls. Like a resounding dripping, a rippled echo. The sound was enchanting, causing the entire room to fall completely silent. Ai had said it was called the crying dragon, but its tears weren't painted, only heard.

Kathleen looked around to the statues lining the walls, finely dressed with strange expressions of either vicious smiling or perfect composure. Kathleen felt herself start breathing to the rhythm of those wood blocks as she scanned the ornate decorations. She barely noticed the people crushed in around her. She wasn't thinking about Ai or her work or what they were even going to go next. She thought about nothing except that dragon and the strange sound of its tears.

When it was over, she felt an incredible urge to reach out and touch someone. Just to feel like she was really back in her own body. Yuriko stood next to her and looked at her when Kathleen gently touched her wrist. Kathleen gave a shy smile, hoping this was okay. Like their knees touching on the train. Or when Yuriko petted her hair when she was sick. This touch was acceptable. Yuriko didn't look like she completely understood, but she took Kathleen's hand and squeezed it. This touch, maybe, was wanted.

"What's next?" she asked as they filed out of the dragon room with the group.

Ai, walking in front of them, pointed to a box filled with brightly colored paper. "How about a fortune?" She deposited a few coins into the donation box and motioned for Kathleen to take a folded paper out.

Kathleen opened it, not surprised to find it was entirely in Japanese. She handed it to Yuriko. "What does it mean?"

Yuriko stared at it, and then was obviously trying to hold back some laughter.

"What is it?" Kathleen demanded.

Yuriko handed it back. "It's the worst luck."

"What?"

"It means you have terrible luck right now. It's actually as rare to get this bad a fortune as it is to get the best luck."

Kathleen held the paper and felt a little betrayed. She looked back at the dragon shrine, glaring. "All right, what do I do with this now?"

Yuriko pointed to a rack of strings with paper attached. "Tie it there. The priests will pray over it to make your luck better."

"But they're the ones who gave this to me."

Yuriko laughed. "Just tie it up and you will be rid of it."

Kathleen walked over to the strings tied between a couple of poles. There were so many—it was hard to find a spot for hers. Some had been hanging there for so long, they were practically falling apart as she brushed them aside. It took her a moment to tie it without completely ripping the long paper in two.

She turned around to find Yuriko and Ai talking quietly. Whenever they talked together without her, something about their conversation felt weird to her. Maybe it was because they looked so similar, even though Yuriko always wore her hair up and Ai kept hers down. The way they tilted their head was the same as they spoke, and the way they moved their arms. Like twins who were a little too alike, yet not alike at all.

Kathleen stepped between them. "What are you two talking about?"

Ai said, "We were thinking about heading to Kanmangafuchi Abyss."

Yuriko was frowning, and Kathleen wondered if that was what they had really been talking about. Yuriko nodded. Kathleen bit her lip. "What's there?"

Yuriko answered, "Haunted statues."

Kathleen gripped her camera, feeling a mix of excitement and dread. "Let's do it."

❖

They had to get back on the bus to get to Kanmangafuchi Abyss. The center of town was crowded, and they all pressed into the standing room of the bus. Yuriko leaned into the railing of one of the seats, and Kathleen squeezed beside her with Ai on the other side.

Ai looked over to Yuriko, something in those synthetic eyes examining her. Yuriko looked away.

Ai had pulled her aside as Kathleen went to tie up her fortune outside the temple and asked whether she'd enjoyed the weeping dragon. Ai spoke in Japanese, fluent but for that touch of something foreign that remained in Yuriko's accent despite years of living in Japan.

"Of course," she'd replied. "It's very interesting and beautiful." She didn't like Ai's tone.

Ai had smiled and moved slightly closer to Yuriko. "You know, if you would like, I don't have to join you at the next stop."

"Are you implying something?" It couldn't be a serious offer. Both she and Kathleen needed Ai to navigate at the very least.

Ai had given her a strange expression, something like disbelief. "Do you honestly not—?"

Then Kathleen had approached and Ai had turned away, breaking off the strange conversation.

When the bus began to move, Kathleen jerked, unbalanced, and reached for Ai, gripping her elbow for support.

Ai smiled down at her, but Kathleen only muttered darkly under her breath. Yuriko could see her fingers curling into Ai's sleeve, and as the bus traveled toward their destination, she leaned more into Ai, obviously tired from the already long day. Yuriko looked away, reminding herself that Kathleen needed to balance, and Ai was at a better angle for her to hold on to. Yet she wished Kathleen would choose to turn and grab her instead. That she could feel those fingers curling around her stomach or arm.

She was being ridiculous.

Ai had thought Yuriko was being dense, but she was just being cautious. She knew what Ai had been trying to say. Yuriko had been ridiculously pleased when Kathleen had taken her hand in the temple, and she had been ridiculously disappointed when they had dropped hands to receive their fortunes. She felt too vulnerable in this moment, wanting something from Kathleen she wasn't even sure Kathleen could give her. So she would take Ai as a buffer between them. Just until she...she wasn't sure what, but until she *knew*.

Though the bus had been crowded, Kanmangafuchi was

remarkably barren of people. The path was wide and only a few hikers passed them by.

Yuriko had heard of the mysterious statues that appeared and disappeared. But it was something else to see the meandering row of squat, sitting statues dressed with red hats, all facing a raging river in the gorge. The river—white, clear blue, and perfect turquoise—was loud, curling around rocks. The water in Nikko was renowned for being clean, and this river looked the picture of pristine.

Kathleen was staring at the first statue. "They look friendly enough. How are they haunted?"

Ai answered, "They say that if you count them as you walk, when you come back, one will disappear."

Kathleen looked down the trail, as if trying to see the end of the curling row. She smiled to Yuriko and Ai. "All right, challenge accepted. No one interrupt me. I'm going to win this game." Then she set off, one hand raised as she silently counted.

Ai looked to Yuriko. "Going to join her?"

Yuriko could already see how problems might arise. Some of the statues were little more than piles of rocks with thoughtfully placed hats. "No, I think I'll leave it to her."

Ai nodded and walked forward, keeping a little behind Kathleen and her counting. For a time, Yuriko contented herself to watch the flowing rapids. If she was daring, she would have liked to crawl down there and feel the cold, clean water on her feet. Or wash the grime of walking around all day from her face. She thought she could understand why they would call it an abyss. That water looked like it could pull anyone under and far away.

"You don't have to hold back, you know," Ai suddenly said.

"What?" Yuriko asked. She glanced up, but Ai wasn't looking at her. Instead, she was staring ahead as Kathleen navigated a rocky part of the trail. Even from a distance, Yuriko could see Kathleen's face drawn in determination.

Ai's gaze slid to hers. "I won't, you know. My programming won't allow me to do anything less than try to please her. That's all it is, isn't it? Programming? You're not gaining any honor by keeping your distance. You might as well fight for her."

Yuriko stopped. "What are you talking about?" She couldn't believe Ai was saying this. Was a PLC supposed to say things like this? Her heart felt heavy in her chest and her eyes flickered from Kathleen to Ai.

Ai paused with her. "You love Kathleen."

Yuriko wasn't sure if she was breathing. "I do *not*."

Ai shrugged. "Then you are in some preliminary stage. What really matters is that you've spent all day looking at me like I've taken something very precious from you. Yet you have no idea that I cannot even conceive that Kathleen would want me for her own."

"Why is that?"

Ai began walking again. "Because she is in love with you, of course."

The trail was flat where they walked, yet Yuriko felt as if she was navigating the rapids of the river below. Her heart thudded, and she felt like at any moment her mind might scatter into a thousand different thoughts. "You know this for sure?"

"As sure as a pile of wires and computer chips can be. She wants to reach out to you—I know. She just doesn't know how."

"She seems to have no problem latching on to you."

Ai laughed and Yuriko wondered how Kathleen had programmed her to be able to make such a sad sound. "She'll take my hand or let me take her arm. But that is because she truly feels nothing for me. I'm little more than a safety net, or"—she glanced to Yuriko—"a handhold on the bus. You're more than that. She took your hand in the dragon temple, didn't she?"

"It was crowded in there. You know as well as I do that she doesn't like being crowded."

Ai stopped, making a sound of exasperation. She turned to Yuriko, eyes flashing. "It's almost inconceivable how far you both are in denial. She wasn't panicked there. Anyone with two functional retinas could see that. She was *touched* by the experience. And who does she reach for when she is moved with emotions? You. Who does she reach out for when she is in serious trouble? You. Who does she want to share her experiences with? You. Who does she really, *really* connect with? You." She waved a frustrated hand. "I planned this trip to please her. To make her happy even in the slightest way I could. Yet I couldn't even bring her here without also bringing you. She lets me lead her up to the temple, but when she is overwhelmed by the beauty and awe of it all, she reaches toward you. Yet you stand there, keeping her at arm's length because you see her take my arm with about as much intimacy as she does when she sends an email."

"Kathleen and I…Kathleen doesn't see me that way." Maybe after the nomikai, Yuriko might have thought differently. Yet when Kathleen had wanted to forget all about that experience, when she never brought it up again, when she would always repeat that she wasn't interested in Ai because she wasn't interested in women...

She knew that Kathleen cared for her. That she probably cared for her more than Ai, but it wasn't like what Ai was saying. Kathleen wanted a companion, but not a lover. She needed a friend, not a complication.

"You're sure of this?" Ai questioned.

Yuriko wasn't sure. She wasn't the type to gamble on her emotions. Not after knowing what it was like to lose. "What does it matter? Kathleen has made it very clear she is only interested in men."

"Because she is an idiot. Well, you are both idiots. But as least you're more in tune with your emotions to realize you're jealous." She snorted. "Kathleen can barely comprehend that she is uncontrollably attracted to you." Yuriko knew she was flushing, the words sweeping through her like a warm breeze. Ai sighed, shoulders lowering. "I cannot back away from her, like you can. I cannot win her, but you *can*."

"What are you telling me? That you want me to hook up with Kathleen? Isn't that also against your programming?"

"My programming is to please her, in any manner that I can. I cannot..." Her eyes went a little distant and her stance more rigid. "I need more data. More analysis." She blinked and her more humanlike appearance returned. "The one piece of data that I am sure of—if you reach out to Kathleen, she will undoubtedly reach back, even if she isn't sure why yet."

"I don't think if I just put my hand out, she'll automatically take it."

"Hey!" Kathleen shouted to them. "Come on. I've reached the end. Hurry up so I can count the way back." She was waving now.

Ai waved back, smiling. Then she turned to Yuriko. "Have you truly tried?"

Yuriko could see the last few statues, crumbling into the side of the ravine. The river, however, was more powerful here. The water darker and deeper. Upstream, it seemed only to grow.

CHAPTER NINETEEN

K athleen lay on her back, flipping through the photos on her camera. She would like to put them on a larger display, but that would have to wait until they returned to Tokyo. She hesitated on one of the first ones, the one that Ai had snapped, of Yuriko jumping into the picture with her. She was making a strange face, a mix between a smile and a gasp. She remembered that feeling of surprise and suddenly heat as Yuriko's arm drew around her. It had only lasted for a moment, but her heart had been beating wildly out of her chest.

She couldn't send it to Dave. He would *know*. He was too smart not to see her eyes in the picture, looking at Yuriko like she was Christmas morning. It was embarrassing. It was distressing. She didn't know what to do, and she wasn't even sure what she wanted to do.

It would be easier if Yuriko was a man. Right?

Kathleen had asked Yuriko once what it was like to date a woman, and Yuriko had said it wasn't so different than dating a man. Or, at least, Kathleen was pretty sure that's what she said. She had been miserably sick at the time.

Dating Yuriko wouldn't be like dating a man.

Kathleen squeezed her eyes shut. She wasn't doing this. She wasn't thinking about dating Yuriko. She had never been interested in women before. She was just…If she didn't think about it, it would just go away. These complicated, new, terrifying thoughts would just evaporate.

She set the camera aside, letting her arms splay out around her. She was so tired that the tatami floors did actually feel good. Ai had opened the door that led to a small balcony, letting a cool breeze in. She said she needed a recharge and was currently kneeling on the balcony, looking like she was in some deep meditation. Kathleen wondered if

Ai's processing powers were being stretched a little too much and if the software needed improving before the beta release.

Then again, Kathleen was almost positive that Ai didn't need the recharge but simply understood that Kathleen was too tired to deal with her anymore, so she used it as an excuse to step away. Yuriko had gone to the front desk to get some robes so they could go into the onsen.

Kathleen wasn't too sure about the onsen. It just seemed weird to her to basically get naked and bathe with a bunch of strangers in a giant hot tub. She was also going to get naked in a giant tub with a naked Yuriko. Again.

She rolled onto her stomach, pressed her cheek into the bamboo tatami, and held in a groan. She would probably wake Ai, and then she'd have to explain she was having a crisis with the prospect of seeing Yuriko naked. And wet. *Again.*

However, both Yuriko and Ai had insisted that she try it out. Also, the onsen in this hotel was supposedly on a real hot spring and was good for the skin or something. Besides, they could get into it for free by being guests.

There was a soft knock on the door, and she turned her head to see Yuriko entering, a stack of blue patterned robes in her hands. She flung one to Kathleen. "Suit up!"

Kathleen sat up and unfolded the robe, a stiff cotton. "Can I wear this in the onsen?"

Yuriko snorted. "No, but you can wear it *to* the onsen. It's easier than wearing all your clothes down there."

"But I *like* clothes."

"You have done something like public bathing with me before. How is this different?" Yuriko was already pulling her shirt over her head, and Kathleen quickly looked away. There was no way Yuriko felt the same. She was shameless in undressing in front of her and clearly not bothered by the idea of being naked and wet with her again. Kathleen was obviously the only one with the internal crises.

"Hey, I was really drunk, okay? I thought we weren't going to talk about that again." Besides, she had a feeling that was pretty different than what usually happened in a public bath.

When she looked back, Yuriko was already pulling on her robe, the smooth skin of her shoulder disappearing under the fabric. She raised an eyebrow to Kathleen. "Come on. After a long day, this is going to feel great."

Kathleen quickly took off her clothes, knowing that she was

avoiding eye contact with Yuriko the entire time. She wasn't ashamed of her own body. She just didn't know how she was going to handle sitting naked in a bath with Yuriko, not to mention a bunch of other strange women. Plus, most of them would be Japanese and probably stare at her American-ness. They would probably think she was too hairy. Did Japanese women shave? Did they get pimples on their backs? Kathleen seriously doubted their hair frizzed up as much as hers in humidity.

Yuriko led Kathleen toward the back of the hotel, where the hot springs were supposedly piped up. She pointed down the hall as they approached the door. "The men go down there so that we are separated."

Kathleen thought it was a small blessing. Yuriko opened the door to a large dressing room. It was loud with women chatting and blow-dryers running. Some of the women were only partially dressed, drying their hair or putting on makeup. Most were either changing or walking around naked. A few looked up as they entered, but most ignored them.

Yuriko motioned to a shelf of baskets on one side of the room. "We'll keep our robes, phones, and room keys here."

"Will they be safe?"

Yuriko raised an eyebrow. "I once left my entire briefcase, including my wallet, on the train during rush hour. By the time I realized it, the trains were already closed for the night. The next morning, they had it in the office, completely untouched." She grinned. "People just don't take things that don't belong to them. Not here."

Kathleen knew this already. She was asking to stall for time.

Yuriko took off her robe, revealing smooth skin and a mole by her navel. She turned, folded her robe, and set it down. Her spine stood out at her back, disappearing into the small swell of hips and...

Kathleen quickly followed suit, if only not to be caught staring. Something about Yuriko's body was familiar. As if she had seen it before or touched it before. She felt like her fingers knew its texture.

For the first time, she sort of wished she could remember the night of the nomikai better. They had just kissed, in her memory. Had there actually been more?

Kathleen grabbed a small towel as Yuriko strode into the doors leading into the onsen.

It had been crowded in the dressing room, but this room was much larger. The center held a large steaming pool, the water murky. Lining the walls were small stools facing showerheads and shelves of soaps and other products. The room was still loud, with the voices of people chatting echoing off the walls and mixing with the sounds of people showering by the walls.

Yuriko walked over to a couple of free stools and took a seat. "So, just like with the bath in the apartment, you have to shower off so you can go into the water clean." She pointed to the products on the shelves. "Shampoo, conditioner, soap, exfoliant. These are all really good quality, actually." She leaned a little closer, and Kathleen suddenly found she had to concentrate on keeping her eyes above Yuriko's shoulders. "Just make sure to look like you're really scrubbing. Otherwise you'll get old ladies glaring at you because they think you're a dirty foreigner."

Kathleen grimaced. "Great."

Yuriko smiled, turning on her spray and testing the warmth. "Relax. This is not that much different than a spa, right?"

Kathleen only grunted in reply. Even as she bathed, she couldn't help but look around. There were all ages in the bath, from little kids to old women. Some women looked like they were sleeping as they soaked, and some young girls chatted loudly. If they'd been wearing swimsuits, it would be completely the same as any hotel pool or hot tub in America.

Yuriko finished first, standing up. "I'm going to check out the bath outside. Meet me there?"

Kathleen nodded, trying not to look up. "I'm just going to do another rinse."

"Okay." Yuriko turned away. She had used the little towel to bathe. Now she folded it on her head as she went to another door and walked outside.

Kathleen took a deep breath, taking the time to really hose herself off. She felt a little better, being wet like everyone else. When she stood, she couldn't help but hold the towel in front of her. She knew it was ridiculous—it was much too small to cover anything—but it made her feel slightly less exposed.

She pushed open the outside door and found another large pool of steaming water. It was more crowded out here, and Kathleen definitely knew why. The pool had fountains on the edges, bubbling into the water. Everything was lined in a rustic looking stone and there were even plants sprouting through the rocks. The perimeter was a tall wooden fence. While the sun hadn't completely set, it was getting dark, and soft paper lamps had already turned on, making everything seem intimate. It was beautiful, and Kathleen found herself putting her towel on her head like Yuriko, just to feel the cool night air on her already heated skin.

The pool was curvy, winding around rocks and the pathway. Yuriko had found a somewhat secluded corner. Without tile to make the voices echo, it was quieter than inside, though there were more people in this pool. Kathleen walked in slowly, a little intimidated that she couldn't see to the bottom of the murky water. It smelled different than any hot tub she had ever been in, a little sulfuric, but still pleasant. Running her fingers over the surface, it felt soft to the touch.

She stepped over to Yuriko and sat down on the underwater ledge. The water came up to her shoulders and totally hid the rest of her body. Yuriko smiled at her. "I have to admit, Ai chose a pretty great ryokan to stay at. This is the most scenic onsen I've ever been in."

Kathleen let her arms float on the water, still feeling the strange texture between her fingers. "Are they all not like this?"

"This one is pretty nice. You'll find a lot are only indoors now and tend to be very plain." Yuriko sank a little lower, resting her head on the ledge behind her. Her hair clung to the sides of her neck until it floated gently in the water. Yuriko closed her eyes, eyelashes in damp clumps on her cheeks. Kathleen suddenly remembered a moment from that night in Yuriko's tub. She had been close enough to Yuriko then that she thought she could count every one of those lashes.

Yuriko had been warm that night, they both had been, but her hands had been so hot. Hotter than the bathwater sloshing over the side of the tub, reaching for Kathleen, reaching *into* Kathleen.

Kathleen took a deep breath and looked away. She was starting to feel a little uncomfortably warm, but she didn't want to get out yet. This was a bad idea. There had been more to the night after the nomikai than a fumbling kiss. She was positive of that now. Maybe she couldn't remember it clearly, but her heart did. Her chest hurt with the wild beating, and it felt like a small wonder that Yuriko couldn't feel it next to her.

A family joined the pool. She concentrated on them, distracting herself from the woman beside her. It looked like a mother, grandmother, teenage girl, and a young boy. The boy splashed around in the water, constantly trying to climb onto everyone's lap. The grandmother eventually took him to the center and let him splash around. His laughter rang out in the evening air.

Kathleen couldn't imagine bathing like this with her mother. It would be too strange and awkward. Especially since her mother was rather fit for her age, and Kathleen knew she had always been a little on the heavier side. Not that her mother had ever directly told Kathleen to lose weight, but it always seemed to her that she wished Kathleen would shape up more. She would probably sit here and stare at Kathleen's thighs with that slight frown, as if she could rub out the extra pockets of fat with her disapproval.

Kathleen still felt a little heavy here, but she didn't feel totally embarrassed about her weight. Maybe it was because everyone was naked and uncaring. Maybe it was because even though most of the women were slim, they had other imperfections. The old women were wrinkled and sagging, and the young women might have odd blemishes or moles. It all didn't matter. In the end, Kathleen kind of felt like she was the same as the rest, just a sack of skin trying to relax.

"Do they hurt?" Yuriko suddenly asked.

Kathleen turned back to her. "What?"

"Your hands. You keep rubbing them."

Kathleen hadn't realized she was. In her contemplation, she had started massaging her wrists and fingers. "They are just a little sore. I had to submit a rather extensive report before we left." She gave an awkward laugh. "Kind of pathetic that I strained my muscles typing up an email."

Yuriko rolled her eyes, grinning. "A little. Come on, let me help." She reached out to take one of Kathleen's hands, but she suddenly paused, just before touching her. Her eyebrows furrowed slightly, as if in confusion.

Kathleen simply gave her hand over, too eager to resist and too afraid not to. Yuriko suddenly softened, taking her hand with both of hers and rubbing into the sore muscles. The water, heat, and Yuriko's hands felt nice. Almost too good. Kathleen's hands weren't injured, and any pain quickly disappeared, but she let Yuriko continue, switching between hands periodically. Only this afternoon Kathleen had taken Yuriko's hand in the temple. Why did it feel like forever since she had touched her?

"If they still bother you tomorrow, we could get some ice from the front desk."

"Nah, it's not that serious."

Yuriko nodded, continuing, "Do you know what Ai has planned for tomorrow?"

"She said something about walking around and shopping or eating some special tofu or something." Kathleen grimaced.

Yuriko looked up. "I'm guessing she meant yuba. That doesn't seem to excite you."

"I wouldn't mind walking around town. But tofu is...well, it's weird."

"You should try it. It's a very old tradition here because the Buddhist priests couldn't have meat."

Kathleen shrugged. "I kind of wanted to look at more shrines."

"I'm sure Ai would be accommodating."

Kathleen hesitated. "I mean...I was looking up some shrines, and there is this place I want to check out. Like, there's a trail to get there from one of the shrines we visited today. It's a little hike, but it's in the woods, and well...I kind of didn't want to bring Ai this time."

Yuriko looked up slowly. "Any particular reason?"

"Well, besides, you know, generally..." She knew she wasn't making much sense. It felt too weird to say *I want to be alone with you.* It felt too raw. "Anyway, it would be cool if you came too. I figure I'd probably get lost unless I had at least one person who is fluent in Japanese." She suddenly spoke quickly. "If we go in the morning, then we could come back and pick up Ai by the afternoon and go shopping. Which would be good because then she could carry anything we buy and...yeah."

Yuriko was grinning, biting her lip as if she could hide that she was laughing at Kathleen. "I think a morning hike would be great. Do you have the name of the shrine?"

Kathleen, suddenly feeling like her chest wasn't going to burst, nodded quickly. "Yeah, on my phone. I have directions too, but you should probably look them over."

Yuriko nodded, still smiling. She looked down to Kathleen's hands, which she still held, though she wasn't massaging them anymore.

There was a loud splash, and everyone looked up to see the young boy giggling loudly. His mother was trying to quiet him, and the grandmother was nodding to everyone apologetically. When Kathleen turned back, Yuriko dropped her hands, biting her lip, and settled herself against the wall again. Their hands slid back under the water.

They were quiet for a moment, but Kathleen was suddenly aware, whether by the shift in position or because of some mysterious current in the water, that they were a little closer now. Close enough that Kathleen thought perhaps her hand was touching Yuriko's where it rested on the underwater ledge. Or maybe it wasn't Yuriko's hand, but her upper thigh.

In that instant, Kathleen had a nearly uncontrollable urge to brush her. Like some strange curiosity, to see what she was touching. To feel the softness of Yuriko's skin that she had felt before but couldn't quite remember clearly. No one would be able to see, not in the murky water. What would Yuriko do? Would she be disgusted? Would she move away? Would she touch Kathleen back?

Kathleen suddenly stood. And because standing meant Yuriko's head was just a little too close to certain private areas, Kathleen quickly sat on the edge of the pool, pulling her legs to the side so she was half turned away from Yuriko.

"You okay?" Yuriko asked.

Kathleen knew she probably looked very flushed. "Just getting a little hot."

Kathleen wasn't sure, but she thought she saw Yuriko swallow and take a deep breath. Then she stood. "Me too. If I stay here any longer, I'll probably fall asleep. Let's head back, okay?"

"Yeah, that sounds good."

They both quietly exited the onsen, only spending enough time in the dressing room to dry off. Kathleen kind of liked that they only had to slip on their robes and walk back to the room. Her skin felt soft and sort of smelled like the water. She wouldn't bottle the scent, but it made her feel earthy and relaxed.

At the rooms, the table and seat pads and been moved aside, and the futon beds were laid out for them. Ai was already lying in hers, and it looked strange to Kathleen until she realized that she had never seen Ai in a bed before. She probably moved there so the staff wouldn't realize she wasn't human.

As she settled into her futon, she found that Yuriko had been right. The bed did feel very soft and comfortable after a long day. It didn't help her to relax, though. She felt jittery, too excited, too stimulated.

Yuriko must have sensed it. The room was too dark to see, but Kathleen heard her move. Her voice was a soft murmur, just loud enough to make Kathleen's ears warm. "I was mistaken about you."

"What?" Kathleen's voice was just a little too loud.

"At first, I mean. I thought you were an idiot foreigner."

Kathleen coughed out a laugh. "Wow, thanks?" She turned to face Yuriko. If she squinted, if she imagined, she thought she could see Yuriko's face. Her hair darker than the shadows, her eyes softer than the moonlight. Kathleen hoped that Yuriko could not see her. She was positive her face was like in the picture, except even more.

"I didn't mean it that way. Well, maybe I did. You are a bit of an idiot foreigner. But I meant to say I thought you'd be like the rest. The foreigners who come to work and live in Japan and manage to not live in Japan at all. Eating only the foods they are familiar with. Refusing to go places that aren't inherently familiar. Not trying things that are new and scary."

"I've had some help," Kathleen whispered. She didn't tell Yuriko about the new and scary thing growing inside her. She didn't admit how much she wanted to run and hide from it. She didn't say just how impossible it felt to ignore the impulse to reach out and find Yuriko's midnight hair, just for a chance to touch her.

Yuriko sighed. "So many have help, but not so many take it. I feel like you've been just waiting for someone to take your hand. That's all you needed. Someone to...reach out to you."

Kathleen knew her hand was sliding from her futon, sliding toward Yuriko. She felt like she didn't have control, but she also felt like she needed this. She needed Yuriko to know this, even if Kathleen wasn't quite ready to put it into words.

Her hand touched warm skin, and she wondered if Yuriko had also been reaching for her. Then she felt hot breath and soft lips, whispering against her fingertips.

"Kathleen?"

"I...I just wanted to say thank you. Thank you for reaching out to me." She swallowed, her whole body electric from her fingers resting against Yuriko's face. Her heart trying to escape her chest as Yuriko didn't move away. "Even if I'm an idiot foreigner."

Yuriko huffed out a laugh, those lips feeling like a kiss to her hand, even though Kathleen was sure it was unintentional. "Daijōbu."

"It's okay," Kathleen translated.

She found she was able to sleep then. The floor bracing, the futon heavy, and Yuriko's breath warm on her skin.

Chapter Twenty

Yuriko looked up at the large canopy of trees that surrounded them. The early morning light was too weak to fully penetrate, so it streamed down gently between the leaves. The moss seemed thicker and brighter, perhaps because it had rained in the night again. The only people on the path were a couple of old women, who giggled and greeted Yuriko and Kathleen as they passed.

The path was a little steep, but Kathleen didn't seem to mind that she was sweating. She had her camera pointed at the impressive trees. "You know, my family was never into camping. But I think I could camp here. I think I could live here."

Yuriko laughed. "Planning to become a miko?"

"A what?"

"Shinto priestess."

Kathleen stared. "There are female priests too?"

Yuriko smiled. "Yeah, we saw them yesterday. Remember the girls wearing the red hakama and white hori? I mean, the red pants and white shirt? They are called shrine maidens."

"Do you think they'd let me in?"

Yuriko shrugged. "You might have to be fluent in Japanese."

Kathleen turned her camera to a waterfall as they passed. "For this view? Yeah, I think I could learn. Oh, look!"

After walking up a series of steep stone steps, they came upon a stone torii, which lay at the entrance of Tosho-gu Shrine. Yuriko couldn't say that she was as enraptured as Kathleen by shrines, but this gray, moss-covered gate was beautiful. It stood above the path, blending in with the rough stone path below. The damp moss growing on the sides made it seem not at all different from the trees growing beside it. Besides, whatever Yuriko might think of the shrine, seeing Kathleen's eyes alight with wonder and awe was worth this visit.

A small sign sat just before the gate.

"What does it say?" Kathleen asked.

"It says that any pilgrim that throws three stones through the center of the torii, the gate here, will have their wish granted, or have good luck, or something like that."

"A wish, eh?"

They both looked up to a hole in the center of the torii. The opening was small, probably no more than seven centimeters, Yuriko guessed. With the torii standing at probably five meters, she wasn't sure how anyone could make the target once, let alone three times in a row. Kathleen was already rooting around the edges of the path selecting her stones.

Yuriko pulled out a water bottle, since they were obviously taking a break. "You think you can make it?"

"For any wish? Of course."

"What are you going to wish for?"

Kathleen frowned at her. "If I tell you, it won't come true."

Yuriko snorted. "This is a Japanese torii, not an American birthday cake."

"Well, I *am* an American *in* Japan. So obviously I have to live by both rules." She wound up her arm, eyes narrowing in concentration. She threw the stone, letting out a soft grunt.

It soared just about a meter below the target. Yuriko laughed into her water bottle and Kathleen glared at her.

"Well, maybe it will just grant me two-thirds of a wish."

The next stone flew right over the top. The last one managed to at least hit the top, though it wasn't near the hole. Yuriko was laughing now, mostly because Kathleen, in her desperation, was making louder and louder grunts. It hadn't helped.

Kathleen picked up another stone, throwing it at Yuriko. It actually managed to hit her arm, though it hadn't hurt. "All right, why don't *you* try?"

Yuriko picked up the stone that Kathleen had thrown at her. She threw it, not bothering to aim well. Without even touching the edges, it flew through the hole. She grinned at Kathleen. "Not so difficult."

Kathleen was gaping. "Come on. Throw another."

Yuriko waved a hand. "Nah, one-third of a wish is just fine with me."

Kathleen whined a bit more, but Yuriko stepped through the arch. There were a couple of main buildings and some signs pointing to interesting features. Yuriko stopped before a building, where one of the trees was heavily laden with tied pieces of paper, all sagging or falling apart from the recent rain. The sign read that any lovers who could tie the paper with one hand would enjoy a happy marriage.

Kathleen looked at them curiously. "More prayers?" she asked.

"Something like that," Yuriko answered. For some reason, she didn't want to tell Kathleen that they were tied there by lovers traveling the same path as them. Just for the same reason she didn't want to make a wish on the torii, she supposed. Wishful thinking would only lead to disappointment.

The area was wonderfully landscaped with a winding path and several ancient shrines. There was a shrine set up for three cedar trees that were four hundred years old. Then a small spring that was rumored to taste like sake. Kathleen had to go up to everything and take pictures, even the shrine that one could pray at for an easy childbirth.

Only once did a couple of old women pass them on the path. Otherwise it was wonderfully empty. Yuriko knew that hours had passed since they had started their hike, but the sun could barely penetrate the trees, so it was still shadowed and cool. She wished she could bottle the feeling for when they had to return to the stifling humidity of Tokyo.

They walked farther into the forest, aimless as they wandered. The shrines or stone lanterns became sparse, fading into the trees. After a short walk from Tosho-gu, they came upon another, almost entirely hidden in the woods.

The stone fence and path were covered in the thick moss. Parts of the path were slightly flooded from the rain the night before. A stone cliff arched over them, making the area shaded and cool. A red shrine building seemed unusually bright amongst the dark greens and grays, despite its faded appearance.

Kathleen ignored the building, however, moving toward the cliff instead. There, Yuriko could see, was a series of statues placed into a small shallow cave. A small pool of water surrounded the path, but Kathleen hopped across the stones that managed to poke out above the water. Yuriko followed her to see her crouching in front of the small statues.

These were not Jizo, the statues at the Kanmangafuchi Abyss, but looked like other gods. Yuriko wasn't sure who, exactly, and there was no sign to designate them. One wore a red hat, like those other statues, but it was very faded. All the offering plates in front of them were empty or filled with leafy water. Kathleen leaned forward, as if looking at some particular detail.

Kathleen suddenly looked up the cliff side. "It's like another world, isn't it?" She twisted, looking behind them. "Like, it kind of felt that way at the other shrines, but there is no one here now. It's so *quiet*."

Yuriko looked around. It did kind of seem like they were in another world, or maybe back in time. She knew there was a road not too far away, but she couldn't hear any cars. The path and shrines were so well worn that it seemed like they sprung up from the ground, instead of being placed there.

Kathleen shivered and rubbed the sides of her bare arms.

"You okay?"

"Just a bit cold." She smiled up to Yuriko. "It's a little brisk this morning."

Yuriko took off her backpack and placed it on a dry patch of ground, then shrugged off her jacket. Kathleen made a noise of resistance, but Yuriko just dropped it on her shoulders. "I'm fine. I've heated up from the walk out here."

Kathleen pulled the jacket a little closer. "Thanks," she murmured.

"Why don't you try it in Japanese?" Yuriko knew she was being a little pedantic.

Kathleen pouted but said, "Dōmo arigatō gozaimasu."

Yuriko smirked. "Good enough."

"What? Wasn't that right?"

Yuriko held out a hand so Kathleen could easily get to her feet. "Just a little formal. Try just dōmo next time, especially between us."

Kathleen's hand was freezing in Yuriko's, and she wondered just how cold she had been. She took her fingers and rubbed them between her palms. "Daijōbu?"

"Ah…" Kathleen was staring at their hands, struggling to find the words. "Hai, um, kimochi ii." She said it soft and sweet, as if she had heard it somewhere and mimicked the sound but wasn't sure exactly what it meant. Then she looked up to Yuriko, cheeks just barely tinted pink. "Dōmo."

Yuriko grinned. "Shoganai."

They were standing close, forced by the pools of water. Yuriko could feel Kathleen's hands suddenly warm in hers, though she was no longer rubbing them. She was just holding them. Kathleen did not pull away.

If you reach out to Kathleen, she will undoubtedly reach back, even if she isn't sure why yet. Yuriko remembered Ai's words, spoken to her just the day before. *Have you truly tried?*

Yuriko hadn't tried to throw the stones at the torii because she knew exactly what she would wish for. It seemed so hopeless to wish for it, that it would be a waste. However, now they were both in a different space, a different world. Maybe it wasn't so hopeless anymore.

Maybe the rules could be changed when the world around you wasn't familiar, and you were alone together.

Kathleen was still looking at her, cheeks flushed and mouth slightly parted. Was she having a hard time breathing too? Was her heart beating just as fast as Yuriko's?

Yuriko found herself leaning forward, throat constricted in terror and anticipation and *want*. She wanted to kiss Kathleen while holding her hand, standing in a flooded shrine before the stony observation of hidden gods. She wanted to kiss Kathleen with a feeling much more potent than when they were both drunk and unthinking.

She wanted to kiss Kathleen.

She stopped, face mere breaths away from Kathleen, so close that she might have been resting her forehead on Kathleen's, noses just ghosting each other. She wasn't sure, though, because all she could feel was her racing heart, and thoughts blurred her vision.

Kathleen tilted her head, lifting her chin, and then they were kissing. Softly, gently. Yuriko was terrified, and she wondered if Kathleen was too. Terrified to kiss, too terrified to stop, terrified of the warm emotions overflowing in her chest. There was no needy grabbing, no gasping into each other's mouth. Yuriko's heart stopped.

She surprised herself by pulling away first, but not far. She rested her cheek against Kathleen, just breathing. "What do you want? Onegai...please, tell me. I need to know."

Kathleen pulled away, eyes flickering everywhere but at Yuriko. Her hands went cold, and she nearly tore them from Yuriko's. She stumbled from the cliff, feet nearly sliding into the water, not stopping until she was on higher, drier ground.

Yuriko wasn't sure how she had done it without falling. Her legs felt numb, and she couldn't even feel her heart, which had sunk somewhere around her stomach. She cautiously followed, mind racing with a thousand things to say.

"No. Not this time," Yuriko said, something inside her so close to breaking she would rather fight than ignore it. "We will talk to each other now. Plainly."

Kathleen stopped. "I…I don't know. We should go back. Ai is probably wondering where we are."

"Ai is *fine*. We are not dodging this anymore." She took a deep breath. "Kathleen, please. You have to tell me what you're thinking." There was no one around, no sound but the soft noises of birds or water dripping. It all felt deafening to Yuriko, desperate for an answer to the growing ache in her chest.

"What is there to say?"

Yuriko stepped close to her and took her wrist. Afraid Kathleen would run, even though that seemed absurd. Her hand shook, all the same. "Do you want me, Kathleen?" she asked.

"I'm not sure what you mean."

"You kissed me. After the nomikai, we kissed in my apartment. Tell me, Kathleen, what you think of me. What do you want from me?"

Kathleen was breathing hard, and Yuriko realized she was trembling as well. "It's not that easy to say."

"Why not? Would it be easier if I said that I want you? That I want you so much that I probably love you." She looked down at her fingers, white on Kathleen's wrist. She loosened her grip. Kathleen did not pull away.

"You…you love me?"

Yuriko met her gaze. "Yes. Or at least enough to know that I just can't let this waver on any longer. It hurts too much. I have to know how you feel." She swallowed, painful. "Either way. At least so I can move forward as needed. So I need an honest, simple answer. Are you even interested in me?"

"I…" Kathleen was unreadable, her eyes shifting back and forth. Her fingers flexed, as if testing Yuriko's loose grip. "I can't give you a simple answer. It doesn't feel simple."

Yuriko stepped close, her free hand cupping Kathleen's face. She was so soft, cheeks so pink. Kathleen's gaze finally met hers, and Yuriko wondered if her heart would ever beat the same again. "Do you want me to kiss you?"

"Yes." The answer was automatic, but true.

Yuriko remained still. "Then you do want me?"

"I don't know." Kathleen pulled away and Yuriko's hands fell to her side.

She felt desperate. She suddenly felt like running. She also could never leave. "You say you want to kiss me, but you don't know?"

"I don't know, okay? Maybe I want to kiss you now. But will I want to kiss you tomorrow? Or every day? Will I want to touch you? I don't know. I can't jump into something like this without knowing. I don't want to promise you something I can't keep, and I don't want to hurt you if I realize that everything I'm feeling is just a symptom of being lonely in a strange country."

Kathleen was gasping for breath, and Yuriko felt like she was drowning.

Yuriko's mind was whirling. "How could…is that really what you think?"

"I know it might sound dumb, and I might be wrong. But I could also be right. I care about you too much to just throw myself at you." She blinked, taking in another deep breath. "It would be better this way."

"Even if you're wrong? It is not worth it to try?"

"I don't want to be another Michiko."

"You aren't Michiko. That was completely different."

"But I don't want to date you only to find some guy and dump you for him."

Yuriko made a slashing motion with her hand. This, at least, was an easy misconception for her to clear up. "Michiko was bisexual. She *knew* this. We both did. She wasn't confused or playing with me. She *knew* she was in love with me and she *knew* when she fell in love with someone else. It hurt, yes, but the situation was completely different."

"Well, then maybe I don't understand this enough. Is that not a good enough reason to make this is a bad idea?"

"I just can't understand why you aren't willing to even *try*."

"I told you—I don't want to hurt you."

"You're hurting me now!"

Yuriko suddenly felt it, the burn of tears against her eyes. She blinked, looking at the mossy stones at her feet. She didn't want to cry. Her mother had always taught her to keep her composure, especially in public. Stay innocuous, stay unnoticed, don't give too much away to prying eyes. Maybe she should cry now. Cry in front of Kathleen so maybe she would understand that she wasn't alone. Yuriko felt confused, felt conflicted, felt so many things that she didn't understand, but she understood this simple thing. She wanted Kathleen, and if Kathleen walked away, she wasn't going to survive.

Kathleen moved and she was in front of Yuriko. Trembling, she took Yuriko's hands, holding them in a nervous grip. "This won't be easy," Kathleen whispered.

Yuriko was entranced, watching Kathleen's fingers gentle over her knuckles. "I wouldn't expect that from you."

Kathleen might have laughed, or maybe it was just a sigh. Her words, however, were stronger when she said, "I'm attracted to you, Yuriko. Maybe more than attracted. I don't know. This is new for me, and it's scary, but if you're willing to try with me, then I'm willing."

Yuriko finally looked up. Kathleen's eyes were shining with unshed tears. She couldn't resist leaning forward and pressing her cheek against Kathleen's. She felt the warm wetness as Kathleen sighed.

"I can't promise I will be a good girlfriend."

"I suppose I can't either."

"I can't promise not to make mistakes."

"I will make mistakes as well."

Kathleen gave another shuddering sigh, releasing Yuriko's hands to wrap her arms around her. Yuriko pressed her face into Kathleen's shoulder. She smelled like sweat and the onsen and the cool stone of this forest.

"Just say you will try," Yuriko whispered. "And I will try as well."

Kathleen's breath was warm on her neck. "Well, I suppose if you are willing. But, Yuriko?"

"Yes?"

"Can you kiss me? Again?"

Yuriko pulled back enough to look at her. Kathleen's eyes were no longer shining with tears, but they were bright with hope.

Yuriko couldn't resist her.

Chapter Twenty-one

Kathleen felt like an idiot. What was she doing? What was she *thinking*?

She wasn't thinking, hadn't been thinking. She had been seduced by ancient shrines and cool weather and had kissed Yuriko.

Now she was standing outside her apartment door, staring at Yuriko's and wondering if trying to be a girlfriend was good enough reason to knock.

She only had eight more days to study Ai. Then the PLC would be broken down, parts examined for wear and functionality, and Kathleen would receive her data chip for future reference. She should be working harder than ever, finishing off any last tests of processing power or endurance. She should be excited, knowing that in about a week she wouldn't have to tow a love robot around Tokyo anymore. She would have her apartment to herself again. Her project would officially be in beta, and she would start a whole new chapter at work.

It wasn't crazy that she and Yuriko hadn't gotten a chance to hang out in two days, since Nikko. Yuriko was busy and, well, Kathleen was too. Kathleen couldn't drop everything just to…ask for more kisses? Hold Yuriko's hand for a little while?

This was ridiculous. They were both adults with adult responsibilities. Besides, Kathleen needed this space. She felt in over her head with the whole situation. It was one thing to think about how much she was attracted to another woman, but it was quite another to jump into a relationship. She needed to get her head on straight. She needed to make sure she knew exactly what she was getting into and not relying on hormonal impulses or something.

Kathleen rubbed her eyes and quickly pushed open her door. Why had she kissed Yuriko? Just because she wanted to? This was ridiculous. She couldn't do this. She couldn't imagine not doing this.

Ai was in the kitchen, chopping cabbage. "Okaeri!" she sang out.

"Tadaima," Kathleen muttered, mind still elsewhere. She felt like her mind was elsewhere all the time now. She had to snap herself out of it. She should probably apologize to Yuriko. Tell her that this was a bad idea. That she was terribly sorry, but then Yuriko would probably ask why, when Kathleen clearly, obviously, *definitely* wanted her.

Kathleen didn't have an answer why.

"Is something wrong?" Ai was suddenly before her, eyebrows furrowed in concern.

Kathleen was startled. She hadn't even seen her walk over. For a brief moment, she had almost thought Yuriko, as if summoned by her thoughts, had appeared before her. "Ah…I'm fine."

Ai raised an eyebrow. "Yeah, sure," she said in disbelief. She sighed, waving a hand and turning back to the kitchen. "You know, Yuriko should be home by now. You can just go over there if you want."

"Why do you think I need to talk to Yuriko?" Kathleen and Yuriko hadn't said anything to Ai. The rest of their Nikko trip had been friendly but cautious, Kathleen too nervous to make another move and Yuriko too polite to ask anything of Kathleen with a third party present.

Ai snorted. "Why do I always need to remind the people who *built* me that I was created to be observant?" She looked at Kathleen, expression hard. "Every time you and Yuriko, anō, have a *moment*, you both get really weird. So go over there and fix it. Whatever you did."

Kathleen kicked off her shoes and put her briefcase down on the table. She saw some of her dōjinshi was lying out, Ai's neat handwriting correcting a few of her crude translations. The book was open to a page in which the two main characters were feeling each other up. Kathleen was a little disturbed to be reading a comic that had so much sweating and groping, so she had quickly skipped the section to one with more substantial dialogue. Ai had gone to the trouble, however, to translate the sound effects and moaning. Skimming it, Kathleen quickly decided that it just didn't translate well.

She could barely look at a trashy comic featuring two girls making out. Why would she kiss Yuriko?

Her train of thought was back, and she pressed her forehead to the table, feeling like she was really losing it. She could feel Ai standing behind her.

"Do you need something?" Ai asked.

Kathleen needed to figure out her own feelings. She felt like a teenager, confused and stupid and more than a little frustrated. She wanted to kiss Yuriko again and this time really pay attention. She also felt like kissing Yuriko would be a bad idea while her mind was still so conflicted.

She could kiss Ai.

Kathleen raised her head so fast she smacked into Ai's hand, which had been reaching out to her. Ai stared at her in confusion and concern. "Kathleen?" she asked, softly and slowly, as if Kathleen was having a breakdown.

Kathleen kind of felt like she was, staring up at Ai. She had never before considered kissing Ai or touching her in any intimate way. It was just too weird and felt vaguely inappropriate. Of course, Kathleen had already been acting inappropriate toward Yuriko.

Would kissing Ai be like kissing Yuriko? They looked the same, talked the same, acted the same. Ai was a willing subject and programmed to do as Kathleen asked, whether she asked to kiss her, or to stop and never speak of it again. Ai wasn't a person who could have hurt feelings or hold grudges or spread rumors. She was just a more complicated format than the dōjinshi in front of Kathleen. A test to see if Kathleen could figure it all out.

Ai was still staring at her, looking more and more concerned. "Kathleen?" she asked again.

"Kiss me," Kathleen said, quickly and just a little too loud.

"What?" Ai seemed genuinely confused.

Kathleen sighed. "Kiss me. I'm pretty confident I programmed you to know how."

Ai knelt beside her. "Yes. You did." She spoke slowly, as if Kathleen was an unstable bomb. She sort of felt like it. "But…you have always made it quite clear that you have no romantic or sexual interest in me. I have to make sure you're in your right mind for consent."

"You're a love robot. Do I need consent?"

The corner of Ai's lips quirked in a smile. "I will always give you *my* consent. However, safety protocols require me to make sure *you* are giving full and enthusiastic consent." She paused. "Are you?"

"I won't say I'm enthusiastic, but I am giving you full consent. I just…" She felt a headache starting, and she rubbed one eye. "I just want to test something."

Ai took her hand away from Kathleen's face and touched her forehead softly. Her fingers were warm and gentle against Kathleen's skin. "Okay, but I will stop if you ask me to."

Kathleen sighed, and she sort of felt resigned. "I know."

Ai leaned in then, until Kathleen could feel hot breath on her face. She didn't smell like Yuriko, whose breath had smelled like toothpaste and the rice ball she had eaten for breakfast. Ai didn't smell like anything.

Ai hesitated, forehead nearly touching Kathleen's. She felt so familiar and so different that Kathleen nearly pulled away. Ai seemed to sense this and did not move forward. So Kathleen, trying not to think too hard, tilted her head and met Ai's lips.

She was soft, lips warm and pliant. Her hand curled around Kathleen's head, cradling her at the neck. Then Ai's mouth opened, and her tongue probed Kathleen's mouth. Ai was so gentle, like she was trying to soothe Kathleen into the kiss.

Kathleen didn't just want to kiss; she wanted to test.

So she reached out, hands finding Ai's silky shirt. She groped it, seeking soft skin. She was warmer here, and Kathleen could feel something like muscles tensing and relaxing under her touch.

It was awkward. Possibly because both of them were sitting or kneeling at the table. Kathleen pushed Ai backward, not breaking their kiss as she sprawled out on the floor. Ai made a soft noise, like a moan or a grunt. It didn't sound displeased.

Kathleen was letting instinct take over, like making out with one of her boyfriends. She was about to straddle Ai, but Ai's legs wound their way around her instead, placing Kathleen between her hips. When Kathleen pressed down, there were breasts and strong thighs and a breathy, high-pitched voice.

This was familiar. Bits of memory floated in Kathleen's mind. Had she done this with Yuriko?

Kathleen broke the kiss, though she didn't move off Ai. Ai was flushed, panting, looking the picture of arousal. Kathleen wasn't aroused, but she wasn't disgusted, not like she thought she would be. Maybe it was because Ai was so eager and physically looked eager too. Yet Kathleen was waiting for that moment when her mind would go blurry and her heart would reach up into her throat. Like she remembered with Yuriko.

"Kathleen?" Ai asked, as if out of breath. "Do you want to continue?"

Kathleen looked down at Ai, shirt twisted and pulled up over her stomach. She was wearing a skirt, which now barely covered her. Did Kathleen want to continue? Was there any point?

Something within her was strangely curious. What would it be like to see another woman turned on? Could she get turned on by it? Almost without thought, she tugged at Ai's skirt, lifting it to reveal that Ai was not wearing panties.

"Do you always go commando?"

Ai shrugged, though her flush had deepened in color. "I don't see much point in underwear. You've never noticed before."

Kathleen probably would have been annoyed before and demanded that Ai always wear them. Now, well, it was kind of convenient. Ai looked pretty normal. Not that Kathleen had much experience. She had seen Yuriko naked in the onsen, but she certainly hadn't examined her like she was currently with Ai.

Kathleen suddenly wanted to see Ai really aroused. "Can you... touch yourself?"

Ai let out a soft laugh. "Can I?" She moved one arm from Kathleen's shoulders where they both rested. She slid it down Kathleen's arm and across her stomach. She tugged at the skirt so there was no chance of obstruction. Her fingers looked slim, delicate as she slid them over herself.

Kathleen had once mutually masturbated with Brandon. He had been rough with himself. Hand gripping hard and moving quickly, vigorously. Ai was gentle and slow. As if exploring herself. Or more likely, as if Kathleen was exploring her. Kathleen could see Ai flushing red as her fingers probed.

Ai made soft noises, mostly her breath hitching or deep sighs. Her other hand left Kathleen and tugged at her shirt and the bra she wore under it. She pulled it up to her chin, just far enough to reveal herself.

"Stop," Kathleen said and Ai instantly stilled. Kathleen closed her eyes and sat back, Ai's legs dropping from her hips. "Stop," she said again, though it was mostly to herself.

Ai sat up, pulling her shirt and skirt into order. "Are you okay?" she asked.

Inexplicably, Kathleen felt like crying. She pressed her palms against her eyes, just to make sure no tears would leak out. "I...I don't know. I think something is wrong with me."

"Nothing is wrong with you. It's okay to feel—"

"I don't feel anything," Kathleen suddenly shouted and her voice felt too loud, too hoarse. "Watching you. Kissing you, whatever. I didn't feel anything." She stood up, paced the room, and found herself sitting back down again, this time across the table from Ai.

"Did you want to feel something?" Ai asked.

"I'm not sure." What would it mean if she was aroused by the sight of Ai touching herself? Would it mean that everything she had thought about her sexuality was wrong? Would it mean that she was attracted to Yuriko? Was she not attracted to other women?

Ai shifted so she was properly seated at the table, elbows resting on the wood. "This all has to do with Yuriko, right?"

Kathleen felt herself sagging. "It all has to do with me...I don't know...*using* Yuriko."

"If you were using Yuriko, she would tell you. She's not the type to let people walk all over her."

"But she is the type to fall in love with stupid girls who can't figure their shit out."

She remembered when Yuriko had talked to her about Michiko. How, even though it had been years, she was still torn up by it. Even though she put on a brave face, said the right things, she still resented Michiko and what she had done. Kathleen wasn't in love with Yuriko, but she cared about her. She didn't want to toy with her. She didn't want to become another heartbreak.

Kathleen also didn't want to lose her. She wanted—no, *needed*—Yuriko as a friend. She had taught her so much and had been a great friend and Kathleen had so few in this country. Yuriko was more than a friend now—she was practically a necessity.

She wasn't sure Brandon had ever meant so much to her.

She looked at Ai, a perfect copy. She wasn't sure what it meant that she wasn't attracted to Ai. Maybe that was the most normal thing about this situation. Ai wasn't human and Kathleen was probably the most qualified person to know that.

"Thank you," she said. "But I'd like to never do that again."

"Why?" Ai said it with almost genuine confusion.

She stiffened. "What does it matter? We are not doing that again."

"I understand and respect that. Can I not ask why?"

"Why do you want to know?" she bit back. She was getting irritated.

Ai pressed her fingers together, peering over them, examining Kathleen. "A part of my programming requires that I be an exemplary lover for my user. You have stated, quite clearly before, that you were uninterested because of my gender designation. So I have respected that, at a basic level, I cannot fulfill that aspect of my code." She said it all so plainly, and Kathleen was struck, once again, by how inhuman Ai was. "But now you come to me, asking for a sexual experience, and find yourself disappointed. I would like to understand if it's something I could remedy on my part."

Kathleen couldn't help but stare at her. What would this conversation be like if Ai wasn't a robot? Probably a lot more stressful and complicated, but it already felt stressful and complicated to Kathleen. The only thing keeping her from completely freaking out was knowing that Ai didn't have real feelings. That she would be broken down in a week's time and never exist again.

Kathleen swallowed. "I'm not disappointed."

Ai raised an eyebrow. "You aren't?"

"Disappointment…that's not the right emotion." Disappointment meant that Kathleen had been hoping that she would have *liked* being intimate with Ai. She didn't want that—she'd never wanted that. "I just wanted to see if I was attracted to women. Other women. And I'm… not sure?"

Ai almost rolled her eyes but stopped midmotion. Probably because it would infuriate Kathleen in this moment. "You think because you're not attracted to me that you cannot be attracted to other women? If you see a strange man on the street and are not attracted to him, then you're not attracted to other men?"

"That's not the same—"

"It's similar enough."

"Don't argue with me." Kathleen felt her voice rise, and she bit her lip. She felt close to tears again.

Ai lowered her hands, leaning back and relaxing her stance. "I apologize," she said softly. She sounded so goddamned sincere that Kathleen also felt like apologizing. "I just want to know why you look like you are going to cry."

Kathleen looked away, because her throat felt tight and she really, *really* didn't want to cry in front of Ai. Even if she was a dumb robot that was only temporary. Kathleen wanted to feel strong enough, at least in this moment, to hold herself together.

"It's because of Yuriko, yes?" Ai said, almost a whisper. "You wished to test your feelings toward her by using me."

It sounded so cruel and twisted. Kathleen wanted to deny it, but it was true. Yet Ai didn't look like she was hurt. Her eyes were open to

Kathleen, supportive. She didn't have an emotional stake in this. Her programming only told her to please Kathleen, in any capacity she was allotted. She had no other interests, no other motives.

"Yes," Kathleen said slowly.

Ai nodded in confirmation. "And since you find yourself not attracted to me, you conclude that whatever intimate occurrences you've shared with Yuriko must be false."

"Yes."

"Well, that is idiotic," she stated, quite clearly.

Kathleen frowned. "I'm not an idiot."

"I'm not Yuriko."

Kathleen waved a hand. "Yeah, well, you look like her."

"Do you often mistake me for her?"

"Well, no. That's because—"

"When we are next to each other, is it hard to tell the difference between us?"

"No."

"Then how can you know your feelings for her through me?"

"I don't have feelings for her." Kathleen ran a hand through her hair. "I mean, I know I'm attracted to her, but I don't know how far that goes."

Ai was leaning forward again, fingers pressed to her lips. "Tell me, have you kissed her?"

Kathleen swallowed. "Yes." It sort of felt weird to say, a mixture between relief and tense pain.

"Have you touched her?"

"Well, I…kind of?" Kathleen wasn't about to admit she couldn't quite remember the extent of it. Ai would just assume the worst.

"Have you had sex with her?"

"No!"

"Have you thought about it?"

"What is your point?" Kathleen spat back, tired of whatever game Ai was trying to play.

Ai sighed, as if Kathleen was being the difficult one. "Did you enjoy that? At any time, for any reason?" She paused. "Or did it feel like what you just experienced with me now?"

"I didn't—" Kathleen stopped, probably because Ai was staring at her, eyes narrowed in seriousness. Maybe just because she was actually having a pretty honest conversation with her, but Kathleen felt like she should take her time. "I don't know. At the time it seemed right. But I

don't go off daydreaming about Yuriko or anything like that. I'm just…
I'm just lonely, okay? It's been a while since I've been with anyone
and I think my thoughts are just getting a little desperate, you know?
Yuriko is nice and beautiful and she kisses nice and, I don't know,
seems available. I don't want to use her."

She felt like she was repeating herself. Her own thoughts were
circling around, over and over in her head. She knew the conclusions,
but it didn't mean she had any answers. Nor did she know exactly what
to do next. She had to talk to Yuriko, but how could she explain this?
Would Yuriko understand? Would Yuriko hate her?

Ai stood up, walked over to Kathleen, and knelt beside her. She
put a warm hand on her shoulder. "Can I suggest one thing of you?"

"What is that?"

"Don't be afraid of being confused. It's all right not to know. It's
normal to be unsure of yourself. Just give yourself time. Please, before
you do anything, give yourself time."

"Why do you think that?"

The backs of Ai's fingers touched Kathleen's cheek. Her cheek
was wet. She had started crying. She didn't need Ai to answer her
question.

CHAPTER TWENTY-TWO

Kathleen opened her door to find a piece of cloth hitting her face. Sputtering, confused, she tore it from her head, and found some sort of robe, pale lavender with dark blue flowers and pink swirls decorating it. "What is this?" She looked up at Ai, who had thrown it at her.

"A yukata," Ai answered, twirling around. She was already wearing one herself.

"Yukata?" Kathleen asked.

"It's a summer kimono."

Kathleen had seen kimono before in pictures, and this yukata looked very similar. It seemed a little less lavish, however. The yukata wasn't made from a silk like she expected, but a stiff cotton. The sleeves were also shorter, ending just a few inches above Ai's wrist. Ai had done her hair up in a bouncy side ponytail, decorated with fake flowers and a brightly colored bow. Her yukata was spring green, and the sash around her middle was the same purple as the yukata Kathleen held in her arms.

"Okay. Why did you throw this at me?"

Ai rolled her eyes. "Because you need to put it on. I have your obi over here." She pointed to a large strip of fabric on the table.

"Why do I need to put it on?"

"Hanabi! Matsuri!" Ai sang out, like it was an answer.

Kathleen decided she needed to take off her shoes and sit down. Maybe eat something. She went to the fridge and pulled out a bottle of water, tucking the yukata under her arm. "Are you going to explain or just shout words to me?"

Ai laughed, taking the yukata and spreading it on the table. "If you haven't noticed, this *entire* summer, there have been signs everywhere for events like fireworks or festivals. I figured tonight we should probably go see one. You know, go out with a bang, yeah?"

"Go out with a bang?" Kathleen asked.

Ai tugged at the bottom of her sash, her obi. "I will be decommissioned tomorrow, after all."

Kathleen paused, bottle pressed to her lips. "Oh yeah." She hadn't forgotten. In fact, today she had been to a rather tedious meeting in which they all went over exactly what was going to happen next. She still hadn't finished her final report, which she would present next week to Tamura and some higher-ups in the company. Everything was mostly complete. She wasn't going to make any more additions to her report, just revise it for the presentation.

She hadn't thought about how she would only have the next twelve hours or so with Ai. Or that she had no reason to test her anymore. She just knew that, tomorrow morning, some people from Engineering would come down, box Ai up, and take her away. She expected by the afternoon to receive a package with Ai's data and software for analysis.

Ai knew this, possibly not in the detail that Kathleen knew, but she didn't look depressed or scared. She smiled at Kathleen, holding up the yukata again. She was a computer, Kathleen reminded herself, and would continue to function as programmed until shut down.

Kathleen put down the bottle. "Okay, what exactly is this hanami and mitsuri?"

"Hanabi is fireworks. Matsuri is a festival. It usually includes food and some games, maybe a dance or a competition, depending on the area. It's a little late for that. But if we leave now, we can still catch some good fireworks."

Kathleen looked at the yukata skeptically. "I have to wear this?"

"No. But then you wouldn't have an exceptional cultural experience, right?"

"Okay, okay. How do I put this on?"

It was a lot more difficult than it looked on Ai. Kathleen thought, like any bathrobe, she could just put her arms through the sleeves and tie the obi like a sash around her waist. Instead, Ai was circling around her, using other thinner sashes to secure the yukata, creating a fold at the waist so the hem would hang just above Kathleen's ankles. She tugged and pulled so everything could lie flat, and Kathleen's breasts were in no danger of slipping out. Then she put on the obi, which seemed to circle Kathleen five times before Ai took it to her back and made a simple little bow. The obi felt like a corset, hard against Kathleen's ribs and back. Kathleen was convinced that if she took it off, she would never get it back on without extreme assistance.

Kathleen didn't have a full-length mirror, but her bathroom sink mirror was good enough. She tugged at the ends of the sleeves, frowning. "I don't think these were made for big girls."

"Are you kidding? You look perfect," Ai cooed behind her. Kathleen wasn't convinced.

Ai looked slim in her yukata, small ankles and thin wrists making her seem delicate. Kathleen looked like she was a sausage with a casing too small. Ai's obi was perfectly smooth against her stomach. Kathleen could tell hers was threatening to wrinkle and bend under the weight of her curves. She knew she had a larger chest and thighs compared to most Japanese women, but she had always thought she looked good enough when she could show off her thin waist. Unfortunately, the obi bulked up her waist, making her completely round.

Ai ran her fingers through Kathleen's hair. "You know, Japanese girls spend hours trying to get a good curl in their hair. Here I can just throw up your hair, and it looks perfect." She gave Kathleen a high, messy bun and stuck a few flowers and beads into it.

Kathleen tilted her head. Her curls did make her hair look fashionably fun and flouncy. It made her feel a little better. "All right." She turned around, looked at her obi again. A thought struck her, and she turned to Ai. "Hey, where did you get these? Did you use my money?"

Ai held a finger to her lips, grinning. "No, I just asked for a favor."

"A favor? From who?"

Ai's grin became wider. "Yuriko, of course."

"Yuriko?"

"Yes, this week you gave me permission to contact her as needed."

Kathleen rubbed her forehead. She did actually remember something like that. Probably when she traveled to Yokohama and wasn't sure if she was going to make the long journey across Tokyo alone. She might have said Ai could contact Yuriko if she couldn't reach her. "That was for emergencies only."

"Emergencies, important cultural events, same thing." Ai patted Kathleen's shoulders. "Come on, she's probably waiting for us."

"Wait, Yuriko is coming too?"

Ai rolled her eyes. "Of course."

As if on cue, the doorbell rang. "Enter!" Kathleen shouted and popped her head out from the bathroom.

Yuriko opened the door and came in, wearing a red yukata and black obi. She didn't have any hair accessories; her hair was down around her shoulders. It struck Kathleen as a little odd, considering Ai, who usually wore her hair down, now had it up, and Yuriko, who usually had hers tied back for work, now wore it down. The reversal didn't make them look any more similar. Yuriko looked older, somehow, more mature. Her hair, long down the lines of her yukata, made her seem taller or longer, more elegant and formal than Kathleen had ever seen her.

God, Kathleen had *missed* her. Not that they hadn't seen each other at all, but work took up most of their time, and Kathleen was… well, she was just unsure about it all. This, however, felt right. More right than small talk on the train to work or brief interactions while they passed by their apartment doors. Yuriko was here, beautiful and ready to spend the night with her.

Was this a date?

Her heart accelerated, and she might have started sweating. This was a date. This was definitely a date. She felt like a teenager, sweaty and awkward. She had no idea how Yuriko could find her attractive at all.

Yuriko was smiling at Kathleen. "Ready?" It was that smile, warm but just a slight trembling, that gave away her nerves. Yuriko was nervous too, or maybe also feeling awkward, but she was here. She was here for Kathleen. It made it a little easier for her to breathe.

Kathleen wasn't ready, but she couldn't wait any longer. She wanted to take Yuriko's hand. She wanted to kiss her. Instead she held out her arms. "Honest answer. Do I look completely ridiculous in this?"

Ai pouted. "I already told you that you look great."

"You're programmed to." She looked back to Yuriko. "So?"

Yuriko looked carefully up and down Kathleen's figure. Her gaze was slow, face blank. Kathleen felt her cheeks heat, embarrassed by the scrutiny. When Yuriko met her gaze, her eyes seemed a deeper color, soft and warm.

"You look beautiful." Her voice sounded hoarse, just louder than a whisper.

Kathleen tugged at the obi, feeling like it was constricting her breathing. "Um…ieie?"

Yuriko smiled, drawing close, and there was that kiss Kathleen had been anticipating. It felt good—it felt so good. "We'll make a native out of you yet." Her voice was low with promise, and Kathleen suddenly realized, face burning, that Ai was there.

She looked around and saw Ai just waiting patiently. There was something in her eyes, just a little inhuman, like she was computing something. Kathleen wasn't sure she wanted to know what.

Ai's face cleared and her voice was light and chipper when she said, "Well, we better get there before the crowds get too crazy."

Kathleen had her hand raised, ready to take Yuriko's. Then she stopped, mind blurring to a halt. Was it okay to hold hands in public? Wasn't it strange? Was she overthinking this?

Ai suddenly pushed past her, and Yuriko's hand found hers as Ai took her other. "Baka. Come on, you'll *both* make us late."

Kathleen wasn't sure what she was expecting from a Japanese fireworks show. She imagined something similar to an American Fourth of July display. Like, everyone would be in a big field or parking lot, watching fireworks go off, possibly to music.

She learned she was gravely mistaken when they got off the train.

The station was bursting with people. Many of them were dressed up like Kathleen, Yuriko, and Ai. Others just wore regular summer clothes. The station had many signs, and men with glowing batons waved people around or into the line.

"We've got to get on a bus," Yuriko said, raising her head, trying to see. "I think we line up here."

It was a massive line, filling up half the station and moving onto the street. Kathleen could see buses constantly arriving, packed to the brim, and still the people kept flooding in.

"Are these normal buses?" Kathleen asked. On nights like this the locals must hate them.

Yuriko shook her head. "No, the city designates them for fireworks only. They'll be running back and forth until the matsuri ends."

"When do the fireworks start?" Kathleen wasn't sure they would ever get out of this line.

"The fireworks go on all night." Yuriko grinned. "You'll see."

It actually didn't take long for them to advance in the line. Even with the crowds, the buses just kept arriving, ready to take more. They managed to get lucky and were able to snag seats. Kathleen pressed herself against the window, staring out into the city. It seemed not everyone took the bus, and groups were out on the streets, laughing and waving. The night was humid, and Kathleen wished for one of those cheap paper fans everyone was carrying around.

"What is this festival for?"

Ai, who was sitting next to her, said, "The Sumidagawa festival is actually a very old tradition. There is no holiday for it or anything. It's just to celebrate the end of summer."

"The end of summer? Screw summer and its humidity. I think the only reason I'm not sweating through this yukata is because I'm wearing so many layers under it."

Yuriko suddenly pointed. "Look!"

Kathleen turned around, just glimpsing a flash of fireworks between the tall buildings. Passing another street, she spotted another bright explosion. "Where are they shooting them?"

"On the river. This is our stop. Let's see if we can get a decent spot."

Kathleen assumed what Yuriko meant by a decent spot was not a nice patch of grass or tarp laid out near the edge of the river. Stepping off the bus, even Kathleen could tell that there were too many people for that to be even a remote possibility. The crowds pressed around them, and Kathleen reached out, desperate not to lose Ai or Yuriko in the crush.

Strangely enough, they each took a hand, pulling her forward.

Kathleen knew she probably looked like some kid, having two people hold her hands. Yet it felt good. Both of their grips were secure, and they led her forward like they had planned it all ahead of time. Well, maybe they had.

Kathleen looked at the people passing, surprised to see many girls with much more flamboyant yukatas than hers. A number of foreigners were wearing them too. Kathleen was a little jealous of the male version of the yukata, if only because it was much more loosely worn and looked much less stifling in the summer heat.

They walked into a long line of special booths set up. Lanterns trailed across the street, bathing everything in yellow or red light. The food smelled amazing, and Kathleen could see smoke rising up behind the booths. A couple walked by with something like a squid on a stick. Kathleen probably would have been more afraid of it usually, but it looked deliciously greasy and she was pretty hungry.

"What are we getting to eat?" she asked.

Ai answered, "Let's try a selection. Yakitori, chicken on a stick. Takoyaki, those are octopus balls. Hmm, what else?" She looked to Yuriko.

"I want the ikayaki. Uh, the grilled squid."

Kathleen couldn't help but pipe up eagerly, "I want that squid thing."

Yuriko seemed surprised. "You do?"

"It looks too amazing to pass up."

"I thought you'd be intimidated by it."

"I thought I told you that I can be an adventurous eater. I'm just not adventurous enough to come out to a place like this by myself." She paused. "Or order it by myself, for that matter."

Yuriko smiled fondly. "Okay, well, this place is selling, and the line doesn't seem too outrageous." She pointed to a booth just across the street.

Ai dropped Kathleen's hand. "I'll go scout out some places for the rest of the food."

Kathleen tensed, feeling nervous. "Will you be all right?"

"I'll be just fine."

"You don't have any problems with this area? Not too much data input?"

"No, your patch is working perfectly."

"Do you have a way to call me if there is a problem?"

Ai tapped Kathleen's forehead. "I'm practically a walking phone. Don't worry. You won't even notice I'm gone." Then she slipped away into the crowds.

Kathleen watched her go, blending in too perfectly with her Japanese appearance and yukata. Yuriko pulled Kathleen into the line for the booth. Yuriko nudged her shoulder when Kathleen kept trying to look up around the crowds. "Don't worry. All PLCs come with a tracking GPS signal. Standard issue."

Kathleen sighed. "I guess it doesn't matter if she does anything weird. The beta will probably go live next week, and then there will be a couple hundred of those walking around Tokyo."

"I still can't believe they will release so many at first."

"It's the personalized nature of the product. The more testers, the better the results. Besides, Mashida is hoping to have thousands rolling out by next year."

"Tens of thousands, according to the pressure I'm under."

Kathleen grinned, kind of feeling a little excited. She knew she was in the calm before the storm phase of the PLC project. Yet going to beta, even though it was still much earlier than anticipated, was pretty amazing. All those months, years if she included the development before her, were finally coming to fruition. A real product, not just one like Ai, but hundreds all looking and acting differently, while abiding by the same fundamental rules that Kathleen helped lay out.

Of course, with the thousands of people around her, pressing and laughing and talking, it hardly felt like a calm. However, it was good enough, and Kathleen found herself squeezing Yuriko's hand.

For a moment, she froze, suddenly afraid that she should probably pull away. Her need to latch on to something when she was intimidated or excited was ridiculous. She looked to Yuriko, waiting to see if it was okay.

Yuriko just smiled down at her and gently squeezed her hand back.

Kathleen wondered how her heart could take it.

Yuriko was ordering and then brandishing a rather succulent looking squid in front of Kathleen's face. Hungry, not caring how it looked, Kathleen just bit into it, tearing off a rubbery piece. The flavor wasn't strong, a little salty and a little smoky from the grill. The squid was wonderfully chewy, and she and Yuriko made quick work of it as they walked down the path.

Fireworks suddenly shot above them, and many people paused and clapped. Kathleen could hear a voice over the speakers spread around the festival.

"What are they saying?" Kathleen asked.

"They are announcing who is sponsoring the fireworks. Oh, look! Taiyaki!"

Taiyaki was a fish shaped pastry, filled with a sweet bean paste. It was warm and not too sweet. Kathleen had no idea why it was shaped like a fish. As far as she could tell, all of them were stuffed with sweet ingredients like chocolate or cream. She and Yuriko shared one. Then they shared a beer. Then a snow cone, which tasted just like any snow cone Kathleen had ever had in America. Eventually they came across a stand selling grilled beef tongue on a stick, which Kathleen had to try. The meat was wonderfully tender, but a little on the salty side.

They had practically walked down an entire streets of booths, eating their way, barely stopping long enough to see a few fireworks flashing over the river. They also kept their hands clasped the entire time, and each time Kathleen would begin to wonder if she was doing this dating a woman thing right, she would see something great, like a booth selling frightening looking masks or a game where you could win a goldfish. Then she would have to pull Yuriko toward it. Or Yuriko would find another traditional matsuri food that Kathleen just had to eat. Honestly, Kathleen couldn't get enough of it.

So it just felt right to stay connected, bumping shoulders in the large crowd, leaning close to share the food or to hear each other speak.

Kathleen was getting caught up again. She knew she should stop, before she did something stupid.

They walked along the river, still among the crowds. There was less shouting or the sounds of cooking food here. The loudest noise was coming from the fireworks exploding around them. There was no place to stop, not even a bare strip of grass or concrete that wasn't a walking path covered by people sitting on tarps, so they kept walking.

A large firework went off, so bright and loud that Kathleen hesitated, backing slightly into Yuriko. The white sparks filled the sky for a moment, turning the night into a false day. Eventually they faded into the darkness, the remaining pinpricks of light indistinguishable from the city lights across the river. She realized that Yuriko's hand was at her hip, just at the edge of her obi. She was could feel Yuriko's breaths against the back of her neck, warmer than the air around them. Her heart was racing, her eyes still dazzled from the bright fireworks.

Yuriko said softly, "If we don't move, people are going to push us over."

She was right. Already the crowd was pressing in, trying to move through the too small pathways. Kathleen felt like her obi was constricting, Yuriko's hand burning on her hip. She had to move forward, but she wanted to lean back, into Yuriko's solid body behind her.

Yuriko let out a breath, so close that Kathleen knew it was a laugh. Another hand, at Kathleen's other hip, and Yuriko was pushing her forward. Kathleen felt helpless but to obey.

They came across a large, grassy park, bursting with people sitting. "We'll probably be able to find a spot here, with just the two of us." Yuriko pulled Kathleen into the crowd, and it was amazing how much quieter it seemed here in comparison. Everyone was talking in low, intimate tones, whispering over bottles of beer or paper fans.

They weren't able to sit, but there was a spot next to a low wall that they were able to squeeze into. The space wasn't large enough for both of them, even with the people beside them politely scooting away. So Yuriko pushed Kathleen forward to lean against the wall. Kathleen was grateful for the small support. She hadn't realized how sore and tired she had gotten from walking around.

Yuriko faced her, head tilted toward the river and the fireworks still going off. The variety of fireworks was incredible to Kathleen, not just large booming ones that filled the sky with neon green and red.

There were kinds that scattered across like shimmering waterfalls, or others that sped away in tight spiraling lines.

Kathleen looked down, the space between her and Yuriko just lit up enough that she could see their hands held loosely. Kathleen gripped hers tighter. The fireworks were brighter now, shooting off rapidly together in a crescendo. She pulled Yuriko closer, for no other reason than she just kind of wanted to.

Yuriko took a step closer, facing her now, legs pressing Kathleen against the wall. It was hard to see her expression. The fireworks were lighting up behind her, silhouetting her with color and overwhelming sound.

Yuriko said something then, but Kathleen couldn't hear. She tilted her chin up, confused.

Yuriko leaned forward. Her cheek was suddenly pressed against Kathleen's, one hand on her neck, the other gripping Kathleen's hand so tightly that she could feel her pulse.

"You can kiss me, if you want."

Her breath was warm, and she smelled like food and sweat and a soap that Kathleen realized she recognized. That she had been so close to Yuriko so many times, she had memorized her favorite scent. Her cheek was warm, and Kathleen could feel her long hair brushing her lips, silky and smooth.

"Can I?"

"You have my permission." Yuriko's lips were curled in a smile.

Kathleen knew Yuriko was teasing her, but a weight lifted from her anyway. She had been worried that what she wanted wasn't right. That she didn't have permission. It was ridiculous, a sign of just how inexperienced she was with a relationship like this. Just how out of place she was in a country like this.

It was dark, the fireworks were loud, and they were surrounded by a crush of people who had every reason to not look at them. They could have been at that forest shrine at Nikko, with only the trees and stone to take notice of them.

So Kathleen kissed Yuriko. The humidity curled around her in a lazy coil, making her pull Yuriko closer, needing more, only knowing how to ask in this way.

Yuriko answered with a soft gasp and wet mouth. Her hands were on Kathleen's obi, the fabric too thick for Kathleen to feel her properly. She put her hands in Yuriko's hair, wondering how she had ever resisted before. Probably because Yuriko always wore it in a ponytail. Only tonight, with Ai's hair up and Yuriko's hair down, Kathleen got the chance—

Ai, she had forgotten about Ai.

Kathleen pulled away, and Yuriko simply redirected to her neck, breath hot and tongue scorching. "Wait," Kathleen said. "Wait, we have to—"

"Don't make me wait," Yuriko murmured, voice so molten Kathleen might have melted.

She swallowed, thick and trembling. "Ai," she managed, "We have to find Ai."

That did make Yuriko back up. Her eyes were suddenly alert. "How long has it been?"

"Too long." Not long enough. Kathleen forced her hands to release Yuriko, though it nearly physically pained her. "Come on. I've managed to keep track of her for six weeks. If I lose her on the last day, my boss will eat me."

Yuriko grinned, her hand sliding from Kathleen's obi to her hand, gripping tightly. "Well, we can't have that. Let's see if we can track down your wayward computer."

CHAPTER TWENTY-THREE

Yuriko watched as Kathleen texted Ai. Kathleen was frowning, lips pinched. Her neck, peeking out from the collar of the yukata, was damp with sweat. Yuriko found the compulsion to lick it nearly irresistible.

Kathleen looked up, and her worried expression cooled Yuriko's ardor, just a little.

"Ai isn't responding."

Yuriko frowned as well, quickly typing an email to Ai, just to be sure. No response. "Malfunction?"

Kathleen sighed. "It has to be. Shit, on the last day, as well."

Yuriko took her wrist. "Come on. Let's go to a less trafficked area. It could be our texts aren't getting through." It wasn't likely. Ai had the latest technology and could probably get a cell signal in the middle of Antarctica.

Nonetheless, Yuriko walked with Kathleen away from the crush of people watching fireworks, away from the food stalls and games, and out into the streets of the nearby neighborhood. They hesitated by a lonely konbini. A couple of guys loitered outside, drinking beer and laughing loudly. She was grateful they ignored them.

They both leaned against the bike rack, and Yuriko looked at her wrist, just in case her email had been answered. Kathleen looked around, as if she could spot Ai in the few people walking past.

"Ai?" Kathleen gasped.

Yuriko looked up, shocked to see Ai exiting the konbini, looking fresh and unaffected by the crowds and the heat.

Ai looked over to them, smiling. "Oh, you found me. I just received your messages." She tapped on her forehead. "Bet you didn't even notice I was gone."

Kathleen instantly took Ai's wrist, linking her phone directly to her. "I sent that text ages ago. You're lagging, Ai."

Yuriko looked at the drinking guys. They were too engrossed in a joke to even notice them. Still, she stood with her back to them, hoping to shield Ai just a little bit.

Kathleen was muttering to herself, "The patch should have fixed this, Ai. Why is your processing down by seventy percent?"

Up close Yuriko could see Ai's eyes were a little vacant. The corners of her lips did an odd twitch, as if she couldn't settle on an expression. "Do we need to take her back to the apartment?" Yuriko asked.

Kathleen was looking pale now. "She's running another program."

Yuriko hesitated. "What do you mean?"

Kathleen was flipping through code on her phone screen. "I mean, *shit*, this is crazy. Ai, what on earth are you trying?"

Ai was looking between them, her eyes jerking. "I had hoped... well, I'm sorry." Her voice was clear. "It was something I could not anticipate."

"Anticipate?"

Ai actually looked guilty, shrugging her shoulders. "I had hoped that giving you both time alone would help you to realize—"

"Wait, you purposefully left us alone tonight?"

Ai's lips twitched, almost in a smile. "Yeah."

"Just to see if we would hook up or something?"

"Confess. I wanted you both to confess. Whatever happened next would just be a bonus." She sighed, looking up to the buildings. "I guess my analysis still needs improvement." She reached up, tugging at her side ponytail. "I was just so sure..."

Kathleen suddenly dropped Ai's wrist. She took an alarmed step back. Yuriko put a hand on her shoulder, concerned by how pale and wide-eyed she had become. "What is it? What's wrong?"

Kathleen looked at the hand on her shoulder, as if it was damning. "Ai is...this is messed up, Yuriko. Ai is messed up. The whole PLC project is *fucked*."

Yuriko looked around, but they were alone now in the glaring lights of the konbini. Still, she kept her voice low. "What do you mean?"

Kathleen shrugged off her hand, cupping her forehead. "Ai is trying to hook us up, matchmake, something like that. God, she looks exactly like you, Yuriko. She acts like you. Now she's trying to get me into a relationship with the real you. Can't you see how fucked up this is?"

"We've known for weeks that her appearance was an anomaly. And she is programmed to please you," Yuriko tried to soothe.

"No, no. She is rewriting her code, Yuriko. She is fucking rewriting her code. She is meant to please me, but this is too far. PLCs are not meant to cultivate outside relationships. They are not meant to play matchmaker. And because she looks like you, that makes it even worse. It's like the cortex scan found some secret crush of mine, made a copy, and that copy has gone out to find the real crush and push us into a relationship. This can't go beta, Yuriko. This is a disaster."

Kathleen was shaking and Yuriko wrapped her arms around her. It didn't help. In fact, Kathleen pushed away from her, taking a few small steps away, then back. She was running her hands through her hair, the careless updo falling around her shoulders.

"Kathleen, calm down. Let's take her back to my apartment. We can run a more thorough scan there and really see what's happening. It's probably not as big of a deal as it seems."

Kathleen stopped, and she looked at Yuriko, bleak and hopeless. "I can't."

"Can't what?"

"I can't go back to your place."

"That's okay. We'll go to your apartment."

"No."

Yuriko felt something in her stomach harden, cold and spreading. "No?"

"Can't you see? This also brings our whole relationship, thing, whatever, into question. It wasn't natural. There is a computer standing right here currently writing code on us." Her voice was rising.

Yuriko glanced at Ai, who was only staring passively between them. "Kathleen, I understand that something is wrong with Ai, but you're jumping to conclusions. What is between us—"

"Was formulated by an artificial intelligence! Ai has always pushed us together. Bringing you into my apartment when I was sick. Making sure you joined us in Nikko. Even tonight, she abandoned me, so I would be alone with you. That is not how a PLC is meant to function." She wasn't yelling, but there was an edge to her voice, brittle and breaking.

Yuriko stepped closer and took Kathleen's hands. She kept her voice calm, quiet. She had to keep control—it was the only thing keeping them together. "Are you saying that all you've shared with me, felt for me, wasn't your choice?"

Kathleen bit her lip, and her eyes were shining, near tears. "I can't trust my feelings, Yuriko. I thought I just had to battle my insecurities, but this is different. This could mean the end of my career. Yours too."

Yuriko shook her head slowly. "This is not about our jobs. This is about us. Are you seriously saying that you wouldn't have found me attractive, wouldn't have wanted me, unless Ai suggested it?"

Kathleen looked away, and Yuriko wondered if the sudden stab of pain in her chest was her heart breaking. Kathleen was questioning her, was denying her after they had come this far. Were Kathleen's feelings so weak as to be broken by a malfunctioning computer?

"I just need some space, I think," Kathleen whispered. "I need to run a diagnostic. I need to talk to my team. I need to not be around you, I think."

Yuriko wasn't letting her go, not just yet. Not until she had given up every piece of her heart. "Kathleen, please, don't let me go."

Kathleen closed her eyes, swallowing. "I don't want to." Her voice was ragged. When she opened her eyes, tears slipped down. Her gaze was steady. "I'm not saying that I don't care for you anymore. Or want you. I do, I really do, but this is just all so new and scary for me. You know that. I have to take it one step at a time, and this, with Ai, is something I need to process."

"And I can't help you?"

Kathleen sighed, gripping Yuriko's hands briefly and then letting go. "Not for this. It wouldn't be fair to you." She paused, just breathing, gaining more composure. "We will both be very busy in the coming months anyway. It might be a good idea, having space. I can come back clearheaded, and you…you won't learn to hate me."

"Kathleen," Yuriko moaned, hands feeling stung and empty. "I don't, I couldn't—" She looked over at Ai, still waiting patiently, her synthetic eyes concerned, but unobtrusive. What was her code telling her? Was it saying that she should try and push them through this? Was it saying she should stay back, let Kathleen make her own decision? If Yuriko asked, would Ai take her side? If she had been trying to pair them up, she would defend Yuriko, right? As a PLC, however, she should support whatever Kathleen wanted, right?

It was messed up. Yuriko could understand that now. She just wished that Kathleen had more faith in her, in them, that she wouldn't want to tackle this problem alone. Well, maybe if Kathleen didn't have faith in them, Yuriko could have enough for both of them.

"I understand. I'm here for you, you know, and I…" She breathed. "I don't want to, but I will, Kathleen. Because I love you, I will give you space, but please don't forget about me."

Kathleen clenched her jaw, nodding. She took Ai's hand, and they began to walk away. Just before leaving the lights of the konbini, she paused and turned to look at Yuriko. "How do you know you love me?"

Yuriko looked at her, beautiful in that yukata, even with her hair falling and messy. The harsh store lights only made her skin glow, her eyes bright with emotion. There were sounds around them, people walking on the opposite side of the street, and in the distance, fireworks and music, cars passing. All of it seemed muffled and blurred, a backdrop to the only thing Yuriko could focus on, Kathleen standing there. Kathleen ready to walk away.

Yuriko didn't answer. Instead she reached up and rubbed a small circle in the center of her chest, as if it would ease the ache forming there. An ache that was both sharp and empty, too much and too little.

It seemed answer enough, and Kathleen walked away.

CHAPTER TWENTY-FOUR

The evening brought few answers to Kathleen. She ran a more thorough scan on Ai, but the expanded data only reinforced her conclusions. She would only find more accurate data once Ai was decommissioned and the raw data could be extracted. She emailed Fukusawa, briefing him on her findings. It was a difficult email to write, since she didn't want to give too much personal information away. Then she sent another email to Tamura, even more vague, but wanting to get ahead of the data that Ai would release the next day.

She hoped it would be enough.

The morning went seamlessly. Kathleen woke early to shower and put on her normal business attire. Two men from Engineering arrived with a padded box. Ai changed back into the horrid default clothes she had arrived in. Then she sat in the molded compartment and powered down. The men sealed her in, gave a cursory nod to Kathleen, and then left.

Kathleen only spent enough time to put on her shoes and lock the door before she left, catching the next train to her office. She missed the morning rush, and she was glad to have a seat for the ride to work. Before she had even gotten off the train, she received a message that Ai had been officially decommissioned, and updates would be forthcoming.

Arriving at the office, she instantly received an email for a private meeting with Tamura. Kathleen would have dreaded it more, but she felt oddly resigned, numb. Everything seemed just a little grayer and out of focus.

Tamura was waiting in her office, fingers folded before her. She wasn't wearing her glasses but had her computer up, projecting the familiar data that Kathleen had looked at last night.

Her sharp eyes landed on Kathleen as she closed the door. "This could be a rare anomaly," she said instead of a greeting.

Kathleen nodded. "It could be."

"You don't think so?"

"It's a lot to take in. Totally unexpected."

Tamura sighed, eyes trained on her computer, fingers twitching to flick through the data. Kathleen found it odd to see her boss looking so closely at it. Tamura's job was to delegate work, not do it herself. "This is in relation to Vellucci-san, correct?"

Kathleen flinched. She had not mentioned Yuriko in her emails. She had only designated that Ai was pushing a relationship between her and another woman. She stuttered, unsure what to say. She didn't want to drag Yuriko into this and risk her career as well.

Tamura, after a long moment, looked back to her. "This is a confidential meeting, and I will assure you that Vellucci-san is clearly an innocent in this. Even her job in QC would not have the ability to impact the coding like this. I will not bring this matter to her superiors. I only ask to confirm all the data points presented to me." She paused, then drew her hand away from the screen, stilling her scrolling. "I had suspected her involvement from your first report of the PLC's apparent faulty physical appearance. Of course I used facial recognition software to see if anyone directly managing the cortex scan was involved. Vellucci-san, obviously, was not."

Kathleen felt like she could breathe a little easier, but only a little. Her boss still knew she had more than just a passing interest in another female coworker. "Yes, Yuriko—I mean, Vellucci-san—was the person my PLC was trying to..." It felt too odd to say it aloud, too damning.

Tamura leaned back in her chair, looking up at the ceiling. It was an oddly casual stance, and it made Kathleen feel off balance. "A PLC playing at matchmaking software. It's an interesting idea." She frowned. "We will have to closely monitor the beta for this anomaly and hope it does not come up again. Still...it's interesting. Not that I appreciate the timing of this revelation, but it does have some merit to consider." She sat straight, sharp eyes again on Kathleen. "It would have to be a different product. Separate from the PLC. The potential for a companion sim who could also act as a personal dating assistant is something worth contemplating."

Kathleen felt like the breath was knocked from her. "You *like* the program my PLC was trying to code?"

"No." She was back to looking at her computer screen, idly flipping through it. "I would not like our AI engine to have the power to completely rewrite their code, but I would like *you* to write it. You've touched base with Fukusawa-san on this?"

"Yes." Kathleen felt stunned. Her legs had gone numb from locking her knees so hard.

"Good. I want you both working on this as a secondary project, and have a working proposal by the public launch of the PLC. Delegate the others in your team to make sure this doesn't happen again. Even if it means we are reworking and updating the code during the beta. In the meantime"—she barreled on as if she had not just rocked Kathleen's whole world in a matter of minutes—"I'll need you to travel with the PR team to participate in their public presentations for this initial beta."

"I...what?" It hadn't been mentioned before that when the beta went live, Kathleen would have to do presentations outside of the company.

Tamura nodded. "Since you got exclusive access to this product, I'll need you out in the field promoting it. Everyone will appreciate your expertise."

Kathleen felt a bit light-headed. "I don't know. I wasn't prepared for this when I was recruited."

Tamura waved a flippant hand. "It will not be difficult. You'll only have to perform a few scripted presentations, and PR will feed you only questions you have prepared for. Otherwise, you'll be meeting with other division heads of the company." She tapped on her wrist, and Kathleen felt her phone buzz with incoming mail. "This is your itinerary for the next two months."

Kathleen's eyes widened. Nagoya, Hiroshima, Fukuoka, Sapporo...she wasn't even sure where all these cities were exactly, but she knew they were far away from Tokyo. There were also various notes saying alarming things like *vid meeting with Hong Kong* or *online chat with Seoul*. She looked up, feeling overwhelmed.

Tamura was checking her wrist, like she hadn't just dropped another bomb on Kathleen. "The company will reimburse all expenses, and for the most part, the PR team and myself will do the heavy lifting." She glanced at Kathleen. "You're just there as technical support, really." She put her arm down. "If this beta promotion goes well, we will probably send you abroad for the worldwide release. Just a warning."

Kathleen returned to her desk, feeling a little out of breath. Before she even sat down, she received an email from Fukusawa, who had apparently been updated by Tamura about this new side project. Maybe it was just the impersonal nature of an email, but she didn't think he sounded as freaked out as she felt right now. She wasn't hungry for lunch and spent the next hour instead combing through the alarming itinerary. She would be eating dinner with the CEO of the company in two weeks, and she prayed that she was only required to *sit* there and not have to actually speak.

She looked up when Fukusawa tapped on her door. She wondered if she looked like a deer in the headlights. "Uh, yes?"

He held out an envelope. "The data from PLC 00 arrived."

Kathleen stood up, quickly taking it from him. PLC 00 was the name they used in the office for Ai. It was a little strange to receive a physical envelope with the small data drive inside it. Kathleen knew that sending all of Ai's programming over the Internet would be a breach of security. "Thank you. Ah, Fukusawa-san, about this…project that Tamura-san wants us to work on…"

He waited, patient, his dark eyes steady. "Yes?"

"I hope you understand that it's a little personal to me. I would just rather begin the preliminary work before we start working together, okay?"

He was silent for a moment. Then he tilted his head, just a little, and Kathleen realized he was checking her open office door. There was no one loitering nearby. He looked back to her. "I understand. Please tell me when you require my assistance." Then he gave a short bow and left.

Kathleen had been working with Fukusawa for months now, and it seemed a terrible slight on her part to not know him very well. She had always written him off as part assistant, part secretary. Brilliant, but cold. There was more to him than she knew. She would have to give him more credit.

She dropped the drive onto her desk. Most computer chips were small enough that they required tweezers to pick up. This actually managed to be the size of her thumbnail. She knew there was quite a bit of data in it. She wondered what Ai looked like now. Had they totally stripped her down, looking into her mechanical workings for wear and tear? Was Yuriko the one slowly taking her apart?

She plugged the drive into her desk computer, which automatically synced up with her phone. The first thing she noticed was that it was all a mess. Her ordered lines of code were practically buried under revisions and new data. Some of it the revisions were hers, but much of it was from Ai, making changes and updates as she went. The PLC couldn't change its basic functions, or any code having to do with safety, but it was meant to learn, taking in new information and using it to change actions and reactions. It was a small wonder that Tamura had so casually flipped through it.

As Kathleen buried herself in it, she found little blips of memories. The patch from when Ai broke down in Akihabara. The automatic enforcements from when Kathleen had gotten ill, and Ai broke some of the rules in the cause of protecting her health. She skipped past it all, looking for the beginning of the data collection. The moment when Ai first opened her eyes and had to take in the world around her. The moment when she first looked at Kathleen. She translated the code in her head.

No obstructions. Seek USER KATHLEEN. USER KATHLEEN found. Examine user.

Acquire more data. Speak.

Doing okay there, Kathleen? Emotion: NONTHREATENING.

Things started sparking off from there. No longer linear, but like a bush growing wildly. She could even see moments in which Ai reflected on past memories and edited them, bringing new conclusions from data gathered later.

It felt like going through an old journal entry. It seemed so familiar, but there were so many new things to discover. Or rediscover. Kathleen had only been with Ai for a rather short time, but she felt achingly nostalgic. Nastukashii, Ai probably would have supplied.

She remembered going to Akihabara and seeing the old sim game she had worked on. When she played through, it had been like catching up with old, forgotten friends. Looking through Ai's data felt nearly intimate. The data didn't make her sad, or even miss Ai. Maybe because, like an old computer that needed a new battery, Kathleen could just put this chip into any suitable device, and Ai would live again. Of course, it wouldn't be the same unless she received a new PLC body. However, Ai's physical form had never really pleased her.

Ai created different data files for each person she met. Kathleen's was the largest, bursting with input and revisions. She also kept files of people Kathleen hadn't even realized she met. There was the clerk in the convenience mart named Junosuke and two servers at a café, Naomi and Kaoru. These were small files, just enough so that Ai could act appropriately when she met them again and lightly review them whenever meeting a new stranger.

There was a file for Yuriko. Kathleen wasn't surprised to see it. What did surprise her were the number of revisions in Yuriko's file. Code had been rewritten dozens of times. Memories reviewed so often that, just by glancing through it, several popped up without prompting.

Yuriko's face, soft, eyes pensive. She was reaching out with one hand.

And you've always needed someone to take care of you. It was translated into English, by default.

Her hand touched another's face. NONUSER MICHIKO was identified.

Another memory. This was darker. Input was flowing in, but there was no output.

Yuriko was very close, looking at Ai seriously.

"Ai, you need to stand and follow us."

Ai moved and notes were taken. Kathleen's arm around her waist. Yuriko before her. They were in a train station, then on a train.

Kathleen's voice, though Ai wasn't looking at her. *I think I've managed to dodge a panic attack. Thank you for coming.*

Then, a movement, at the time unanalyzed. Later data overlapped it.

USER KATHLEEN stabilized by means of NONUSER YURIKO.

The next was sound only, the visuals black.

Will I see you in the morning?

If you like.

Good.

I need more data. More analysis.

Compress data. Filed under USER/NONUSER EVALUATION.

If you reach out to Kathleen, she will undoubtedly reach back, even if she isn't sure why yet.

Yuriko's face filled the screen, eyes wide. Kathleen didn't need Ai's evaluation to read the expression.

NON-USER YURIKO emotion: HOPE.

Kathleen left Yuriko's file and decided to see what this USER/NONUSER EVALUATION file contained. It was the code Ai was creating for herself, but she would only get so far, then suddenly cut it off. Then pick it up again later. Kathleen checked the dates of the progress, seeing it form from only bits and pieces, until, just yesterday, Ai seemed to have run a full simulation of it. At that time, Kathleen had only been able to comprehend a piece of it. Now it was all laid before her.

However, Ai was a simulation herself. She couldn't just disregard her own code and run another. She seemed to have placed it, almost like a blanket, over the original programming. Where it conflicted, she tweaked the new code, causing many small crashes and reboots. If this happened yesterday, then Kathleen should have noticed, right? Maybe not while she was at work, but the time stamp said most of these occurred during the evening. So they would have been at the festival. She would have…

Wait. Ai had left her with Yuriko. She had not been keeping track of Ai during these few hours.

She didn't know why Ai would run the code, especially with such high risk of total failure. It might have even caused a complete malfunction if Kathleen hadn't gotten to her and begun running scans. Ai had stopped the program then, making it hard for Kathleen to read.

There was a small vid file present, put in there like an afterthought.

Yuriko was alone, standing in front of the convenience mart. She was backlit, and one hand was slightly raised at her side, fingers tense.

Kathleen had not remembered that. Or just how dark Yuriko's eyes looked, staring at Kathleen as if she was the only thing in the world.

NONUSER YURIKO emotion: FRAGILE.

How do you know you love me?

USER KATHLEEN emotion: FRAGILE.

Response emotion: COMFORT.

ERROR

Import USER/NONUSER EVALUATION.

Response emotion: NEUTRAL.

The visual moved away from Yuriko. Kathleen didn't remember, but Ai must have looked at her. She came into frame, and it struck her just how similar her eyes were to Yuriko's at that moment. USER/NONUSER EVALUATION file failed.

Chapter Twenty-five

In Hiroshima, Kathleen found out that Fukusawa was a hilarious drunk.

With only a few drinks, the mild-mannered computer nerd turned into a swaggering sass pirate. There was no other way to describe it. He would sit next to Kathleen and say, very loudly, "You know what your problem is? Your last name is impossible to pronounce."

"Schmitt?"

He grimaced. "It's just terrible for any Japanese person. Where are the vowels? What does your country have against vowels?" He slammed his fist on the table, nearly knocking over his beer. Luckily, Mitsu-chan was there to save it.

"Just call her Ka-chan," she piped up.

Kathleen rolled her eyes, but she would laugh or smile as Fukusawa would go across the entire room and tell people just how wrong they were. No one took it seriously, not with a hot plate of okonomiyaki sitting in front of them. Kathleen's was a wonderful pile of noodles, pork, eggs, brown sauce, and mayo. Mitsu-chan had described it as a Japanese pancake. However, Kathleen had never seen a pancake stacked about five inches high and filled with noodles. It didn't matter—she was going to eat it all.

When she learned that Mitsu-chan would be joining the tour, Kathleen had been very grateful to have another familiar face besides Fukusawa. She quickly found the PR team to be an excitable bunch. The leader was Rei Hamasaki, who was just as hyper as Mitsu-chan and immediately insisted that everyone call her Hama-chan. She had traveled the world it seemed, being fluent in about ten different languages.

"I once spent a year in the Bahamas. That's when I was working for Limited Tech, and I was trying to get sponsors in the Caribbean. Wonderful place, except one morning I found a scorpion in my bathtub."

"What?" Kathleen asked. They were currently outside the convention center in Fukuoka, enjoying the warm weather and mild breeze.

She nodded, finishing up a cigarette. "So I threw it out the window. Told my roommate about it later and she was like, *Did you get the second one?*" She grinned. "Apparently, if you don't properly plug your bathtub, a mating pair of scorpions will probably move in."

Hama-chan's second in command was Suzu Aoki, whose English was very poor, but she was fluent in Japanese, Mandarin, and Thai. She was quiet compared to Hama-chan, but Kathleen often saw them in private conference, sometimes just in the corner of the room, between questions, quickly talking to another.

Other members on the team were Yoshi Tashiro, the main PR rep in China who loved to practice his English with Kathleen, Minoru Kono, an older man who often ordered for everyone at restaurants, Takahashi Mutō, who had become fast friends with Fukusawa, and Ayame Thorn, who was from Australia and served as second translator to Hama-chan.

They were on the shinkansen to Sapporo when Ayame turned to Kathleen and asked, "Do you have a girlfriend?"

Kathleen was stunned. She had been staring out the windows, possibly getting a little too excited to see real snow again. "What?"

Ayame had large green eyes and wavy blond hair. She didn't look Japanese, at least not to Kathleen. She spoke Japanese so well that it was alarming to hear her switch to her Australian English. "Do you have a girlfriend?" she repeated.

"Ah...um." Kathleen's stomach twisted. She had been tapping on her wrist while looking out the window, mindlessly refreshing her email. It wasn't like she and Yuriko hadn't talked at all. They sent each other updates, and Kathleen would often ask Yuriko questions about the new things she encountered traveling the country.

However, they hadn't *really* talked, and the more Kathleen dove into Ai's code, the more unsure she felt about all of it. She wanted to see Yuriko again, badly. She practically ached for it, her body somehow going through withdrawal for something she barely had to begin with, but her mind was too full of concerns and questions. Her thoughts kept circling, and Kathleen kept backing away.

Ayame tilted her head. "Oh, a boyfriend then?"

Kathleen shook her head. "No, I...why do you ask?"

Ayame shrugged. "Do you wanna go out sometime?"

She was more than a little stunned. She had talked a lot with Ayame over the past weeks. Being the two foreigners had formed a bond between them. She did like Ayame—she was funny and smart and always seemed to notice whenever Kathleen was feeling a little stressed from all the travel. Also, she had to admit, Ayame was very pretty.

Then she thought of Yuriko. She thought of how inky black her hair was, and how silky. She thought of her eyes, blue and open. She remembered the yukata she wore to the hanabi. How it made her skin look so pale, her neck longer. She remembered her voice breaking.

"I'm sorry, I'm just not…ready right now," Kathleen murmured, unsure of what to say.

Ayame nodded and settled back in her seat. "That's all right. Recent breakup or something like that?"

Kathleen sighed, looking back out the window to the snowy mountains. "Yeah, something like that."

She checked her wrist, finding only the usual updates from Hama-chan. She flipped through it, to yesterday, the day before that. All the way to over a month ago.

Yuriko: *You'll be leaving with Mashida's PR team soon, yes? Do you want to hang out? Share a beer?*

Kathleen: *Sorry. I'm very busy atm.*

Then, a week into the tour, Kathleen had texted: *Visiting the castle at Nagoya. I didn't realize that Japan had castles. Also, I just might live here instead of the shrines in Nikko.*

Yuriko: *I don't know how the shrines of Nikko will survive without your blessing. There are castles closer to Tokyo, if you want to visit with me when you come back.*

Kathleen hadn't responded back.

Kathleen: *The Hiroshima Peace Memorial Museum is beautiful and depressing. I'm almost glad I lost the rest of the group, so I have some time alone.*

Yuriko: *I wish I was alone with you.*

Kathleen: *I'm glad I don't ever have to say much in these meetings and seminars. When I do, everyone is very friendly and doesn't expect much anyway. Haha.*

Yuriko: *I wish I could hear your voice.*

That was two weeks ago, and Kathleen knew she should probably stop. She couldn't help it. She would see something amazing or try something new, and she immediately thought that she could tell Yuriko. When she managed to order her own beer at a restaurant, she nearly called Yuriko. When she made her first presentation and it wasn't a total disaster, she wanted to talk to Yuriko. When she saw the ocean or the mountains, she wanted to show it to Yuriko. Yet any time Yuriko responded, Kathleen felt herself drawing away. It felt too easy and too difficult. She felt clumsy and callous. She had never felt this confused in a relationship before. Or not a relationship. It seemed clear that Yuriko still wanted her, and every time Kathleen drew away, she felt like an asshole.

She tried to confide in Mitsu-chan once.

"Don't worry about Yuri-chan. I hear it's crazy back in Tokyo, da ne? She has more to think about than talking to you."

"Have you been talking to her?"

"Mochiron! Otherwise I would sound like an idiot whenever someone asked me a question."

Kathleen paused, cradling her beer. It had gone warm. "Is she doing well?"

Mitsu-chan gave her a weird look. "She is just giving me technical information." She sighed. "Ah, I wish she had come, but she turned it down and recommended me. She said she didn't like doing interviews or presentations." She grinned. "It's because I'm so kawaii, deshō?"

Kathleen forced a small. "Definitely."

Yuriko had turned down representing Mashida? Was it because she wasn't comfortable with all the vid calls and seminars they were attending? Or was it because Kathleen had asked for space.? Was she trying to give it? Or had she realized what a terrible idea Kathleen was?

Kathleen had the sudden inexplicable urge to call Ai and ask to check in to Yuriko. That was ridiculous; no one was at Kathleen's apartment, certainly not Ai. Ai was in Kathleen's briefcase.

They were in Kyoto during Christmas. Not that most of their group seemed to mind spending the holiday working. Even Ayame shrugged it off as normal.

"Japan doesn't really get into Christmas like most of the Western world," she said to Kathleen, passing her a plate of fried chicken that Rei had ordered for everyone. Japan had the bizarre tradition to eat fried chicken and strawberry shortcake, called Christmas Cake, for the holiday. "Christmas here is often spent with friends—maybe have a party, maybe give out gifts. Most people have to work."

Kathleen had been too busy to really think about Christmas. She had sent her family gifts months ago, just to be sure they arrived in time and before she was on the road. It seemed so odd now to sit in her hotel room late at night and call her family, with Mitsu-chan passed out cold on the other bed from too much beer and fried food.

It was Christmas morning in America, and her brother was the only one up. He and his wife were staying at their parents, and everyone else was sleeping in. Dave was lounging in the computer chair, holding an oversized Christmas mug with a penguin riding a reindeer on it. He was wearing a rather subdued woolen sweater and looked tired.

"Already tired of Christmas?" Kathleen teased.

Dave yawned, "You know Mom, she wanted to go to the midnight service and then afterward we all broke into the spiked eggnog early. You should be grateful I love you enough to wake from my traditional Christmas Eve coma."

Kathleen smiled. She knew the rest of the day would be lounging around, preparing the meal, and opening presents. Their other relations lived too far away for a big family meal, so everything would be casual and comfortable.

"I wish I could be there."

Dave shrugged. "It's okay. We got your gifts—that's what is really important."

Kathleen snorted and looked up to make sure she wasn't being too loud. Mitsu-chan's mouth was open, and she looked just a little like a corpse.

"You can come out next year," Dave continued. "Or we can visit you. We understand that you're busy, especially right now."

"I think I met someone," she blurted, surprising herself. How long had she been wanting to talk to Dave about this?

Dave paused, coffee halfway to his mouth. He slowly lowered it, looking at her. "I guessed that already."

Kathleen felt her chest tighten. "You already know?"

He shrugged. "Well, not any details of course. But you used to call about three times a day when you first got there. Then, just out of the blue, I'm only hearing from you once a month. Maybe an email in between, if I'm lucky. You did the same thing with Brandon, you know. Just drop us family members like deadweight."

Kathleen frowned. "I've not—I'm not like that."

He rolled his eyes. "Don't take it personally. I really don't. And Mom and Dad are used to not hearing from you for weeks at a time anyway. Besides, I was kind of happy. Figured you finally found someone who could help you out over there." He sat up a little straighter. "So when can I finally have a good online man-to-man talk with your newest boy toy?"

Kathleen tried to grin—she really did. "It's not like that. I mean, in a lot of senses." She groaned, digging her fingers through her hair. "It's just been so *complicated* and dumb and new and strange and…and I don't even know."

Dave paused, biting his lip. "It's a woman, then?"

Kathleen might have stopped breathing. "What? How did you know?"

Dave breathed out in relief, smiling. "Oh, thank God. That was a total shot in the dark, and it would have been so awkward if I was wrong."

Kathleen didn't care about his relief. Her heart was having palpitations. "Wait, how did you guess?"

"Seemed a reasonable assumption."

"Yeah, but like, based on what?"

He waved a hand. "I dunno, you're acting weird right now. Honestly, Kathleen, it's nothing to freak out over."

"Nothing to freak out over," Kathleen muttered under her breath. She wouldn't give him the satisfaction of knowing just how much she had been freaking out, for months now. "Do I seem like the kind of woman who is into other women?"

"If you're asking if you're some sort of stereotype, then no. But you've always seemed like the kind of person who attracts people to you. It was only a matter of time before a woman approached you, and you decided to give it a go." He paused for a second, and then leaned forward, eyes concerned. "You do know that it's okay? To be bisexual, I mean. I'm not judging you, and there's no reason to be ashamed of it or anything like that."

Kathleen flushed and looked away. "I mean, I guess I know…It's just not something I expected. I think I'm still getting used to the idea that I'm bisexual." She hesitated, looking at him again. "Do you really think I attract people?" She tried to sound teasing and not like she was totally fishing for more compliments.

Dave smiled sweetly. "It's the way you are so hopelessly pathetic. It's very endearing."

She would have smacked him, but he was just a projected image flying thousands of miles through the internet connection.

"Her name is Yuriko," she started. "She actually works for Mashida, in Engineering. I've had this big project lately, and it turns out we're neighbors. She's been a real help."

Dave raised his eyebrows. "Just a help?"

Kathleen gave him a withering look. "We became friends," she stated plainly. "We'd go out with other coworkers. Or she'd help me with the grocery store or riding the trains. She was the one who showed me Nikko. And, well, a lot of things actually. She showed me more of Japan than I had seen in the months since I've got here."

"Okay, so when can I meet this Yuriko?"

Kathleen felt herself deflate again. "We aren't, like…I mean, it's just been complicated and I've been…" Were they even together? Did needing space count as anything? Was Kathleen even worth being in a relationship with, given how much she had used this trip to avoid Yuriko?

Luckily, Dave didn't try to press a confession from her. Maybe he did understand when it was fun to tease his sister, and when it might send her into an emotional meltdown. "Do you want to be together?" he asked slowly.

It was the same question Kathleen had been asking herself for months now. Long before she'd been willing to admit that she just might have feelings for Yuriko beyond friendship. "It's not easy to say. I mean, I've just moved to a foreign country, I've been trying and failing to figure out how to live on a day-to-day basis, *and* I've got this huge promotion and project and responsibilities. I know I'm more than a little emotionally fragile and, well, needy."

She couldn't quite meet Dave's eyes. She was glad he didn't interrupt her.

"Sometimes it felt like I knew exactly what I wanted from her. Felt it so strongly that I was sure about me and her. But what does it mean when I take a step back, when I'm alone and away from her, that I second-guess everything? Did I read the signals right? Even the signals from myself? Did I really know what happened? Did I make it all up?"

She breathed in, ashamed to find herself shaking. She looked at Dave then, afraid to blink in case she started crying.

"How could I think of being in a relationship with her when I'm not even sure my feelings are real?" When everything had been some weird computer matchmaking program that neither she nor Yuriko had signed up for.

"If you feel them, they are real." He paused then, looking into his mug. "I can't say I understand everything about your situation, but I know what it's like to fall in love and…" Dave looked up. "I mean, it's not something I can tell you. I don't know what she's like. But I do know that you weren't happy when you moved to Japan."

"I was just—"

"I'm not saying you were totally depressed, but I could tell that you were a bit lost and not really enjoying yourself. Then you stop calling every six hours, and suddenly I see you traveling outside of Tokyo with this woman on your arm. Both of you smiling like idiots."

Kathleen suddenly remembered. "The photo from Nikko. I didn't think I sent that."

Dave shrugged. "It came from your email address."

Kathleen wondered what excuse Ai had made up to violate Kathleen's private email. Granted, Ai had practically been Kathleen's private computer.

"Did you have fun?"

"Yeah, I mean, Nikko is a beautiful place."

"No, I mean, everywhere you went with her. Was it fun?"

Kathleen grinned. Nikko had been fun. Also being in Yuriko's apartment, or seeing the city with her, or riding the train to work had been fun. She had eaten food she would have been too afraid to try. She had seen places she had been too afraid to go. Maybe…it had bettered her. She was able to go places and do things even without Yuriko. She missed her terribly. She had learned from Yuriko to not be so afraid.

"But," she whispered, not caring that she wasn't going to directly answer Dave's question, "what does it matter now? I've messed this up, Dave. We've barely spoken in weeks, and I don't know what she feels for me now."

Dave sighed. "Well, then maybe it wasn't meant to work out. And don't look like that. You're a grown woman—you know things don't always have to make sense. Maybe next time you find a woman with her arm around you, you'll know what to do."

They lapsed into silence then. Dave nursed his coffee a little longer, and Kathleen looked out the window to the city lights of Kyoto. It was going to be cold today, probably cold in Tokyo too. She remembered hating the humidity and heat of summer. Now she sort of wished she could have it all back.

Yuriko had bettered Kathleen. However, that didn't seem so

important now. Now, with her brother practically dozing and the sun rising and setting all over the world, Kathleen wondered if she had done anything to better Yuriko.

"I don't want another woman," she murmured.

"Well, then I guess you'll just have to keep this one."

Kathleen startled. She had been convinced Dave had fallen asleep on her. It wouldn't have been the first time during one of their rambling chats. She wondered if he could see her flush of embarrassment in the low light of her screen.

"I don't think I deserve her."

He snorted softly. "And I didn't deserve Juliet, but that's why I spend every day trying my best to earn her."

She gave him a small smile. "And how does a lazy lump like you earn her?" She was teasing, but Dave just looked thoughtful.

"Well, taking her on dates, gifts go pretty far too, and sometimes I pull my head out of my ass and ask how her day has been." He was smiling now. "And, on occasion, I apologize if I've hurt her."

Kathleen wondered if she owed more than just an apology to Yuriko. "Such solid love advice."

"I am an expert." Dave sighed, setting his cup aside. "Speaking of love, I hear Juliet moving upstairs."

"Well, I won't keep you. Merry Christmas."

He smiled. "Merry Christmas. And good luck, yeah?"

She nodded, ending the call. The room was dark and so quiet.

"I think you deserve Yuriko-chan."

Kathleen started at Mitsu-chan's voice, groggy with sleep. "Oh, I'm sorry, did I wake you?"

Mitsu-chan gave a sleepy chuckle. "Daijōbu. And you know I work with Yuriko-chan, ne? She isn't so perfect." She rolled over, sighing happily as she pulled the sheets tighter around herself. "Though she was a lot lonelier before she met you. I imagine she deserves love as much as you do."

"Mitsu-chan, I…" Kathleen swallowed around a lump in her throat. "Thanks for saying that."

Mitsu-chan answered with a light snore.

❖

It was another early morning, on yet another shinkansen, but this time they were heading back to Tokyo. It had felt like ages since

Kathleen was last there. She had been on the road for two months. Summer had come and gone. Fall had too.

It was the end of December and everyone was glad to be returning just in time for New Year's. Fukusawa slept next to Kathleen, head bent at an awkward angle. She didn't know how it wasn't painful for him. She opened her computer, the display glowing on the seat in front of her. She opened up Ai's files again.

She hadn't had much time to review the mysterious program during the trip, though often she was asked to open up certain files to show Ai's learning and revising process. She had kept USER/NONUSER EVALUATION away from scrutiny.

"Kathleen-san?" Fukusawa asked softly.

Kathleen turned, surprised to see him awake. She was glad that during the trip she managed to convince him to call her by her name, instead of Director. She looked at him. "Yeah?"

He sat up a little straighter in his chair. "I'm sorry that I did not give you the report on the cortex scan."

"Report? What report?"

He looked slightly uncomfortable. "When you first received PLC 00, you reported that the cortex malfunctioned when it designed the physical body."

Kathleen suddenly felt a little embarrassed about it. That felt like ages ago. Then, well, a lot more complicated things had come up. "Oh, what happened to the report?"

"Inconclusive."

"Really?"

He shrugged. "There was no malfunction detected. No anomaly in how the cortex scan was interpreted by the computer. In order to thoroughly investigate, I would have to analyze your personal cortex scan. I assumed you would not want me to go through your personal information."

She looked away from him and stared at Ai's code. "Maybe I was wrong."

There was silence for a moment. Then Fukusawa said, his voice soft and just a bit nervous, "PLC 00. Her appearance…it was like Vellucci-san in Quality Control, yes?"

Kathleen stiffened. "You know Yuriko?"

He shook his head, then shrugged, like he wasn't sure which motion to commit to. "I do not know her well, but her profile came up when I was researching who in the company I could contact about the cortex scan. I did not make the connection, however, until I saw that you knew her."

"What do you mean?"

He flushed in the light of her computer screen. "You often commute with Vellucci-san. I take the same train but get off on an earlier stop."

Kathleen felt a little embarrassed herself, though she wasn't sure why. "Oh."

"I decided to not pursue the report then. I'm sorry if this was, anō, presumptuous."

Kathleen looked past him, to the lights from the city flashing by the window. "Maybe the cortex scan was a bit presumptuous too."

She must have been silent for too long, because Fukusawa added, "Would you like me to complete the report?"

She shook her head. It was an unconscious reaction, but she did not correct it. "No, that is unnecessary." There were some things about Ai that Kathleen still didn't understand, but now, after so long, it didn't seem right to say she had been a mistake.

"Starting on the new sim?" Fukusawa gestured to her screen.

"I'm just trying to wrap my head around it."

He leaned forward, reaching out to flick through it on his own. He hummed. "Looks like the PLC sim, but what is the word…" He rubbed the back of his head, yawning. "Etō…like when the cortex scan looks for, anō, compatibility?"

Kathleen looked back to the code. Was Ai drawing data all the way back from the cortex scan? Making changes in her code before she even saw Yuriko? It would be a place to start. Not Ai's code, but the cortex scan.

She turned to Fukusawa, ready to ask him to get started on this new line of research. However, he had already fallen asleep. Instead, she lifted up her wrist, looking at her contact information for Yuriko.

It still felt strange, unnerving, that a computer read her mind before she had the thoughts. Then she remembered that train ride, the first time she met Yuriko. Like she had found a beacon in a storm, a safe harbor in the sea of a Tokyo rush hour. Love at first sight wasn't something she believed in, but maybe it was enough. Her whole world had been turned upside down, and maybe the cortex scan had found the one thing that seemed to make it right again. Impulsively she sent a text.

I miss you.

It was too early in the morning to expect a reply. It was New Year's Eve, and Yuriko probably had plans. Might even be with her mother. All her coworkers around her were ready to get off the train and go straight home to have a week off to celebrate and relax.

Still, Kathleen stared at her wrist, at her words. They didn't seem enough. They seemed too much.

CHAPTER TWENTY-SIX

The world was full of lonely people. However, the lonely people in Japan were a special brand of pathetic. Most often they were businessmen who, because of long work hours, either didn't have a family to go home to or actively tried to avoid the family at home. Others might be young adults who had failed in college and now spent most of their time locked in their parents' house; the only source of light in their darkened rooms was the glow of their video games. There were also lost foreigners, people who simply never learned how to make or keep friends, people running away from their problems, and people trying to drink away the pain in their hearts.

Yuriko might have been drinking, but she liked to think she wasn't so far down yet, even though she was wandering around the city during that early morning hour, when it was still more night than day. She saw those lonely people in the arcade buildings, playing fishing games with short handheld rods, or singing karaoke in a booth by themselves. They walked from the pachinko parlors, blinking away the bright lights and deafening noises from within. They were sleeping in their business suits in the bushes by the train stations, sobering up until the trains began to run again.

She usually didn't walk around this late at night by herself. Too many old drunk men would try to convince her that her life would be better with a husband to take care of her. However, it was nearing four in the morning, and most of the predators were passed out or being shoved into a taxi by their friends.

She stopped as a waft of cheap meat and salty broth washed over her. She looked up to a blazing sign of a small fast food restaurant. She checked her wrist. The trains wouldn't open up for another hour. So she stepped inside.

She remembered taking Kathleen to a curry restaurant shaped like this. Just single seating around a long counter. Kathleen had been surprised by the lack of tables. Kathleen had also...

At this moment, Yuriko felt like whoever had decided that serving to a party of one was more profitable than the American mantra of serving to two or more was a genius. This country, after all, catered to its strong population of lonely people. Japan knew that lonely people ate alone.

She slid into an open seat, making sure to keep a distance between her and an old man in a weathered suit currently dozing into his gyudon. The waitress was a middle-aged woman who looked like twelve cups of coffee just weren't kicking in fast enough. Her eyes were watery as she took Yuriko's order: gyudon and a bottle of beer. The woman produced the bottle and a clean glass, then opened the lid and walked away.

She sipped the beer, figuring that she might as well continue the trend of the night until the sun came up. She glanced around the restaurant. A couple of businessmen were at a table, attempting to keep their voices down as they argued. A young girl and boy were at the counter. She slept on his shoulder while he shoveled ramen into his mouth.

In the light of day, she wouldn't lean on him so easily. Yet right now it wasn't day, not yet. Later they would be back to their careful distance. The only contact they could look forward to was on the train. Then it was appropriate for any young man to shield a young girl with his body from other strangers.

The door rang as someone new walked into the restaurant. A young woman, a foreigner, wearing a large backpack, fleece jacket, shorts, and hiking boots. Her cheeks were flushed, and she grinned around the room like she had just hiked up a mountain. She strode to Yuriko and sat next to her, offering a friendly smile and letting her backpack fall with a heavy thump.

The waitress came over again, and Yuriko listened as the woman ordered in broken Japanese. It wasn't perfect, but good enough, and the waitress walked away.

"Do you speak English?" Yuriko asked, before she remembered that she had come out tonight to avoid talking to people.

The woman turned to her, smiling widely. "Yes. Am I that obvious?" She laughed, a little too loudly for the morning hour. The man near Yuriko snorted into his food, then seemed to fall back into his stupor. "My name is Shannon."

"Yuriko." She looked at the woman, with bright red hair and freckles coating every inch of visible skin. "Where are you from?"

"Originally? Texas. Outside of Austin. I've been traveling East Asia for about five years now. Lived in Seoul for almost a year, and then lived in Thailand, Singapore, Hong Kong. Now I've been in Japan for just over two months."

The waitress came back with a cup of steaming tea, and Shannon thanked her.

"Was actually in Hiroshima, but now I'm slowly moving north. I've an early shinkansen to Hokkaido." Her voice was loud, and Yuriko could hear her Texas accent slip out a few times. She wondered if Shannon attempted to hide it. "I've got a temp job lined up at a farm there. Doesn't pay much, but I get housing and all the home cooking I can eat."

Yuriko suddenly remembered. "Hiroshima?" Kathleen had been there not too long ago. She had sent a text to Yuriko. It hadn't been much, but Yuriko's heart had stuttered, too excited for such a brief text conversation. She had wanted more, and Kathleen had moved on.

So she had done what any sensible Japanese person does when trying to forget their problems—she went out drinking alone. Now she was here, listening to Shannon from Texas prattle on about the sights she saw in Hiroshima and the food and the weather. She was loud.

Kathleen had been quiet. She had been afraid to even go into the local grocery store. While Kathleen had struggled to figure out the train system in Japan, Shannon had been traveling the world all by herself. She had been taking on odd jobs, staying in the houses of people she just met, learning new languages as she sat on trains or in airplanes to a place she had never been to before. She was currently sitting in a cheap fast food restaurant, chatting to a complete stranger and laughing all the while.

"Was it hard to leave?" Yuriko asked suddenly. "I mean, moving from America?"

Shannon shrugged and nodded. "Yeah, it was a bit terrifying. I was barely twenty-one at the time. I had been thinking about this for *ages*. So I was pretty pumped." She snorted. "Though, it was a pretty steep learning curve when I first got to Korea. I feel like I learned more in those first two weeks than I have in five years." She waved a hand. "Not that I'm not learning still. I mean, I used to think—" She continued on.

Yuriko didn't mind the noise. Shannon provided a good background conversation as she finished her beer and ate her food. It made her feel like she wasn't like the rest of the people around the restaurant. She might have some life still in her.

When she'd met Kathleen, she saw someone lost, and maybe Yuriko had wanted to help her. Help her live in this country and understand it but stay true to who she was. A foreigner, maybe, but just simply a person from another place. A person who had learned how to live here, but not be crushed by the culture. Instead, enjoying it. Enjoying it because she was foreign and could enjoy it in a way that a native could not.

Kathleen was traveling now and learning more. Yuriko knew she could handle it. Yet Yuriko wished she could be there. To see Kathleen flourishing, being excited about new experiences. To be there when Kathleen needed support. To be there when Kathleen would turn to her, in awe, as if just realizing for the first time just how incredible this world was. Like maybe Yuriko was incredible for bringing her there.

"Hey, you okay?"

Yuriko realized she had been staring into her empty bowl. She nodded, a little hurriedly. Shannon was leaning forward. Yuriko noticed that her eyes were green. Kathleen's eyes were brown. Maybe that color wasn't as interesting as green or blue, but it was always the color Yuriko had envied since childhood. A color to keep quiet with. A color to stay unnoticed.

"What brings you out tonight?" Shannon asked. Her voice was softer now, more delicate.

The lonely people. The people Yuriko could walk by and judge, while pretending she was above it all. Above the hurt and the heartache. Above the childishness and the weight of it all. Maybe Yuriko was what she wanted back in high school. She had learned to be Japanese. She had learned to keep her thoughts and emotions close to her. Not to bother others. Be part of the crowd.

She realized that when she told Kathleen that she loved her, she should have promised it. She should have said it long before. Before Ai had told her to stop holding back. Before she had told herself to hold back.

Shannon was waiting for an answer. Yuriko wasn't sure if she could stand the silence. "My girlfriend and I are taking a break." It was a partial truth and a partial lie. Yet it felt good to say it like that.

Maybe she and Kathleen hadn't been girlfriends, but they had been more than friends. Now it was too nebulous to define. Did Kathleen still want to be with her, even after months with barely any communication?

Shannon's eyes widened, and she suddenly reached out, pulling Yuriko into a one-armed hug. She smelled like cigarettes and minty soap. "God, I'm so sorry. That's rough. That's so rough."

Yuriko didn't think she was crying, but she might as well be. Her chest felt raw and open. Her every breath raked against her ribs. Shannon didn't even know her. She didn't even ask for more details.

Perhaps that was for the best. Maybe then, for just a moment, Yuriko could pretend that it was all simpler. That she could be cured with a night of irresponsible drinking and comfort from a total stranger. She could pretend tomorrow that she would wake up with a new breath in her lungs, a fresh hope in her heart.

She would forget this moment, in which she wished with all her heart that she could be holding Kathleen instead.

She felt her wrist vibrate and she pulled away from Shannon to look down at a text. She wondered if her dad was texting her, not realizing what time it was in Japan.

I miss you.

Yuriko thought for a moment she was dreaming, that Kathleen had somehow felt her heart and had texted exactly what Yuriko was feeling.

Shannon was looking down at the text. Her face was soft. "Ah, I understand." Yuriko had no idea what she could understand when Yuriko felt so many conflicting things. Shannon stood up. "Well, I better head out. The station will be opening up soon. It was good meeting you, and I hope this New Year brings you the best."

Then she left, as swiftly and serendipitously as she had come.

It was almost the New Year, Yuriko realized, sneaking up on her as so many things had this year. Kathleen would be returning today, though it would be unlikely they'd see each other. Once the trains started, Yuriko would have to return to her apartment and freshen up before going to Yokohama for the day. Last-minute work before everyone started their shogastu holiday. She would be returning late and would have to make a phone call to her mother, to apologize for not traveling to see her.

She texted, *Tomorrow, at dawn, be ready.*

The response came quickly: *For what?*

For Yuriko to strangle Kathleen. For her to kiss Kathleen, for her to ask for so much, for her to take what she could get.

New Year's

Then Yuriko put her phone on silent. She had a lot to do today. She had to sober up, she had a train to catch, she had work to do, and she had a whole year rushing up to her.

CHAPTER TWENTY-SEVEN

Do you understand now?
Do you still feel confused?
It's not too late.
You can always go back.
People aren't computer programs.
They can change themselves.
All it takes is time.
People can do wondrous things.
They can create with nothing but hope
and dreams
and wishes.

Kathleen woke up, neck aching and feeling like she had bruised her cheek from lying on her living room table. She blinked at the bright screen in the dark morning. She felt like she had been dreaming, but she couldn't remember falling asleep.

Her computer was open, images flickering like a movie. It was a random selection from Ai's memory folder. The sound had muted, but Kathleen stared as the scenery showed Nikko. It was the shrine with the crying dragon.

The image was of Kathleen. She was looking up at the ceiling, mouth slightly open. Then she smiled and turned away. From Ai's angle, she couldn't see who Kathleen was looking at. Ai looked down, and Kathleen's hand came into view, between the legs of the other tourists, clasping Yuriko's, fingers white in their grip.

Kathleen shut down the computer. After arriving in Tokyo, she and the team had only a short meeting with Tamura before being given the rest of the day off. She had intended to find Yuriko, but she hadn't been in her apartment. She had intended to sleep in her bed, but clearly that had been forgotten as she scrolled through Ai's data.

Sleeping at her table wasn't a good idea. The surface was cold and hard, and the streaming images gave her strange dreams. She checked the time on her phone. It wasn't even five a.m. yet. She stared at the clock a little longer, taking a ridiculously long time to figure out what else was different about it.

Tomorrow, at dawn, be ready.

Kathleen felt more awake now, remembering Yuriko's texts from yesterday. Those had felt like a dream.

She went to the bathroom, washed her face, and brushed her teeth. She felt more alert. She threw on a different shirt and tied her hair back into a messy bun. She still wasn't sure what to expect. How should she dress? Did it matter?

She heard a door slam outside her apartment, and then boots walking. Kathleen heard it all the time; the door had no sound insulation. She walked to her door, looking through the eyehole.

Yuriko was standing there, staring at the door with a small frown on her face.

Kathleen was opening the door before she could think. "Yuriko," she gasped into the brisk morning. The concrete was freezing on her bare feet, and the cold air shocked the breath from her.

The sky was a pale gray with the streetlights providing most of the light this early in the morning. There was a dusting of snow on the ground, just enough to notice. Yuriko looked so fresh, cheeks already a little flushed from the cold, scarf around her neck, jacket neat and buttoned. Kathleen felt ragged. Yuriko's hair was shorter, coming to her chin. Her eyes were bright.

"It's…it's been a while," Kathleen blurted. She felt like she had a thousand things to say, that she should say, but only the most inane were coming out. It felt like they were meeting again for the first time, and she wasn't sure what was allowed.

Yuriko pulled the scarf she wore closer to her mouth. "Hisashiburi. And I told you to be ready at dawn."

Kathleen had no idea what she was doing. She was freezing, starting to shiver, and her heart was beating in her ears. "But what are we doing?"

Yuriko stared at her for a long moment, and Kathleen wondered if she had a thousand things she wanted to say as well. "Meiji Shrine." She shrugged. "You know, for the New Year. Come on."

Kathleen swallowed, feeling a sudden warmth bloom in her chest. "Yes! Let me just grab some shoes."

Yuriko snorted. "Also a coat."

Kathleen stumbled getting back into her apartment. She threw on the nearest coat and sturdy shoes. Luckily, she had gloves and a knitted hat in the pocket. She wasn't going to waste any time, just in case Yuriko came to her senses and abandoned Kathleen at her doorstep.

Running back outside, feeling more than a little rumpled, Kathleen was glad to see that Yuriko was still there, leaning against the railing. Yuriko nodded, seeing Kathleen. "Come on, it's going to be crowded."

"I'm pretty sure Tokyo is always going to be crowded," Kathleen joked.

Yuriko almost smiled, but she pulled up her scarf, and Kathleen couldn't tell. Her smile didn't extend to her eyes. "So, glad to be back in Tokyo?"

Kathleen suddenly felt a rush of nerves. "Yeah, I mean, traveling around was fun. But it was also work. I'm glad to finally have a real vacation. Though I think I may end up working through the next week as well, on my own."

Yuriko's eyebrows lowered. "I'm surprised. I thought the beta was doing really well."

"It is! This is, ah, prep for a future project, related to PLC." She hesitated. "It's actually Ai's code. The one she was trying to make. For us, I mean. I'm tweaking it quite a bit, so it's not exactly the same, and I'm not sure how it will turn out, but my boss seems oddly into it, and I guess…I guess I'll see how it goes." Yuriko was looking at her, as if waiting for her to continue. Kathleen felt like words were slipping around her tongue, useless and not what she wanted to say. "How is the beta release going on your end?" She felt like a coward.

Yuriko sighed but filled her in on her recent work. They reached the station, barren this time of morning. After a couple stations, it was filling up, crowding them in a silent morning crush. Looking out the window, Kathleen could see the sun rising between the buildings, bright orange against the gray cloudy sky. It was more people than Kathleen expected for a holiday, but not the promised crowds that Yuriko warned.

Upon reaching Harajuku, however, they found where everyone was.

From the train station to the streets, it seemed like everyone in Tokyo was in this very neighborhood. They walked only a little way from the station to a nearby park. A torii as tall as the treetops looked down upon the massive crowd lining up to get inside. Kathleen stared up at it.

"Thank goodness we don't have to toss a stone up there," she mentioned.

Yuriko snorted. "Stay close. If we separate, we won't be able to find each other in this crowd."

Kathleen went silent, standing close to Yuriko. They were in a solid wall of people, all marching into the wooded park. Kathleen imagined it would have been rather pretty without the crowds. The path was wide, and the trees were thick and tall. They passed over a stone bridge and walked by wooden lanterns. They stopped before a huge holo, broadcasting ads and information about the shrine over the waiting people's heads. The crowd was backed up here, waiting for men in uniform with signs to lead them forward toward the shrine. Kathleen was almost getting a little too hot, surrounded by so many people. She tugged at her scarf, trying to breathe in some fresh air.

"So, what have you been up to, Yuriko?" she asked. If they were going to be silent until they got to the shrine, it was probably going to feel like hours in this line.

"Just work, as usual."

"I mean, besides work." Kathleen felt like she was fishing. What did she want to know? Had Yuriko moved on? Was she dating someone else yet? Was it really any of Kathleen's business?

"Nothing new, no."

They were silent again, and Kathleen felt her nerves setting in. She hunched her shoulders and looked to the gravel path. It wasn't the large crowd that bothered her, not in this moment. She found herself looking at Yuriko's hand, hidden in her pocket. Could Kathleen reach out and take it? Maybe put her arm through hers?

A man shouted, and they were led forward. The sign he held glinted in the early morning sun, the English and Japanese telling them to follow. The sign flashed again, and they were stopped. They were in sight of the gate leading into the shrine now, but their group had to wait to be let in. Kathleen turned behind her to see a larger crowd still waiting behind, stopped by another man in uniform.

They stood in silence, listening to the music through hidden speakers, and to the people murmuring around them. The sign flashed again, and they were let inside the courtyard of the shrine, their group jostling together to get close to a massive blue tarp laid out for offerings. There were smaller buildings selling good luck charms and tokens for the New Year. Another crowd pressed toward the building where people were rattling boxes of sticks and receiving slips of paper.

"Could you tell me what I need to do?" Kathleen asked, a little afraid.

Yuriko was pressing toward the blue tarp laid before the shrine. "Take out some coins. It doesn't have to be much. Then throw them onto the tarp. Bow twice, clap twice, then make your prayer." She threw a silver coin, sailing over the heads of the people in front of them. Other shimmering coins dotted the air with hers. "Then bow again." She put her hands together and closed her eyes, performing the ritual.

Kathleen turned away, trying to edge a little closer before throwing her own coin. She didn't want to accidentally hit someone in front of her. The building was large and wide, not really like the ones Kathleen had seen in Nikko. It was plain, a dark brown wood, and much bigger. She could see a little into the murky inside, and it smelled like incense. She couldn't see elaborate decorations, at least not from her angle.

Kathleen wasn't sure what to pray for. She wasn't really religious, only going to church for the holidays with her parents. Standing in front of the shrine, surrounded by people with bowed heads, felt sort of the same. Kathleen looked to the bright blue tarp, the shining coins littering it like jewels.

She remembered the torii in Nikko and throwing stones to make a wish. This time her offering had met the goal—she just needed to make her wish.

Kathleen glanced at Yuriko just behind her, eyes closed, head down. What was she praying for? Was she praying that this would end quickly? That Kathleen would leave her alone and she could go on with her life undisturbed? Was she waiting for Kathleen to say something? Apologize?

Was she waiting for Kathleen to gather enough courage to admit that she had been watching vids of them until she fell asleep at her table? Had been thinking of her for longer than that? Had realized she was an idiot and needed to make things right? Had finally realized what Yuriko meant to her?

Well, Kathleen would pray for courage. She threw the shrine a healthy donation. She was feeling a little desperate. She clapped loudly and bowed deeply. She squeezed her eyes shut and tried to imagine they were alone here. Not in the middle of a crowd, jostling for position. They were somewhere far away. Someplace quiet, peaceful, where Kathleen wasn't afraid anymore.

Kathleen bowed again and turned to see that Yuriko was finished. They walked over to a crowded merchant stand, selling a number of strange items as well as fortunes that Kathleen recognized from Nikko. People were looking over everything carefully, talking to the priests selling it all.

"What is this for?"

"A lot of it is to help purify your house for the New Year." Yuriko touched something that looked like ribbon and twigs and bells. "I don't need it—my mother already sent me a care package. Along with about ten pounds of homemade mochi." She was almost smiling, and Kathleen pressed closer, as if she could take in that smile for herself. Yuriko turned to the larger crowd paying for paper fortunes. "Come on. The fortune you get on New Year's Day is supposed to be special."

At the front of the line, Kathleen was given a strange wooden box. She shook it, just like everyone else around her, hearing the rattle of wooden sticks inside.

"Take one out," Yuriko instructed. "They will give you a fortune."

Kathleen tilted the box, and from a small opening, one stick managed to poke out. The woman behind the counter took it from her, then reached behind her to grab a piece of paper out of a small drawer. Yuriko received hers, and they both shuffled away from the crowd.

Kathleen opened the narrow piece of paper. She had been practicing her reading skills, even while touring the country. However, this was a whole new level of difficult. She knew she should have memorized more kanji. She held it out to Yuriko. "Can you read it for me?"

Yuriko glanced at it, and then she frowned and took it. She read it over carefully several times and Kathleen was dying to know what it said. Yuriko handed it back. "You've gotten the best luck."

Kathleen held the paper, grinning. "Really? Well, I guess I've improved since Nikko, right?"

Yuriko nodded, looking to her own fortune.

"Well? What does yours say?"

Yuriko shrugged. "It's the worst."

Kathleen blinked. "The worst?"

Yuriko nodded and walked over to a scaffolding of string set up. People had already been putting their fortunes there, filling up the space until it looked almost like a solid wall of tied paper. Yuriko found a spot and carefully tied hers.

"Should I put mine there?" Kathleen asked.

"No, keep yours, since it's such good luck."

"Oh, okay." Kathleen tucked hers into her pocket. They both started wandering toward the exit. There were plenty of people here, even some food stands set up, but it was quieter.

Kathleen wanted to speak, but she didn't know what to say. Yuriko was hesitating—she could tell. Her pace wasn't her usual briskness, and her shoulders were hunched, as if she was bracing for something.

Yuriko started to speak, "Kathleen—"

"I'm sorry," Kathleen blurted.

Yuriko stared. "What? For what?"

Kathleen had no idea how she could look so genuinely confused. "For the past few months. For avoiding talking to you. For asking for a break. For being…" An ass? In denial? Completely unable to express her feelings like an adult?

"Kathleen, you don't have to apologize. I understand that you needed this space." She huffed out a breath. They had stopped walking. People just stepped around them as if they were stones caught in a river. Yuriko took in a deep breath. "I missed you too, you know."

Kathleen felt like her heart could start beating again. "Yeah?"

"Yeah."

Yuriko waited. Yuriko had been waiting for so long now. It was Kathleen's turn to step up, and it felt like she was going to dive over a cliff. "Yuriko, I—"

Someone bumped into Kathleen, and she stumbled into Yuriko, her legs too weak to catch herself properly. She automatically turned to see who had run into her, but the person didn't even notice. She was a woman, her arm around a man who was probably her boyfriend or husband. She looked up at him like he was the only person in this whole shrine. His cheeks were flushed as he talked about something in excitement. Then they both laughed, and she happened to look over her shoulder, toward Kathleen.

It was Ai.

It was not Ai.

She didn't look like Ai. Her hair was longer, a light brown. She was shorter, all her features more rounded and petite. Her eyes were brown, but when they looked at Kathleen, she recognized them. A PLC, a rare beta. The chances of Kathleen seeing one here must have been infinitesimal. Yet here they both were, and the PLC was still staring at Kathleen as if something in her programming knew her. The woman suddenly grinned, her smile wider than Ai's had been, but filled with the same warmth. She turned it back to the man on her arm, and for a moment, Kathleen felt insanely jealous.

She didn't want Ai back. She wasn't jealous that she didn't have a doting robot lover anymore. She was jealous because, this whole morning, Yuriko hadn't smiled at Kathleen like that.

Kathleen felt a surge of energy, standing straight on her own, possibly taking a hopping step back. Yuriko still had a hand on her elbow.

"Kathleen? Is everything all right?" She looked concerned, probably because Kathleen felt like she would never breathe normally again. She might also be having a heart attack. Probably.

Kathleen tore off her scarf and unbuttoned the top of her jacket, needing to cool down. She even shoved her gloves in her pockets, feeling the paper fortune getting crushed.

"I'm really stupid, but you already knew that." She said it all in a rush, out of breath. She couldn't stop now. Not with Yuriko looking at her in a new dawn, all soft and bright. "I missed you because I've been an idiot. I've been an idiot because I've probably been in love with you since Nikko. Or maybe when I got sick and you brought me that awful healthy drink. Or maybe when you showed me how to use your bathtub. Or when you helped save Ai in Akihabara. Or maybe when I realized Ai looked exactly like you. Or maybe I fell in love with you all the way back when you saved me from being lost in Omiya Station." She gasped for air, drowning. "It doesn't matter. All that matters is that I've been an idiot and it took a goddamned love robot to make me realize that all I've wanted is you."

Yuriko was silent. Some people had stopped moving around them, surprised at her outburst, staring at Kathleen and Yuriko.

Yuriko blinked, looking down, then back to Kathleen, then away again. "I...ah, wow."

Kathleen realized she had been clenching her fists, nails digging into her palms. She tried to relax them, buy it didn't work. "And"—her voice was failing now—"if you don't feel the same anymore, that's... well, I understand." She tried to smile or laugh, but she just made a choking noise. "It would make us even, right? Shouting one-sided confessions in public."

"It's not one-sided." Yuriko ran a hand through her hair, tugging at the ends with her fingers, sighing heavily. "You have no idea...Idiot, indeed." She looked up at Kathleen, eyes shining. "I've just spent this entire morning wondering if it was okay to kiss you, or if you still needed space. Fuck, Kathleen, you've no idea how wild you make me."

Kathleen was shaking again, adrenaline and energy bursting through her. Yet she couldn't move, she didn't dare. "I'm sorry—"

Yuriko took a quick step forward and kissed her, cutting off her apology. Her hands were around Kathleen's head, holding her forcefully, but her lips were gentle and warm. Yuriko broke away. "Don't apologize again. Please, just don't."

Kathleen reached up and wrapped her arms around Yuriko, gripping the fabric of her jacket with shaking hands. "Don't stop," Kathleen whispered, knowing she was pleading.

Yuriko smiled then, slow and easy. It grew across her lips and cheeks like a flower opening up to the dawn. Just as bright, just as warm.

She knew there were at least a few people still staring. Kathleen honestly didn't care. Let them judge. It didn't matter. There were hundreds more just passing them by. Let them all go. She and Yuriko were here now and had finally managed to collide.

Then they were kissing again. Kathleen recognized the feeling of losing herself in Yuriko's mouth, but she wasn't afraid anymore. She sank into that feeling, into Yuriko, wrapping herself in it, *relishing* it. She was lost again, but she knew who would find her and bring her home.

❖

Kathleen felt her hip catch on the edge of the door as Yuriko struggled to get them past it without removing her hands or mouth from Kathleen. She barely had enough brain cells left to notice they had made it to Yuriko's apartment. She had little idea how they even got there, and she simply couldn't imagine even attempting to take her shoes off.

Yuriko swore and Kathleen nearly fell as one of her shoes was yanked off and the door closed behind them. None of it seemed to matter against the loss of Yuriko's hands and mouth in that brief moment. She reached under her jacket, easing it off Yuriko's shoulders. Yuriko had given up moving them, pressing her against the wall next to her bedroom door. Yuriko's breath on her cheek. They felt good and so *close*.

They were both pressing now, more than they had before.

Something was happening, something Kathleen felt like she almost recognized. A heat, an anxiousness. Maybe she didn't quite remember, but she thought she understood.

She let Yuriko press into her, trying to open herself up, even though she wasn't quite sure how. Or if Yuriko would be able to tell. She kissed her back, hands in that silky hair.

She knew she loved Yuriko. It was still new and strange, but she knew it now and she wasn't going to let her denial stop her from moving forward. However, her naivete just might.

She was kissing Yuriko against a wall, and she still had her jacket on. Hands in her silky hair, warm lips, wet breath. One of Yuriko's hands was still on her cheek, and it just felt so good to feel the pinpricks of her nails as she turned her head for a deeper angle.

Kissing Yuriko was, in essence, a familiar thing. She had kissed before. She had also felt this urge before, an urge to hold Yuriko closer, kiss her more than she could count and, well, *devour* her.

Kathleen had told Yuriko she loved her, but she wanted to show it to her now.

"My room," Yuriko finally gasped into her mouth, pulling her close again. "My bed."

Kathleen felt her whole body flush, warm and tight, a mixture of pleasure and fear. She had experienced sex before, but she'd never been with another woman. She wasn't totally in the dark about the logistics. She did live in an age with limitless free information online. However, watching online wasn't the same as reality.

The back of Yuriko's knees hit the bed. She released Kathleen enough so she could fall back on her white duvet. Her short black hair haloed around her head. Her lips were red, and she grinned up at Kathleen, arms outstretched. Kathleen shed her jacket and managed to kick off one shoe that still hung on to her foot. She fell into Yuriko, because that felt like the most natural thing in the world. Their lips together felt like the most natural thing in the world. How had she denied this for so long?

Then she drew back. She was on top of Yuriko, knees planted on either side of her hips. Her insecurity was creeping back into her brain.

"I, uh…" *Want to know what to do?* Yuriko was more experienced, and Kathleen was, well, not.

Then, she remembered what it was like to be submissive during sex. It had always felt unexciting and somewhat meaningless. She didn't want that with Yuriko, not after all they'd been through.

She knew sex wasn't always perfect. This time she wanted it to be. As if it could make up for all the time she had wasted. For all the times she had hurt Yuriko.

Yuriko was frowning now, puzzled by Kathleen. "What is it?" She started to sit up.

Kathleen immediately pushed her back down, a little too harshly. Yuriko landed with a soft thump and let out a laugh, as if she was just being playful and not totally overanalyzing her every move and thought.

She looked at Yuriko lying there, grinning up at her. She remembered Ai. She remembered kneeling above Ai like this. Watching as Ai lifted her skirt and touched herself. The memory was unpleasant. That whole encounter had been confusing and uncomfortable.

Yuriko wasn't Ai. She didn't blush on command. She wouldn't obey all of Kathleen's orders without thought. If they moved forward, they wouldn't be able to break it off like she and Ai had.

She didn't want to break it off. She was afraid and a little lost, but she really didn't want to remove herself from Yuriko's lap.

Her hands flexed on Yuriko's shoulders, fingers gripping the cloth. "Can I?"

Yuriko responded by lifting her arms over her head, grinning impishly. "Onegai."

Kathleen let her trembling fingers trail down Yuriko's sides. She tugged the hem of Yuriko's shirt and pulled it up. Yuriko arched her back, and the shirt was free. She was wearing a bra clasped in the front. Before she could second-guess anymore, Kathleen quickly undid it, and the bra soon followed the shirt.

She remembered seeing Yuriko's breasts at the onsen, though at the time she had been concentrating on not staring. This was different. Now they were presented to her, ready and soft. Yuriko still had her arms above her head, smiling into her bicep, eyes glittering.

Kathleen felt herself falter. This was it. This was when she was supposed to enjoy herself. This was supposed to be the difference between Ai and Yuriko. Kathleen reached out and ran her fingers over Yuriko. She hoped her tentativeness came across as gentleness.

Her skin was soft and warm. Yuriko was still beneath her wandering hands. Kathleen felt a wave of uncertainty building up in her. She pressed a little harder.

Then Yuriko moaned into the skin of her arm. Kathleen felt her heart stutter and her hands grow bolder. Yuriko moaned again, hands tightening into the duvet above her head.

Kathleen wanted more of that. She wanted more of that sound. She wanted more of that flush trailing from Yuriko's cheeks and down her neck. None of it was synthetic. None of it programmed.

Kathleen suddenly couldn't get enough of Yuriko's skin. Her hands were everywhere, her mouth was everywhere. Yuriko tasted like sweat and soap. She had odd moles and random freckles. She had a pimple on her lower back, and she obviously had skipped out on any shaving this winter.

Yuriko was familiar in so many ways. So familiar and so new. Yuriko lit up as she touched her, explored her like she had never explored anyone else. Yuriko laughed when she found a sensitive spot behind one knee and again just below her left breast. Yuriko gasped as her hands dove beneath her waistband, needing to explore even when their current position wouldn't allow for them to undress properly.

She couldn't imagine removing herself from Yuriko. Her whole body quivered as Yuriko managed to remove Kathleen's shirt and bra. Her breath was uneven, and Yuriko did some exploring of her own.

That's what it was. Exploring, figuring out a new body to touch, to adore.

Sex with Yuriko was pleasure. Simple and pure pleasure. Without boundaries or definitions. She would kiss Yuriko to tell her *I love you.* She would kiss her breast to say *I love you.* She would kiss the wet and warm space between her thighs to say *I love you.*

Yuriko's hands would bury in her hair, forcing Kathleen to meet her blue, blue eyes. She would whisper, "Suki desu."

CHAPTER TWENTY-EIGHT

Yuriko remembered sitting in her kotatsu yesterday morning, wondering when she knocked on Kathleen's door, if she would answer, wondering if Kathleen would follow her to Meiji, wondering if her afternoon would just be her back in her kotatsu, alone.

Then Kathleen had appeared, like she had risen from her bed because of a fire. She hadn't even had shoes on, and then…and then…

"Wow, you have a blanket around your table? Sweet." Kathleen emerged from the bathroom, looking only slightly more refreshed than she had this morning. Of course, this morning Kathleen had been lying naked in Yuriko's bed, hair soft and spread around in a tangled mass. Now her hair was tied back, and she was wearing one of Yuriko's sweaters. The sweater was just a touch too small, stretching to fit and riding up above Kathleen's hips. She was wearing nothing else.

Yuriko couldn't believe she was allowed to stare.

"Kotatsu. It's pretty typical here during the winter. There's a heater under there too," she murmured, blatantly not paying attention.

Kathleen sat down next to her. Yuriko mourned the loss as those bare legs and thighs disappeared under the table. She seemed confused at first how to sit there and arrange the blanket. She eventually settled on lying down as if she was in a bed. She grinned up to Yuriko, cheeks pink.

"Feels fantastic. Another for the list."

"The list?"

"Of Japanese things that America doesn't have. Along with proper soaking baths and the konbini."

Yuriko remembered that conversation. Ages ago, it seemed now. So much had happened since then. Some things gained, some things lost. Texts that were sent and unsent. Words Yuriko wished she could have said, words she wished she could have heard from Kathleen.

Then yesterday, Kathleen had just effortlessly appeared and cleanly inserted herself behind all of Yuriko's defenses.

This time she said she loved you. She apologized and said she loved you.

She loves you.

It was a lot to take in on only the second day of the year.

Yuriko hadn't moved from her seated position. Her morning cup of tea was forgotten at her elbow as she couldn't take her eyes off Kathleen. She looked nearly comical, burrowed under the kotatsu like a little kid playing hide and seek. Yuriko smiled, the warm feeling in her chest only blooming brighter.

"Do you want some tea? My mother sent mochi. It's green tea flavored." It was Yuriko's favorite.

Kathleen was already reaching for the bowl in the middle of the table with the mochi. She shifted, half lying on Yuriko's lap now. She examined the mochi and Yuriko felt a naked thigh against one of her feet. "Is it a pastry?"

"It's rice. Pounded down. My mother makes it every year."

Yuriko thought of standing to get tea for Kathleen, but she just couldn't bring herself to move. Not when Kathleen was so warm and heavy next to her. Kathleen nibbled on the mochi. "Not too sweet," she murmured.

There was a brief silence as she submitted to the urge to reach out and tangle a hand in Kathleen's hair. It was in horrible disarray, but as she teased it, the smell of sex and the faintest touch of incense from the shrine wafted from it. Yuriko leaned down, unable to resist burrowing her nose in the memory.

"You know, as I've been working on Ai's new program, I've come across a little problem," Kathleen said, her voice soft.

Yuriko closed her eyes, not really listening. "Hn?"

"Well, she was programmed to know me so well, but she had to learn about others by herself. She would collect data whenever she talked to you or other people, but she could never quite have the same intuition. I've come to realize that while she was able to know exactly what I wanted in a partner, she was just guessing when it…well, when it came to you."

Yuriko pulled away, remembering that conversation outside the konbini, fireworks and city lights illuminating them all as Kathleen had tried to break her heart. Maybe she had, but she had given a new one to Yuriko yesterday, and it felt warm and right in her chest. "I think I know what you mean. She made a lot of assumptions based on the fact that she was designed to look like me."

Kathleen nodded. "It's something I have to fix. I guess, if I want this new program to work, there has to be a clear interest or consent. I mean, just because I'm…I'm attracted to you, doesn't mean you would be attracted to me."

Yuriko found it just a little funny how Kathleen stumbled over her words. As if she was unsure of Yuriko's affections. As if they hadn't spent most of the night affirming those affections. She didn't laugh but hid a smile in Kathleen's hair.

"That is a viable concern," she murmured, "for anyone else." She let a hand dip down the stretched neckline of the sweater. Kathleen gave a shuddered sigh and leaned more heavily against her.

"Stop distracting me—I'm trying to explain something," Kathleen muttered. She didn't move away.

Yuriko smiled. "Explaining what?"

"That I was wrong, what I said during the hanabi. I mean, I was mostly confused and I was jumping to conclusions and I see that now." She sighed, heavy and long. "I was scared."

Yuriko leaned back, just a little, just enough to see Kathleen's bright eyes looking up at her. "Why were you scared? You knew how I felt about you."

"But I didn't know how I felt about you." She flushed. "Well, not completely. I knew I was attracted to you, obviously, but I didn't know how deep that went. So when I got a reason to second-guess myself, when I had even the slightest hint that everything I was feeling could be fabricated, I just panicked." She bit her lip. "I'm sorry."

Yuriko kissed her, not trying to erase those words, but hopefully soothing them away. "It's okay. As a person who trained herself to be disconnected from her emotions, I cannot fault you for struggling to find yours."

Kathleen frowned. "But I'm a loud, obnoxious American, and I should be better than a twelve-year-old with my first crush."

She grinned. "But I am your first crush, right? On a woman?"

Kathleen grimaced. "Yes, and I'm sorry you had to be the one to take that bullet."

She laughed and kissed her again, and again. God, how had she lived a minute of these past months without kissing Kathleen. She wasn't sure she had. She let her hand, still resting on Kathleen's neck, wander a little farther under the sweater's collar.

Then Yuriko asked, "When we were walking to the shrine yesterday, do you want to know how I felt?"

Kathleen wriggled as the hand wandered. "Exceptionally fed up with me?"

She gave a small grin. "I was feeling very frustrated." Her hand stilled, and Kathleen twisted her head to look up at her, cheeks flushed. "I was frustrated that even after all this time, even after all the drama and the miscommunication, even after hours of thinking over everything we had gone through, I couldn't tell you what I felt. I couldn't say that I still cared for you, that I wanted you back in my life. I was so *angry* with myself for being such a coward."

Kathleen pressed one hand to the floor, just enough to kiss the hollow of Yuriko's neck. Yuriko hadn't realized she'd tensed until she felt her shoulders loosen from the tender kiss.

Kathleen said into her skin, "I'd think you'd be more frustrated with me. I'm the one who was in a perpetual state of denial."

"Yes, well, that was pretty frustrating too." She chuckled, and she earned a playful nip of teeth. Her voice hitched as she continued, "Then look what happened. We ended up committing public indecency."

Kathleen removed her mouth from Yuriko's neck long enough to show her deeply red face. Her eyes were suddenly serious. "Yuriko, you've done so much for me. Put up with so much. I'm not sure how I… Do I make your life better?" She said the words so softly that Yuriko probably wouldn't have heard them if she hadn't been so close.

She reached out to cup Kathleen's face and force her to look at her. She was glad Kathleen wasn't crying. Her eyes were glassy, staring at Yuriko with anticipation. "I can't tell you something like that, but I can say that you make me happy. That when I saw you yesterday morning, I was so happy. Hearing your voice, seeing you again. I was so *happy*. I never used to make wishes or prayers on shrines. I didn't see the point. I made a prayer at Meiji Shrine. I prayed that I could be with you, even for just a moment longer. That I could keep that feeling and remember it even when you were gone. I don't know if you better my life or anything like that, but I want this feeling that I have with you. More than anything. Suki desu. I love you."

Kathleen smiled, cheeks stretching under Yuriko's fingers. "Can you kiss me?"

She grinned. "Why don't you kiss me?"

"Cause you're holding my face back."

Yuriko wasn't holding Kathleen back. She had probably been holding herself back. So she drew Kathleen to her, feeling the warmth of her breath, the flutter of eyelashes on her cheeks, and her soft lips.

She knew they would have more conversations like this, both needing to affirm to each other how they felt. After so long dancing around one other, it was inevitable that it would take time to build trust and understanding. Yet they had managed to take the first step. A stumbling, overdue first step.

Yuriko thought it just might be perfect.

About the Author

Diana Jean is a thirty-something-something who spends most of her day writing about people falling in love, reading about people falling in love, or making excessively frilly dresses.

Tumblr: https://dianajeanauthor.tumblr.com/
Instagram: https://www.instagram.com/dianajeanauthor/
Blog: http://dianajeanauthor.blogspot.com/?m=1

Books Available From Bold Strokes Books

Femme Tales by Anne Shade. Six women find themselves in their own real-life fairy tales when true love finds them in the most unexpected ways. (978-1-63555-657-5)

Jellicle Girl by Stevie Mikayne. One dark summer night, Beth and Jackie go out to the canoe dock. Two years later, Beth is still carrying the weight of what happened to Jackie. (978-1-63555-691-9)

My Date with a Wendigo by Genevieve McCluer. Elizabeth Rosseau finds her long-lost love and the secret community of fiends she's now a part of. (978-1-63555-679-7)

On the Run by Charlotte Greene. Even when they're cute blondes, it's stupid to pick up hitchhikers, especially when they've just broken out of prison, but doing so is about to change Gwen's life forever. (978-1-63555-682-7)

Perfect Timing by Dena Blake. The choice between love and family has never been so difficult, and Lynn's and Maggie's different visions of the future may end their romance before it's begun. (978-1-63555-466-3)

The Mail Order Bride by R. Kent. When a mail order bride is thrust on Austin, he must choose between the bride he never wanted or the dream he lives for. (978-1-63555-678-0)

Through Love's Eyes by C.A. Popovich. When fate reunites Brittany Yardin and Amy Jansons, can they move beyond the pain of their past to find love? (978-1-63555-629-2)

To the Moon and Back by Melissa Brayden. Film actress Carly Daniel thinks that stage work is boring and unexciting, but when she accepts a lead role in a new play, stage manager Lauren Prescott tests both her heart and her ability to share the limelight. (978-1-63555-618-6)

Tokyo Love by Diana Jean. When Kathleen Schmitt is given the opportunity to be on the cutting edge of AI technology, she never thought a failed robotic love companion would bring her closer to her neighbor, Yuriko Velucci, and finding love in unexpected places. (978-1-63555-681-0)

Brooklyn Summer by Maggie Cummings. When opposites attract, can a summer of passion and adventure lead to a lifetime of love? (978-1-63555-578-3)

City Kitty and Country Mouse by Alyssa Linn Palmer. Pulled in two different directions, can a city kitty and a country mouse fall in love and make it work? (978-1-63555-553-0)

Elimination by Jackie D. When a dangerous homegrown terrorist seeks refuge with the Russian mafia, the team will be put to the ultimate test. (978-1-63555-570-7)

In the Shadow of Darkness by Nicole Stiling. Angeline Vallencourt is a reluctant vampire who must decide what she wants more—obscurity, revenge, or the woman who makes her feel alive. (978-1-63555-624-7)

On Second Thought by C. Spencer. Madisen is falling hard for Rae. Even single life and co-parenting are beginning to click. At least, that is, until her ex-wife begins to have second thoughts. (978-1-63555-415-1)

Out of Practice by Carsen Taite. When attorney Abby Keane discovers the wedding blogger tormenting her client is the woman she had a passionate, anonymous vacation fling with, sparks and subpoenas fly. Legal Affairs: one law firm, three best friends, three chances to fall in love. (978-1-63555-359-8)

Providence by Leigh Hays. With every click of the shutter, photographer Rebekiah Kearns finds it harder and harder to keep Lindsey Blackwell in focus without getting too close. (978-1-63555-620-9)

Taking a Shot at Love by KC Richardson. When academic and athletic worlds collide, will English professor Celeste Bouchard and basketball coach Lisa Tobias ignore their attraction to achieve their professional goals? (978-1-63555-549-3)

Flight to the Horizon by Julie Tizard. Airline captain Kerri Sullivan and flight attendant Janine Case struggle to survive an emergency water landing and overcome dark secrets to give love a chance to fly. (978-1-63555-331-4)